Table of Contents:

INTRODUCTION:

Lew and Charlie are the ultimate outdoor adventurers, hunting, trapping and fishing their way from Arctic Alaska south to the jungles of Central America. Along the way they also solve mysteries, catch crooks, and rescue the occasional damsel in distress.

The stories ran as a monthly serial in *FUR-FISH-GAME* magazine beginning in 1926. Over the years, Maurice Decker would write 36 of the novella-length adventures, each broken into monthly chapters with classic cliff-hanger endings. The final chapter of the final story appeared in December 1961.

To mark the magazine's 60th anniversary year in 1985, one of the stories was republished in its entirety, all 11 monthly chapters. When the story was coming to a close, readers who had become hooked on Lew and Charlie flooded the office with letters asking for more, and another of the original serials was republished in its entirety the following year. Thirty-five years later, the magazine's readers are still hanging on every word.

None of the stories had been available in book format until *The Adventures and Lew and Charlie Volume I* collected the first three adventures. Volume 2 took up where Volume 1 left off, and now Volume III continues the long-running tale with Lew and Charlie battling a gang of pearl poachers, solving a ghostly treasure mystery, and battling to survive while locked in a snowbound cabin with a fiendishly clever murderer.

Wardens at Wayne

Chapter 1 – Some Job

A wide grin illuminated Lew's face as he declared, "Some job!"

Their interview with Mr. Sanderson, head of the state game commission, had been brief but highly satisfactory. "Gosh, that was easy," he continued. "We hit this town an hour ago. Now we're game wardens for the Wayne Lake District. Fast work, eh?"

"You're right," agreed Charlie with a grin of his own. "The commissions are in our pockets and our silver badges are pinned to our vests. He handed them out like dealing cards. I'm surprised he didn't try to force the first month's salary on us in advance. Imagine drawing a hundred and fifty per month just to look after the game and fish up at Wayne?" he added.

"He handed us the job like he was doing himself a favor," Lew concurred. "Course, the letter we had from Mr. Harris helped. These Southern mountains are a long way from the good old Northwoods where we had all that fun helping Harris defeat Blake and his gunman Dutch. Good thing he and Sanderson are such good friends."

"Sanderson said the Wayne's all backwoods and kind of rough," Charlie said. "That means there won't be much chance for you to get in trouble, Lew. Want to stick around the city until tomorrow?"

"I should say not!" Lew replied, looking around at the state capital where they stood. "These tall buildings crowd in on me so I can't breathe. I'm all for Wayne Lake and the good old pine timber. I want to see deer tracks and turkey scratchings in the hickory."

They procured a state map at a drug store and then walked back to the Union Depot where they learned a train left for Hicks City in an hour. Hicks City was where they would leave the main line, changing for the mountain train that ran up to Wayne Lake.

They spread out the map and studied it. "Why, Wayne isn't a lake at all," grumbled Lew. "Just a wide place in the river." He pointed to a sausage-shaped swell in the blue line that represented East River.

"The map doesn't show any real towns, either," Charlie announced. "Must be thinly settled country."

Before the train was due to arrive they stowed their two heavily loaded suitcases at the check room. They would travel light to check things out, bringing just hunting clothes. Once they found lodging, they would return for the rest.

It was midnight before they stepped down from the train at Hicks City, a county seat at the foot of the mountain range where Wayne Lake was located. The sleepy-eyed agent informed them the train for Wayne did not leave until nine o'clock the next morning.

"Come on," Lew growled. "Let's go over to the hotel and get a few hours sleep."

The red-eyed clerk at the hotel languidly shoved a brass-tagged key across the desk at them. "Number 28," he droned.

They were halfway up the steps when a man running down the other way collided with them, knocking Lew's bag from his hand.

"Can't you look where you're goin'?" the man cried. Then, before either could answer, he ran on down the stairs.

"That bird had a lot of manners," Lew grumbled as he bent to pick up his suitcase. "Look here, Charlie. He dropped something."

It was a small black memo book. "If he hadn't been so snooty," Lew continued, "I'd try to follow him and give this back."

They found their room with no trouble and entered. Charlie snapped on the light and removed his coat and collar. Lew sat down on the bed and opened the small memo book. Pencil notes were scrawled over the pages. He read aloud:

"Three hundred today." And then, "B laid off a week."

He turned another page, glanced at it and then said, "Guess I better leave this with the clerk. He may need the figures for... Whoa! Listen to this, Charlie:

"New man at W. L. won't come in." When Charlie didn't reply, Lew persisted, "You think 'W.L.' means Wayne Lake?"

"There's a million things with the initials W.L.," Charlie retorted. "I suggest you go to bed and get some sleep before you start hatching up a crazy plot from that nickel book."

"Just the same," Lew answered thoughtfully, "I'm going to hang on to this book until I know what it's about."

The summer night was sultry, and they slept but intermittently in a poorly ventilated room. Up before sunrise, Lew stuck his head out the only window. "I haven't had a breath of fresh air since we left the North," he complained.

They dressed quickly and descended to the hotel lobby.

"Breakfast at seven," the clerk announced, looking even sleepier and more red-eyed than before.

Since it was closer to six than seven, they decided to take a walk around town. It was a typical county seat in the South, with a market square in the center piled high with bales of cotton. Board awnings roofed with corrugated iron projected out over rough stone sidewalks. Listless clerks were just starting to haul out merchandise for the day's business. Sacks and boxes of potatoes and apples and melons, bundles of hoes, cotton planters, one- and two-horse cultivators all were laid out on the sidewalks or stood against door jambs.

Charlie glanced at his watch. "Time to go back for breakfast," he announced. They entered the hotel just as a rush started for the dining room. Squeezing in with the crowd, they seated themselves at a long table. Two girls were making the rounds, bringing steaming platters of fried ham and eggs and thick china cups of black coffee.

A large, heavy man slid down into the chair beside Charlie. He pulled a bandana handkerchief from his pocket and mopped his face. Glancing at them with bright little eyes, he spoke in a friendly voice, "Howdy! Tolerable warm today."

Charlie agreed with a nod. The town sat in a valley below the mountains where cool breezes swayed the pine and cedar tops.

"Strangers in town?" the man asked.

"Yes."

"Staying?" he pursued, and Charlie caught an unexpected trace of persistence behind the question, as if the man was determined to know more about them despite Charlie's short answers.

"We're going up to Wayne Lake," Lew put in.

"Yeah?" the man answered. "That's a fine place. My nephew runs a store up there. If you want to know anything just hunt up Ben Scribbens. Tell him his uncle Asa sent you. He'll help you out alright. Asa Wright—that's me."

"We'll do that, thanks," acknowledged Charlie. Then he introduced Lew and himself.

"We just got the job as game wardens up there," informed Lew, with a trace of pride in his voice.

"Well," Asa replied with a wide smile. "That's dandy. Ben can help you out lots with that. He knows everybody. Don't forget that if you need anything straightened out."

Again Charlie thanked him, and Asa raised his coffee cup, beckoning a girl to refill it. Charlie could barely swallow his coffee; it was stronger than any camp coffee he had ever tasted.

As they left after eating, Asa walked beside them. Outside the door, they sat in chairs on the hotel stoop.

Asa took a handful of long, slim cigars from a pocket. "Smoke?" he invited, but Lew and Charlie declined.

"Goin' up on the mornin' train?" he asked, and they nodded.

"Fine country," Asa went on. "Mighty nice climate. Know you'll like it. Ain't much for a warden to do, I guess. Just trampin' over the mountains and runnin' up and down the river."

Asa lapsed into reflective silence. Charlie glanced at his watch. Their train left in a quarter of an hour.

"We better get started," he announced.

Asa shook hands with them as they left the hotel.

"Looked like a hard-working old fellow, didn't he?" Lew observed with a smirk as they walked to the station. "I'll bet the hardest thing he's done in the last twenty years is sit in that hotel chair."

"We ought to look up his nephew when we get to Wayne Lake," Charlie replied. "It might be handy to have an in with someone we can turn to for local information."

All day the short mountain-train's engine puffed and groaned up the grades. In mid-afternoon, the tracks swung in beside a dark blue channel which they knew from the map had to be East River. Lew leaned out of the open car window to study the deep, gushing flow.

"That's some river," he finally enthused. "First thing, we must order an outboard motor and a speed hull."

"You go ahead," answered Charlie. "I don't want to blow my first four months' salary on a boat."

The mountains grew higher and steeper, covered with heavy forests of pine. The peaks were studded with twisted cedars growing straight out of bare lime rock. Charlie got out the map.

"We can't have over forty miles more to go," he decided.

Only an occasional log cabin squatted beside the river. The only stops on the railroad line were short sidings where cordwood and hand-hewn oak ties were piled up waiting for shipment. They climbed higher and higher as the river also climbed with the road bed, twisting swift and cool, a serpentine ribbon of bright blue.

When long gray shadows began creeping down the mountain-sides and shrouding the valleys below with purple-tinted dusk, the train wheezed to a jerking stop beside a low rambling building with a faded board bearing the words: *Wayne Lake*.

"I don't see the band out to greet us," Lew observed. "Guess they didn't know representatives of the commonwealth were arriving."

A man jumped down from the engine cab, and crossing the tracks at a swift walk, headed for the single row of unpainted buildings that comprised the town. Lew watched with interest.

"That looks like the fellow who bumped me in the hotel last night," he declared. "I told you the initials W.L. in his notebook meant Wayne Lake."

Charlie counted 10 buildings, three of which were small country stores. One larger than the rest stood out in prominent contrast, and walking closer, they read the legend across its front: *Ben Scribbens, General Mdse.*

"Shall we go in and introduce ourselves?" asked Lew.

"Not yet," answered Charlie. "Let's take a walk and look about on our own account first."

A thin old man in wrinkled blue serge was dragging a rather limp mail sack into the station building. A long, scraggly mustache drooped down on either side of his mouth."Howdy!" he greeted them with the customary salutation of the mountains. "You boys got any baggage?"

"Nothing except these two suitcases," Charlie answered. "Where can we get supper and a room for tonight?"

The keen old eyes scanned them from shoes to hats without missing a detail. "I guess you can stay with me if you want," he offered. "There ain't no regular hotel here. I take in some of the folks that visit. Ben Scribbens, he takes the rest. Just as quick as I deliver this mail I'll take you up to the house. My name's Boggs."

Charlie completed the ceremony of introduction.

As they climbed the rock-strewn trail, Boggs explained the train schedule and his job as station agent. One train a day came up into the mountains. After it left Wayne Lake, it rambled farther into the mountains some 5 miles to a large tie-loading siding. Then it coasted back down and then on to Hicks City. It was a dead head line, one of those backwoods lines where a train had to back part of the way out.

He turned in at a pine-sided house with a neat lawn in front and a garden at one side. The garden seemed better kept than the others passed along the way.

A gray-haired woman stood in the door, welcoming them with a friendly smile. Charlie and Lew passed on into the kitchen and washed the travel grime from their hands and faces. They could smell the alluring aroma of fresh corn bread coming from the stove.

Boggs looked in at the door. "I have to go back to the station and wait fer the train to come back," he announced. "She comes a tearin' when she gets started back on the downgrades. I reckon you boys are hungry, so Ma'll set supper fer you now."

After they had eaten a hearty meal, Lew proposed they walk out for that look at the town. It required only a couple of hundred yards of walking, and soon they found themselves at the edge of the settlement with only a rough road or trail leading up the steep mountain away from the river. The outlines of the peaks above were framed by the glow of a rising moon. The air was soft and cool, and the plaintive call of a whippoorwill sounded in the pines.

The click of horse hooves on the rocky trail roused them from dreamy contemplation. The sound grew louder until they could hear rocks knocked from the road plunging over the side of the sheer drop. When a dark shape loomed around the final bend, sparks flew from hooves striking stone. The rider was galloping his mount down the neck-break trail, and Charlie and Lew had to spring out of the road to escape being ridden down. A derisive laugh was flung back to them as the rider swept past.

"Look at that fool!" cried Lew, scrambling back onto the trail. "That's no way to abuse a horse. One slip and they'll both go crashing over the cliff."

They listened to the clattering hooves until the rider reined in at the cluster of houses in the village. Then they walked back down to the Boggs household. As they approached the yard they saw with surprise that a horse stood by the low gate. Someone was talking loudly on the porch. Someone else just inside the door was answering.

Then the door slammed shut, and a tall figure strode out to the horse. With an agile leap, the man landed in the saddle. The door of the house opened, and they heard the voice of Boggs cracking with wrath.

"You come snoopin' around here again, Bill Smead, and I'll turn my shotgun on you!"

A snorting laugh was the answer, the same laugh that had been flung back at them on the mountain trail. Then the horseman wheeled his mount towards them.

"Step back, Lew," Charlie spoke quickly, "or he'll run us over for sure this time."

The rider spurred the horse directly at them as they stepped behind the fence protecting Boggs' garden. "The crazy devil!" Lew cried.

Again, a hoarse, mocking laugh was the only reply.

When they stepped up on the porch beside the station agent, Charlie demanded, "Who in thunder was that?"

"Bill Smead, the biggest scoundrel that ever escaped hangin'," was the angry response. "I got a double-barrel shotgun on the wall filled with buckshot just for him. I'm not afraid of Bill. But I reckon I'm the only one at Wayne Lake that ain't."

"Who's Bill Smead?" Charlie questioned further.

"He's deputy sheriff here," Boggs answered, "and he asked me right out what your business was, young fellows. What are you doing up here, anyway?" the old man asked.

"We're the new game wardens," proclaimed Lew.

A sound that resembled a groan came from Boggs, and it was like a cold breath of foreboding in Charlie's face, a sensation like what comes when one opens a cabin door in the dead of winter.

"What's the matter?" Lew responded. "There ain't nothing criminal about that, is there?"

"You're all right," Boggs assured them. "Only you don't know what you're up against. There's been three wardens in the last year. The first disappeared. Some say he got tired of the job and sneaked out; others say he's on the bottom of the lake.

"The next fellow they sent up, he lasted two weeks. Then one night he came runnin' down to the station just as the train was pullin' out. He leaped for the rear end of the caboose and just made it. I got a good look at his face as he passed. Boys, his eyes was bulgin' out with fear. The third man ..."

"Burt Lee," Charlie interrupted. "We have a note for him from the commissioner at the capitol. Where can we find him?"

Boggs looked silently at Charlie before he answered. "Lee was found shot dead this morning on the other side of the lake. His breast caved in by a load of big shot at close range!"

"Some job!" Charlie unconsciously echoed Lew's words of the day before, but his voice carried an entirely different tone.

Chapter 2 – Night Thrill

"So, that's why we got this job so easy," Lew's voice was somewhat strained as he spoke.

"What's this all about?" Charlie demanded of Boggs. "Who would kill a man over what little game is around here?"

"It's the pearls," the old man's voice lowered to a husky whisper.

"Pearls?" they echoed in unison.

"That's right," Boggs asserted. "I'm going to tell you boys just what I know and also what I think of this business. I tried to tell Lee, poor fellow, but he called me an old fool. That is, he did at first. But I think he finally saw I was right."

"Go ahead," Charlie encouraged. "We'll be glad to hear anything that might help us."

"For five years now," Boggs began, "the river has been closed to pearlin'. The Game Commission got the notion that the mussels was gettin' scarce, so they declared all clams had to be left alone for eight years. They wanted them to grow big and thick like years ago. There's three years to go before the season opens again. But Bill Smead found out the shell beds was already gettin' lousy with pearls, and he started in cleaning up."

"When we took this job there wasn't a word said about pearls," interjected Charlie. "Sanderson did say that the warden here, Burt Lee, would tell us the details of our duties."

"Well, poor old Lee won't be a tellin' nobody nothing now," replied Boggs.

"The pearls must be fine, big ones," suggested Charlie.

"They are," asserted the station agent, "the biggest, clearest river pearls found anywhere in the South."

His voice sank to a whisper again. "Boys, last month I sent out a package for Bill Smead that he insured for $4,000. Reckon his gang was too busy to spare a man to send them down."

"What did he say?" Interrupted Charlie.

"About the box?" Boggs read his mind. "He just grinned and said he was playing a joke on a friend who would have to pay the big charges, so he run up the value. He sent it collect."

"Neat alibi," muttered Lew.

"I figured that little box was a week's work for Bill's gang. The water was low and the moon full, just like tonight."

"How many in the gang?" asked Lew.

"Nobody knows. Or at least nobody's talkin'. All the people know he's poachin' pearls, but he has them scared. Nobody talks about it. My next door neighbor might be in the gang, for all I know."

"What are they going to do with Lee?" asked Charlie.

"Bill Smead had his body sent downriver by boat to his family. Like I said, Bill is deputy sheriff here. Whatever he says goes. He declared that Lee had shot himself, and his own gun was found lyin' beside him. I think different, but Smead's the law, and his report said it was a self-inflicted gunshot while hunting."

"Won't his family start an inquiry?" Lew demanded.

Boggs shrugged his shoulders. "It won't get nowhere."

"How long has this been going on?" Charlie wanted to know.

"About a year. It started when the first game warden came up. Bill was just getting started in a small way, and then he saw he could make real money, so he got some men in with him."

"Is there a money telegraph at the office?" Charlie asked.

"I can send money, but I can't pay none out," Boggs answered.

"Take us down to the station," Charlie insisted as the old man seemed to hesitate. "There's something we need at once."

As they walked together to the station, Charlie scribbled a short message and handed it with some bills to the agent.

"Send this on to Hicks City."

Boggs whistled as he read the note. Then he entered the office and began clicking away with agile fingers.

"Now," said Charlie, when the message had been dispatched, "where does this pearling take place?"

"The best beds used to be three miles up the river. They run on several miles more. I reckon that's where Smead works."

"The trail follows the water?"

"Most of the way," Boggs said.

"You take care of our stuff until we get back," Charlie instructed. "And don't tell anybody in Wayne what our business is here."

"Where you goin'?" the old man cried as Charlie turned from the house. "You ain't goin' up the river, are you? You'll never come back. Bill Smead won't stand for nobody spyin' on him. He has men watchin.' They'll shoot you and pitch you in the river."

"Don't worry about us," assured Charlie. "With a little help at this end, we're just the guys to straighten this thing up."

"I'll do all I can," Boggs said eagerly. "I want to see Bill Smead in jail. He killed my dog last summer. Ran over the little fellow with a wagonload of ties. And laughed."

Boggs' whiskers trembled as he recalled the injury. A mountaineer's dog is like one of the family. One might as well strike down a child as a favorite dog.

"I've got to see what we're up against," Charlie told Lew as they passed swiftly through the settlement towards the twisted trail leading up the mountain. They climbed at a swift pace, dodging the larger stones in the rain-washed dirt road.

"Why rush out in the night?" Lew asked. "Can't we wait until morning when we can see what's what?"

"This is too serious to wait, Lew. More than likely two wardens have been murdered and one scared away. I want to get the jump on Smead and his gang before they know we're onto them, and I suspect there's something bigger back of this."

"Old Boggs might have been stringing us," Lew suggested.

"He might," admitted Charlie. "But I don't think so. I think he may be the only one around here that we can trust. Mountain folk stick together, you know. If Boggs didn't have his own grudge against Smead, he might not have said anything. We can't count on any other help around here."

"Nor from the capital," Lew answered dryly. "I can't understand why Sanderson didn't tell us more."

"He may not have known how bad things were, and then he may have counted on Lee putting us wise. I'm going to write him in the morning. He must know the truth about Lee's death."

"Did you bring a gun?" Lew asked.

"No. I didn't think we'd need one. I just wanted to come up here and take a look around. Now I wish I had brought an arsenal. Smead knows we are here, and his visit with Boggs shows he at least suspects something. If we hadn't jumped aside, he'd have run over us right there in the trail."

After a moment of quiet thought, Lew offered, "I suppose you're right. The gang will work tonight, rake in a bunch of clams, and then lay low to see what we are up to. Maybe if we catch them by surprise we'll find some illegal pearls."

"That's the idea," Charlie replied.

Up and up they climbed until they reached a summit where the road flattened out across the level top of a ridge. The river lay a thousand feet below. Beyond both banks they could see the dim outline of mountains even higher than the one on which they walked.

They tramped half an hour in silence. Then Lew looked over the cliff and commented, "Looks like the river is widening. The lake must be ahead. If Smead is out working tonight, we ought to see boat lights."

The trail led over a steeper ridge and then dipped abruptly just before a steep descent. Charlie edged out as close to the sheer drop as he could and pulled a small pair of night glasses from his pocket.

He focused them and then searched every corner of the sheet of water that lay like an opaque mirror in the moonlight. Suddenly, he thrust the glasses at Lew. "Take a look!"

At first all Lew saw was natural beauty—a moonlit lake fringed with slender pines. But then something else caught and held his attention. Straight out before them, hugging the opposite bank, he could just discern the long, narrow lines of a river boat, such as fishermen or pearlers might use.

"Look below that," whispered Charlie. Lew turned the glasses until he was looking almost straight down. Through the thin-topped cedars he saw two more boats.

"Those are the boys we want to look over," Charlie whispered, pointing straight below.

They followed the road for another half-mile, swinging down around sharp curves along the steep mountainside. When the river lay less than a hundred feet below, Charlie cautioned, "Not a sound now." Then he swung over an edge to climb down through the cedars. But just as his feet dropped off, they both heard a faint click from the rocks in the road. They flattened themselves under a cedar.

A man was walking softly in the moonlight, hesitating between steps as though to listen. At first all they saw was a tall silhouette. Then they made out a broad-brimmed hat drooping. A long object lay across one arm, and Lew thought it might be a gun until he recognized it was a stout club.

The man stopped barely 20 feet from where they lay hardly daring to breathe, and then, after a minute of intent listening, he turned and passed into the shadows down the road, out of view.

"One of the guards," whispered Lew, with his lips right against Charlie's ear.

Charlie nodded then straightened his legs and began to descend. The cedars furnished handholds and places to step, much like a rough ladder. Foot by foot they slipped noiselessly down to the river.

The hollow sound of a paddle striking a boat's gunwale froze them like statues. Then a river boat loomed behind the screen of willows and cane that grew along the edge of the water.

They strained their eyes to see the big craft better, both eager to know if the men inside were really poaching forbidden pearls.

Three men sat in the boat, and as it passed even with their position, they could see a heap of something piled between the seats. Two men plied long, slender paddles while a third sat in the stern leaning out over the water. Was he raking up mussels?

As he leaned out for a better look before the boat was hidden again back of the curving bank, Charlie thrust out his foot to steady his balance and his toe pushed a loose rock. It went rolling with a splash into the water.

The boat stopped, and the rear paddler straightened to look straight at where they were crouching. They held their poise, praying their outlines blended into the shadows. They knew the eyesight of the mountaineer was keen and piercing.

The man raised his paddle ,and they both exhaled. But then a low, sharp whistle rang out. An answer sharp and clear echoed from above. Then they heard a man running on the road. A crash in the reeds at the water's edge warned them the boat had landed. They would be caught from both sides in a second.

"We've got to get out of here," Charlie declared in a whisper.

Side by side, they ran crouching through the undergrowth away from the boat. They heard low-pitched shouts and then a man came over the bluff with 10-foot leaps. They ducked lower and ran even faster through the willows, no longer concerned with remaining silent. More men were pursuing them from the rear, and Lew suddenly stopped and grabbed Charlie's arm.

"There's another boat landing ahead," he panted. "We're cut off both ways!"

Two men sprung out of this boat. One crouched and took a quick turn about a cedar with a mooring rope and then both plunged into the timber, heading straight towards them.

"In the water," Charlie whispered. "It's our only chance."

Charlie slid on his stomach and entered the water headfirst like a snake. Lew followed, leaving scarcely a ripple on the surface of the swift current.

They grabbed overhanging limbs that barely cleared the water and hung there with only mouths above water. Their pursuers ran past without a glance down at the river's edge.

Charlie pulled Lew up and ordered, "Now we get their boat! Move quick. When they meet the other men, the whole gang will be coming back for us."

They drew themselves carefully up from the water. A half-dozen quick steps brought them beside the boat, and Lew cast off the rope. Charlie shoved vigorously as he climbed in, and they shot out into the swift water.

"If they see us and start shooting, duck down behind the gunwale," ordered Charlie, picking up a paddle. The swift current swung them about and carried them at a fast clip downstream. Charlie was working the paddle with all his strength to put more water between them and the men on the bank.

A rifle ball ripped through the boat's side and splinters flew about their knees. Both fell to the floor of the boat.

Out on the moonlit water they provided an easy target. Charlie did the only thing he could. He used the tiller to turn the boat back in to shore, towards the enemy but where they would be shielded by the shadow-cloaked timber growing out from the bank.

Charlie sat upright and paddled faster than he had ever before in his life. He expected a shot any second, but the moments dragged by, and then, with a mighty sigh of relief, he shot them back under the protective bank cover.

"The cliff has been eaten away by the current here," he whispered to Lew. "They can't see us from above."

A volley of shots rang out, and bullets tore through the trees and splattered the water where the boat had been a moment before. They paddled up to the sheer cliff wall. Charlie caught a limb.

"We might as well tie up here," he said. "If we go fifty feet farther, we'll be out in the light again and those rifles on top will make short work of us."

"And then what?" Lew asked.

"I'm still working on that," Charlie admitted. "But at least our scouting party has been successful. Look at this pile of mussel shells."

"Lot of good that's going to do us on the bottom of the river," growled Lew. "Listen! I hear paddles coming."

The other boat was creeping upon them, also hugging the bank.

"Take off your shoes," whispered Charlie. "We must swim past them. It's our only chance."

Lew obeyed and then dropped softly into the water.

"Swim fast, but silent," cautioned Charlie right before they both sank beneath the surface.

Believing the boat would hug the bank to flush them out, they swam out some 10 yards, and then, turning over on their backs, floated downstream with only their noses above water.

Minute after minute passed. Once, Charlie thought he heard a hollow thump as though two boats bumped behind them. Finally, they turned over and swam swiftly with a fast crawl stroke, gradually edging into the bank, agreeing to land at the first suitable spot. Shouts were sounding from the cliff. The pearlers were searching up there, thinking they had taken to land.

As he swam around a sharp curve, Charlie saw a flat bank and tapped Lew's shoulder, pointing to it. They swam in and climbed out.

"We must get away from the river," Charlie said. "A boat will start down any minute. When they realize we swam away, they'll know we went downstream. Nobody could buck that current for long."

They twisted as much water out of their clothes as they could and then crept up to the edge of the road.

"Everything's clear," said Lew. "Let's go!"

But as he stepped forward, a man stepped out of the brush brandishing a club. The man growled a harsh command to stop.

Charlie swept his hand to the ground and, without shortening his stride, swept up a heavy rock and smashed it into the man's face. The fellow keeled over like a ninepin. But then he scrambled back to his feet and started chasing them. More were following, and as they dodged into the undergrowth a rifle rang out.

With Lew on his heels, Charlie dodged through the cedars, never running in a straight line but at top speed all the same, putting as much ground between them and the armed men as he could. The shouts were growing fainter when they turned back onto the road. They slowed to a trot but still ran, with ears and eyes alert. A mile passed under their feet. "I guess we left them," Lew finally panted.

"Quite a busy evening," Charlie grinned, glancing at his partner.

Lew snorted. "Too busy if you ask me. I'll have stone bruises on my feet for a month. We've lost two good pair of shoes, been shot at and half drowned, not to mention nearly getting clubbed over the head. And what have we gained?"

Charlie chuckled. Now that the immediate danger had passed, he was thinking of the pursuers now brooding over their escape.

"I'm satisfied with," he declared. "We knew it was a risk to come here unarmed. But we made two important discoveries. These fellows are pearling. And they're dangerous."

Half an hour later they stood in the center of the village. "Shall we wake up Boggs and get a bed?" Lew asked.

Charlie consulted his watch. "It's past midnight. Suppose we climb up on those cotton bales and sleep here tonight?"

They awoke stiff and cold but cheered to see a thin column of smoke streaming up from Boggs' chimney. He met them at the door with both worry and astonishment in his eyes.

"Where in the Sam Hill you boys been?"

"We got lost on the riverbank," Charlie replied. "It was so late by the time we got back to town we hated to wake you. So we slept on a couple of cotton bales."

Boggs looked into his face with shrewd old eyes. "Find anything interesting before you got lost?" he asked.

"Too interesting," Lew cut in. "We'll tell you later. What I want right now is breakfast and lots of it."

After eating they followed Boggs down to his office. He put forth several shrewd questions about their night's adventure, but seeing they preferred not to talk just then, he dropped the subject.

They lounged about the station until nearly noon. Then, fuming at this inaction, Lew demanded, "What are we going to do next?"

"Let's go see Ben Scribbens," Charlie offered.

When they entered the general store, the town loafers standing around the counter ceased all conversation. Charlie had no trouble picking out Ben Scribbens, a man of about thirty years, solidly built with a red perspiring face—in other words, a younger edition of his uncle Asa Wright back in Hicks City.

They walked up and bought a couple of bottles of pop. Then Charlie casually introduced himself and Lew as the new game wardens, and mentioned their recent acquaintance with Asa. Ben smiled broadly at that and wiped his face.

"Wayne Lake needs a couple of good game wardens," he volunteered. "Folks around here aren't as careful of the game laws as they might be."

"It looks like a big job," Charlie replied in doubtful tones. "I'm not sure we can handle it."

Lew's eyes blinked at that, but for once he held his peace.

"Sure you can," encouraged Ben. "The mountain folk are pretty reasonable when things is put to 'em right. There may be a few that'll act tedious, but they'll all come around."

"Some of them got quite tedious last night," Lew thought to himself. Then he nudged Charlie. "That saddle hanging by the door is just like the one I used last winter," he said.

Charlie turned. He knew Lew had used a saddle the past winter about as often as he had used an ice cream freezer, but he nodded and let his gaze go past the leather article to the man who stood close at the glass window, staring in at them.

"I'm glad you pointed it out to me, Lew." Then he turned to Ben and added, "What do you get for a saddle like that?"

"Thirty dollars."

"We'll be back for it and another just like it after we pick up a pair of horses," Charlie promised.

The stooped-shouldered man at the window turned away, but before he left Charlie noticed a bruise spreading over the side of his face. A bruise, Charlie thought, that could have been caused by a chunk of rock backed by a muscular arm such as he himself possessed.

They set their empty pop bottles on the counter, said goodbye to Ben, and walked to the door. As they stepped out both glanced up and down the street. The man with the bruised face was gone.

"Did you recognize him?" Charlie asked quietly. "He is the same man who bumped into you in the hotel at Hicks City."

As they walked past the corner of Ben's store a hand suddenly shot out and grasped Lew by the shoulder. He turned with a short exclamation, drew back his fist, and stared straight into the face of the man with the bruised cheek.

Chapter 3 – The Phantom Boat

Charlie stepped briskly to Lew's side, shoulders squared for anything that might follow. But the man dropped Lew's shoulder and held up his hand, cautioning them to silence.

"What's the idea?" Lew asked.

"You boys better beat it," said the man in not unkindly tones. In fact, Charlie thought he could detect a note of friendly admiration in the voice. "You got away pretty slick last night, but the big boss won't be happy. There'll be killin' if you push it anymore."

His voice turned grim and cold. "Take my advice and catch the next train down." Then, before either could answer, he whirled about and disappeared behind the store building.

"What do you make of that?" asked Lew.

"I make out that this is bigger than it appears on the surface," Charlie spoke seriously. "There's some deeper reason for murder. It isn't just about poaching mussels."

"Well, what is it?" Lew faced him eagerly.

"I don't know. Not yet. But those boys meant business last night. And now one of them is telling two game wardens to get out of town while they still can. I think we better duck out of town until the train comes in," Charlie added. "I wrote to Sanderson yesterday. But we won't hear back from him for a couple of days."

They climbed up the steep mountain trail until they reached a point overlooking the village and the narrow strip of flat land on each side of the river.

"Gosh, it's pretty country," Lew finally said.

"Pretty dangerous," Charlie replied grimly. "Give me that little book you found the other night."

He sat down and studied each of the short entries. The shadows of the pine trees had lengthened across the valley when a shrill whistle brought them to their feet. The train was pulling into Wayne.

"Let's go slowly and arrive after the crowd has left the station," Charlie suggested.

When they arrived the station house was empty. Boggs handed Charlie a small, square package through the window of his combination ticket and telegraph office. "Quick response," he said.

"It was," Charlie agreed, "but we won't need these now."

Boggs and Lew both looked at him in surprise. Then he further astonished them by saying, "Give us two tickets back to Hicks City."

Boggs pursed his lips.

"Clearing out?" he asked shortly.

"We're taking the next train," said Charlie.

"Too much for you?"

Charlie shrugged his shoulders without replying.

"I sort of hoped you boys would stay," the old man said wistfully.

"How long before the train comes?" was all Charlie said to that.

"She's coming now," Lew interposed as he heard a whistle back of the river bend.

As Charlie stepped through the door he spoke over his shoulder, "Be patient, old-timer. A fellow that'll run over a dog and laugh about it already has too much rope out. It'll tighten up on him soon enough."

They swung aboard as the train settled to a shuddering stop.

"I'm letting you run this expedition," Lew said dryly as they took seats on the single passenger coach hooked up at the front of the train. "You might, though, tell me what's the idea of pulling out so soon and going back to Hicks City."

Charlie glanced around to make sure the coach was empty save for themselves. "Two reasons," he began. "First, I want the folks in Wayne to think we got scared and pulled out. That is going to make it easier for us to dig to the bottom of this business."

"And the other?" prompted Lew.

"After last night I realized we need different equipment. To deal with river men we've got to have a boat, one that will move fast. We're going to get a speedy skiff, but something not so conspicuous that it will draw attention. Then we'll hook a four-cylinder outboard motor on her. If we don't, these pearlers will just laugh at us. We can't catch them with paddles."

"What's in that package you ordered from Hicks City?"

"Something to warm your heart, my boy." Charlie cut the string with his knife. "Two long-range automatic pistols. Load this baby up and shove it in your hip pocket. I saw them in the hardware store the morning we walked about Hicks City before breakfast. I wired extra money to get them up on the morning train. That was before I discovered we must have a boat."

"We going to pay for the boat ourselves?" Lew asked.

"When we buy it, but then I'm going to mail the bill to Sanderson. If he's the sort of fellow I think he is, we'll get the money as soon as he can cut the necessary red tape. We'll probably be the first wardens so equipped on the river."

Charlie spread his state map out on the seat before them.

"My idea is to stay out of Hicks City, because that's where they're going to think we went. This train stops at a siding just before the railroad leaves the river. We'll slip off there without anyone seeing us, if possible. Then we'll find that river skiff. The map shows a bigger burg than Hicks City about forty miles downriver but not on the railroad line. We can paddle down there and buy the motor. I'm sure we can find what we want there. Then we come back and drop in on Wayne Lake, ready for business."

"Good plan," approved Lew. "Why keep away from Hicks City, though? Think anybody down there is hooked up in this?"

"I think the man who dropped the notebook was down there on business," Charlie opened the book, pointed to a page and read:

"New man at W.L. won't come in."

Then he looked up at Lew. "I think the 'new man' was Lee, the warden before us. He wouldn't join them, and that is why he was found shot dead on the riverbank."

"We should have gone to the place where they found him and looked things over," said Lew.

"We should have," Charlie agreed. "Perhaps when we come back we will. It's probably too late to find anything to help clear up how Lee was shot, but you never know."

The train lurched around a curve so violently they were almost thrown from their seats.

"We took that curve pretty fast," grumbled Lew. "I wonder if the engineer saw it coming?"

The train continued rolling down the stiff grade with increasing velocity, wheels clanking and windows rattling like a volley of rifle shots. Charlie stood up to peer out of the dingy glass, but a sharper curve threw him over against Lew.

"Say," cried Lew. "I'm going up front and bust that engineer one with his own monkey wrench if he doesn't slow down."

He was rising from his seat when the car door ahead burst open and a brakeman with a lighted lantern in his hand shot inside, stumbling as the car swayed wildly from side to side.

"What the devil…" began Lew.

Before he could finish, the brakeman shouted, "Help me jam on the hand brakes! The air line's broke!"

He turned and led them out of the door onto the platform. "Hurry! Before she hits Catfish Curve!"

He pointed to the hand brake wheel above their heads. "Get up there and twist her down! Then you'll have to hold her. The lock dog's been broke a week. The cliff is four hundred feet high at Catfish. Remember that, and hold her down!"

Lew leaned out over the platform as Charlie climbed the steel ladder. They were rushing through the night at a furious pace, a heaving thunderbolt of steel.

Showers of sparks flew in his face from the grinding gears of the engine. The engineer had thrown her in reverse, but even the massive locomotive engine was no match for the force of gravity on a steep grade. Charlie was up on top of the rocking car now. Lew grabbed the ladder and pulled himself up, too. They braced their feet, twisting down the wheel of the hand brake with all of their strength. The footing was dangerously insecure, and Charlie ordered,"Wedge your foot under the edge of the walk."

The brake went down an inch at a time as they forced the handle around. A shout in the rushing wind on the opposite end of the car told them the brakeman had locked the brake ahead.

He was coming towards them and said, "If she don't slow, better jump to the mountainside. You'll be dead men if you stay on the train, and you'll be just as dead if you jump over the cliff on the other side."

"I'd say about the same bet either way," answered Charlie, glancing at the wall of rock hurtling past them on the inside of the grade. The roof under their feet started to lean out from the narrow ribbon of steel, sliding until they knew the angle was getting perilous.

"Get ready!" Lew shouted as he gave one more tug at the brake wheel. "She's going over!"

"Stay with her another second," Charlie grunted. "I think we're starting to slow!"

The car leaned out at another swerve, and then they felt the front end pull in as the car rounded the curve. They were slowing, but would it be enough to hold them on the track when they reached the deadly curve still to come?

The brakeman waved his lantern at them. He had passed back to the last brake wheel on the caboose in the rear. Whether his signal was encouragement or a warning to jump, they could not tell. But jumping into a flashing wall of rock at such speed would likely be deadly, too.

The better chance was to hope the train somehow held to the rails.

Then they were on the sharp edge of Catfish Curve.

The car bucked and rocked, groaning and squealing as they skidded into the curve, leaning out more and more as it gave into the momentum dragging the whole train off into space.

But the car settled back into an upright position, and, as Lew put it later, "humped up like a camel" one time before settling on the rails. With a wild surge of relief, they realized the worst was past. They jammed the wheel down another inch, and with the grade flattening out, 5 minutes later the train jerked to a stop.

Lew wiped his face. He was sweating profusely despite the cold night air. The brakeman hurried along the top of the train, his face the color of chalk in the light of the lantern.

"That was as close as I ever want to come," he groaned. "I can't figure out what went wrong with the air. We tested her before we left Wayne Lake, and she was OK."

The engineer and fireman were examining a coupling on the air hose. "Here it is!" the engineer cried. "Line has been cut clean through with a hacksaw!"

"Who would pull a stunt like that?" the brakeman asked.

"I don't know," the engineer replied. "But they must have got off at Crane's Siding, five miles from the curve. Who was it, Pop?" he asked the aged conductor.

"I didn't collect a ticket for Crane's," he replied.

"I saw a man jump down from the front end of this car," the fireman said. "If you didn't get his ticket, he must have been ridin' blind."

"But why?" asked the engineer as he helped install the new length of air line. Nobody had an answer for that.

When they were done with the simple repair, the engineer simply said, "All right—climb aboard. We're late already."

The brakeman swung his lantern. Lew and Charlie climbed back into their car.

"Well," said Lew as he sat down, "more from our friends back at Wayne Lake?"

"I think so," confirmed Charlie. "Their plan seems to be to terrify everybody. I don't think they actually intended to wreck the train. But they miscalculated the results."

When the conductor passed through the car they stopped him.

"Flag her down at the siding where the river leaves the road," Lew said. "We're going to get off there and walk. I got all the train rid-ing in mountains I can stand for one night."

They dropped off, suitcases in hand, and looked about as the train pulled away. As soon as the headlight had faded in the distance, they could see a dimmer light piercing the black night some hundred yards back from the tracks, on the river side of the right of way.

"We'll see if we can buy a place to sleep," said Charlie.

As they approached, a rangy hound dashed out barking. Lew spoke to the animal in a low, friendly voice. It stopped barking but sniffed suspiciously at his legs.

The cabin door opened. "Who is it?" a rough voice called.

"We're travelers, just off the train," Charlie replied, "We need a place to sleep tonight."

The door closed a few inches. "We ain't takin' in travelers," was the reply. "You better be gittin' on."

Lew stepped up to the door. The pungent smell of sour mash filled the air. They had stumbled upon a moonshine still operating full blast under the cover of night.

"We're going on downriver in the morning," Lew replied. "We got money, and we know how to mind our own business."

The man stuck his head out slowly for a better look.

"Waal," he hesitated, and then making up his mind said, "Since you put it that way, you kin come on in."

He pulled the door wide and they stepped into the room. A woman sat beside the fireplace holding a child in her lap. Two more slept in a narrow bed along one wall. A shotgun stood close by the door jamb, and Charlie saw a pistol-size bulge in the man's back pants pocket as he turned away from them.

"I'm runnin' off a barrel of mash," he said half apologetically. "I reckon you can smell it. Revenuers don't bother us much on the river, but we have to be careful of strangers."

"You can run off a tank car of it for all we care," Lew assured him. "All we want is a place to sleep and some breakfast. We'll pay you well for both."

The man nodded. "You'll find a tolerable bed in the attic," indicating a ladder leading up to a trap door in the ceiling.

"We'll turn in right away," said Charlie, already starting up.

"Here's a light," their host called, handing up a tallow candle.

They found a bed on the floor close to a square opening in the peak of the roof. A brief examination by candlelight showed it to be surprisingly clean. With a sigh of thankfulness, Charlie pulled off his shoes. "Don't wake me before five o'clock," he urged.

Lew leaned out of the opening that served as a window. "I could read a newspaper by this moonlight. Say, there's a small creek running right past the yard. Pretty handy to keep a boat in. I suppose our friend downstairs runs a boatload of liquor out every week."

"I suppose so," agreed Charlie. "But I'm more interested in sleep. Come on. Let's turn in."

The tinkle of a cowbell on the mountainside awoke Lew. He turned over impatiently. His muscles still ached, and he was very tired. Then, as he dozed off to sleep again, the door closed sharply below. Lew's eyes flew open at that.

The dog barked a single short yelp. Then there was the sound of a blow, and the animal whimpered before lapsing into silence.

Then a different sound brought Lew's eyes open again: the muffled roll of the exhaust of an idling motorboat. Lew lay in bed listening. Probably somebody coming upriver for the load of moonshine.

But then he realized the boat was coming downriver from Wayne. His curiosity fully aroused, he crawled out of bed to sit beside the open window and watch.

The roar of the boat grew louder until he figured it was even with the cabin. Then the noise died away in a stutter of small explosions.

After half a minute, the motor picked up again, and as Lew leaned out of the open roof peak, he saw the outline of a long, low boat flash past and disappear up the little creek. There was just time for him to catch sight of a dark figure hunched in the forward end. Then the motor died away again.

Lew turned back to bed. "Probably also been picking up a load from stills further up the river," he thought. "What's the matter with me, anyway? I've got to get some sleep."

But as he closed his eyes and tried to slip off, he kept listening for the sound of a starting motor. When everything stayed silent he thought, "They're making quite a stay of it."

Then he sat up as new sounds rent the quiet of the night.

Somebody was cranking up a four-cylinder automobile back of the cabin. It sputtered and then droned as the gear bands tightened. A door closed softly below.

Lew listened for a few minutes longer until he was sure that whoever had come speeding downriver in the racing boat was now driving away in a car.

When he next awoke, Charlie was shaking him.

"I hear folks below. We better go down if we want breakfast."

"I smell coffee and bacon," Lew declared as they pulled on his clothes. Then he told Charlie what he had seen and heard in the night. "Every little noise wakes me," he grumbled. "I suppose you slept through all of it."

"I never heard a thing until five minutes ago," his partner admitted as he finished lacing his boots. Charlie was used to Lew's unnaturally keen hearing and simply accepted it as fact.

"I've a notion to go snooping along the banks of the creek after breakfast," suggested Lew.

"Better not," advised Charlie. "Remember you assured the man that you were not a bit interested in his business."

"This doesn't exactly fit in with moonshine," argued Lew.

"I don't think so, either," Charlie agreed.

They climbed down the ladder, and their host greeted them with a surly growl. His eyes were red, and they guessed he had been up all night. He only grunted when they attempted conversation during the meal, glancing at them with suspicious eyes.

When the food was eaten, Charlie laid two dollars on the table.

"We want to buy a boat," he said as he rose, "something big enough to take us downriver."

At these words the man perked up, "Tate Wheeler makes 'em and sells 'em. He lives on this bank about four miles down. Be sure to tell him I sent you."

They thanked him and left.

"The only time he acted civil this morning was when we said we were going on downriver," Charlie observed. "He was much more friendly last night."

Two hours later, they were bargaining with the boat builder for a slender skiff, beautifully made of sawed red cedar. The outside had been planed and sanded by hand. It was light and buoyant,with a framework of solid white oak. The craft measured 16 feet in length and had a square stern—just the thing for a powerful outboard motor.

Charlie bought it with a twenty-dollar bill. Five minutes later, they were paddling downriver, headed for the city of White Falls where they expected to get a motor.

* * *

On the evening of the third succeeding day, a boat propelled by a lusty out-stern "kicker" chugged its way upriver, breasting the powerful current with a speed highly satisfactory to the pair of men who were its only occupants.

"If I don't shave pretty soon," said Lew, rubbing the stubble on his chin, "folks will think Santa traded his sleigh for a motorboat."

"You leave that beard alone," admonished Charlie. "Whiskers and ragged overalls are the best disguise around here. There's the cabin where we stayed. I wonder how the moonshine business is going?"

"I gather from your comment that we are going to investigate a little," grinned Lew. "Maybe we can camp half a mile upstream."

Which is what they did. Then they cooked supper and took a wagon sheet off the boat to make a lean-to shelter to sleep under.

"I want to see that other boat," announced Charlie. "If it makes regular trips up to Wayne, I figure tonight is as good a time as any."

"And if we don't catch it tonight, we'll camp here until we do," added Lew.

Night fell over the mountains. Another hour passed as they sat quietly beside their fire, waiting. Then Lew raised his head. Knowing how acute his ears were, Charlie watched his face eagerly even though he could hear nothing himself.

"We're in luck!" Lew finally said. "It's coming!"

Twenty seconds later, Charlie picked up the faint drum of a motor. On it came, growing steadily louder, and Lew grinned. "That's the same motor I heard before."

They crouched at the edge of the river. "He's hugging this bank," whispered Lew. "Will he see us?"

There was no time for Charlie to answer. A dark shape burst across the narrow opening between the trees that shaded their camp. It passed so close spray from the sharp prow of the speedboat soaked them both. As the craft shot by, Charlie caught one glimpse of a crouching figure at the helm. Then a helmeted, goggled face turned back for a quick look at them as the boat disappeared upstream.

Charlie leaped to his feet. "Throw our stuff in the boat," he cried. "We're going to follow!"

Chapter 4 – Battling Boats

Three minutes later, they were cruising upriver. The boat they followed was out of sight, but they could hear the motor. They had been lucky finding one of the latest model outboard motors at White Falls, one with a nearly silent underwater exhaust. They were confident the man in the boat ahead could not hear them following.

Charlie sat in the prow, night glasses in hand. At intervals he searched through the dusk. He did not want to run up too close and let the man know he was being chased.

Lew shoved the throttle over to near the last notch, and they went on plane with a third of the boat's length raised above the surface of the river. A tense hour passed before Charlie snapped a warning.

"Shut her down! I see him!"

Lew cut the motor and steered in close to the bank where the heavy shadow of pitch black night provided cover.

"He has slowed to refill with gas or else the motor is giving him trouble," Charlie guessed.

"It's a good thing he isn't hitting it at full speed," observed Lew. "With that motor, he'd leave us behind like a pay car passing a tramp."

The boat ahead sped up again and gradually pulled out of sight. Hour after hour they followed under a full moon that illuminated the center of the river.

Eventually sunrise glowed rosily on the horizon, and a fringe of mist smoked up the eastern bank. Charlie was steering now, and he swung the boat over into that light fog. He had been wondering how they could keep up the pursuit undetected when the sun came up. This band of mist would solve the problem for maybe an hour.

"We just passed Wayne," Lew called. "The village, I mean."

Half an hour more would bring them to the lake.

"He's slowing down—get ready to stop!" warned Lew. The craft ahead was slowing, and Charlie steered closer to the bank and cut speed until they were just holding their own against the current. He felt concealed in the thin mist but could not be sure.

The speedboat, now clearly visible against a background of white limestone cliff, was barely moving. And then, even as they looked, the boat vanished! One moment it was there, and the next all they saw was the rippling surface of the river and the white cliff.

Lew turned an astonished face to Charlie.

"That boat just faded away into thin air!"

Charlie snatched the night glasses from Lew and trained them on the cliff. The powerful lenses easily pierced the light fog, yet he saw nothing to indicate where the boat had gone.

"He had to go somewhere," Charlie said. "Unless he sank."

"Hardly," Lew scoffed.

"I wish we dared go over and examine those cliffs," Charlie said. "But I don't want this fellow, whatever his business, to know we followed him tonight."

They were in the wider length of river known as Wayne Lake. Charlie took advantage of that and steered as far away as he could from where they last had seen the speedboat. Lew pointed out several large piles of mussel shells on the bank. The poachers were making no attempt to conceal their business.

When they were even with the bank where Bill Smead's gang had chased them that first night, they discussed the narrow escape in hushed tones. Then they cruised on until they reached the upper lake, where high cliffs channeled the river back to a channel.

Charlie steered the boat up a small creek and landed it where fallen timber stopped any more progress. It was a good place to lie concealed, 100 yards off the lake. They covered the boat with cane, and when they were finished, a man might walk within 10 feet and never suspect its presence.

While Lew cooked breakfast, Charlie walked inland to see if they had camped too near to some mountaineer's cabin. But he saw no sign of a homestead for half a mile and decided they would be safe enough. After eating, they spread out the wagon sheet and blankets and slept.

"I knew my stomach would wake me up," Lew grunted as he sat up and reached for his watch. It was an hour past noon.

Charlie cooked lunch, and they both ate hungrily.

"Well, Generalissimo," Lew inquired around a mouthful of bacon and eggs, "what's the program for this evening?"

"Why, we're going to swoop down to the lower end of the lake and gather up several boatloads of pearl poachers," grinned Charlie. "Handcuff 'em and ship 'em to the capital for prosecution."

"In that case," Lew replied. "I'm going back to sleep. It should be a rather active evening, judging from our last brush with these boys. But the shooting won't be all one-sided this time," he added, patting the bull-nose automatic in his pocket.

"We might as well force this thing to a head," Charlie continued. "At the very least, we know Smead has been gathering mussels illegally. But I want to catch them actually poaching pearls. Then our case will be bulletproof for prosecution. We will drift in silently, using the bank for cover. When we're sure we have the evidence, we'll crank the motor and surprise them. We can run rings about a paddled boat."

"They can still shoot," Lew observed.

"That's the chance an officer of the law must take," Charlie replied. "But I think if we work fast, you can jump over in one of their boats and order the men to paddle to shore. I'll drive the other boat in ahead of me. That will mean at least four men collared, and if we get them jailed, I suspect the rest of the gang will go back to whatever they did before becoming pearl poachers."

"Sounds good," Lew agreed. "But I'm not shooting blanks tonight. The mortality rate among local game wardens has been a little too stiff lately."

He took the pistol from his pocket and sighted along the barrel. "I wish we could risk a little target practice," he sighed. "I would like to know just where to hold this baby."

"Keep the muzzle low and you'll have no trouble at close range," advised Charlie.

They slept until the shadows of the pines faded in settling dusk. Then they pushed the boat back out of the creek and drifted along, close to the bank. The tank was full of gas. They were all set and keenly alert for the planned raid on the poachers.

Charlie pointed to the bank. "That looks like the place we stole their boat to escape," he whispered. "Suppose we tie up there?"

They headed in and secured their craft to an overhanging limb, letting the length of the rope swing the boat in close to the bank. Then, still as statues, they waited for night to settle.

Lew sat in front, ready to cast off. Charlie's hand was on the starting rope of the motor.

An hour passed, a nerve-racking hour. As time dragged on both worried that the men they sought might not appear. Then Lew glanced over with a smile. "I hear paddles," he announced. "Two boats, I think, coming from different directions."

A fish jumped out in mid-river, clearing the surface with a splash that somehow relieved the tension gripping them. The bump of paddle against wood could be heard plainly now, and the indistinct murmur of voices. Charlie looked anxiously at the sky. The moon had not yet cleared the mountains. There was not enough light for them to see anything the men in the other boats might be doing.

But no doubt the poachers were at work. More bumping and then scraping sounds floated down the river, mingled with splashing and low-voiced commands. Lew looked back, his hand on the rope, his face a white blur in the night.

"Hold tight," ordered Charlie. "We can't see what they are doing, and they could give us the slip."

Minutes passed with the boats drifting ever nearer. Then the strip of dim light in the river's middle widened, and they saw with satisfaction the rim of an almost full moon emerging from back of the steep black mountains.

"There they are," Lew breathed, pointing to a black shape out in the river. "Let's get 'em!"

Charlie's pulled the rope.

The motor spun, coughed feebly once and balked.

With quick fingers, Charlie rewound the rope. The motor must start now. Any more delay would give the men in the pearl boats too much time to escape or dump what they were doing overboard. It was a little surprising they had not reacted to that single motor cough.

This time the sputter was followed by a sharp explosion, and then the motor purred to life. Charlie opened the throttle cautiously so as not to flood the engine, and Lew pushed the nose of the boat out into the stream. In a matter of seconds they were bearing down at full speed on two boats sharply outlined against moonlit water. The first was hardly forty yards away, and Charlie knew they must take that one first. The other was nearer the river center and would be easier to corral. There were two men in each.

Sharp exclamations arose from the boats, and the occupants began paddling like mad for the bank. It was going to be a close race, but Charlie knew they were speeding five yards to their one and would run alongside the nearer craft in a matter of seconds.

"Watch for guns," he warned Lew. Even as he spoke, a stab of fire from a boat ahead launched a bullet that hummed by head-high.

Lew crouched, and leaning out close to the water, leveled his pistol. "Drop that gun!" he ordered. "Or I'll shoot!"

Another shot crashed back. But he saw they would be together in another three seconds. So, rather than fire back, he scrambled to his feet, ready to jump over into the other boat. He already had decided to shoot to kill if he saw a gun leveled at him. But the men were paddling; they had decided not to waste time exchanging gunfire.

Lew wondered why they did not jump in the water and leave the incriminating evidence in the boat, until he remembered that many mountain folk never learn to swim, even those who spend their entire lives near a river. Swimming isn't considered recreation in the mountains. Charlie slipped their boat alongside the other. The pearlers had lowered their paddles, realizing there was no chance to escape. Lew shouted to them to surrender in the name of the law.

Lew's fingers closed on the other boat rail, but as he lifted his foot to step over, a clatter of explosions straightened him in surprise. He loosened his grip as an astonishing sight met his bulging eyes.

A motorboat was roaring through the night, the sharp prow bearing down upon him. In that brief second he remembered the craft they had followed upriver, and he realized it must have been lurking in the shadows on the opposite side, covering the pearl boats.

Charlie saw the danger at the same moment. He turned the helm to dodge the prow that roared straight at them, spray cutting from the sharp stem in two thin lines that curved back like jets from a fire hose.

Charlie realized his only chance to escape a crippling blow amidships was to turn their boat's prow straight into the speedboat. A broadside blow would cut their light craft in two and send them down into the river depths.

Just as the more powerful boat towered over theirs, he flung the steering arm over and swerved to the side. He did not miss the oncoming thunderbolt completely. Yet his quick reactions resulted in a glancing blow that rattled the seams of the cedar planking. But the wood held, and the boats shot apart.

Knocked off his feet by the impact, Lew hung balanced over the water for a perilous second—before tumbling headfirst.

Shouts of triumph came from the men in the pearl boats. But as they paddled shoreward to get clear of the melee, Charlie turned his motor on full throttle and followed. He saw he had no chance battling the faster, heavier boat on the water and determined to land and continue the fight on ground. But before he could gain 20 yards, the stranger came roaring at him again.

In his attempt to avoid being cut in two, Charlie had not noticed Lew's fall. Every atom of attention had been focused on turning the attack. He had recognized the crouching, helmeted figure at the wheel of the other boat, had seen the cold glint of metal as the moon flashed across the thick goggles over his enemy's eyes.

As the keen-edged prow reared up before him again, he had no time to maneuver, so he instead drew his pistol and sprayed bullets into the hooded cowl. In the dim light he saw splinters flying and grim satisfaction filled him as he pressed the trigger until a wide-open bolt told him the clip was empty.

With flying fingers, Charlie dropped out the spent magazine and shoved in fresh loads. As he flipped the gun up for a second barrage, he saw his first had turned the attacker, who now was shooting off into the shadows beneath the overhanging cliff.

With grim satisfaction, Charlie sent a couple of shots into the rear of the craft before it disappeared from view. Then he turned about and, for the first time, realized that the front of his boat was empty.

"Lew!" he called anxiously. There was no answer except the fading exhaust of the speedster roaring downriver. The two pearling boats had landed. He was alone on the lake.

Had Lew been thrown into the water? Or had he leaped into the pearlers' boat, completing their original plan? If he had landed with the pearlers, he might be in need of help. There would be four against one. Charlie headed full speed for the bank, cut the motor and coasted in between the two skiffs.

They were both empty, and Charlie knew he must act fast. Every second of delay would decrease his chance of finding Lew in time.

His partner had either landed with the boatmen or else he had fallen overboard. In either case, his situation was perilous. Lew might be injured, unable to swim. But knowing Lew was a strong swimmer, Charlie decided to search the bank first. Then he would speed downriver, calling as he went. He twisted the boat rope about a bush and sprang out on the bank. Then he climbed up the face of the cliff.

He heard a faint sound ahead as he fought his way up the rocks. Gnarled cedars tore at his hands and clothes. But the rattle among the rocks guided him. Someone was above, trying as desperately to escape as he was to capture. As Charlie scaled the cliff he grimly remembered how a few nights before it had been he and Lew scrambling over this same ground to escape.

He didn't care how many men were ahead. He was gaining rapidly and could hear panting gulps for air.

Charlie leaped, and with that tiger-like spring was able to grasp an ankle with his strong fingers. A mighty heave tore the fellow from the side of the cliff, and Charlie pulled him down where he could sink his fingers into the pearler's throat and choke off any cry.

"Yell, I split your skull," Charlie menaced with upraised pistol.

The fellow looked tall and brawny but young. He was helpless in Charlie's steel grip.

"Where's my partner? What happened after he jumped in your boat? Speak up!"

The pearler gasped and Charlie loosened his grip. The young man was shaking with fear. Something in Charlie's eyes chilled him like a blanket of ice.

"I don't know!" came a whimpering response. "He fell in!"

"Don't lie to me!" Charlie replied in a quietly dangerous voice. He felt sure the man was telling the truth but had determined to sweat his prisoner further.

"I tell you, he fell in the river!" the man whined.

There was truth in his desperation. Lew must be in the river or on its bottom. Charlie quickly shoved his gun in a back pocket and searched the prisoner. The man was unarmed. Charlie hauled him down to the riverbank and shoved him in the motorboat. Then, spinning the motor, he started chugging downstream.

"We're going to search," he said, "and you better strain your eyes. Finding my partner dead or alive is the only thing that will save you from a trip to the river bottom. Try to jump out, and I'll drill you before you hit the water."

Pistol in hand, Charlie swept his gaze between the glinting waves and the prisoner in the bow of the boat. He hugged the bends where he knew the current would swing a crippled swimmer.

The man in front was doing his best, Charlie decided, but as they covered the length of the lake, he was losing the small hope he had held at the beginning. It was the most impossible of wild goose chases, and he knew it.

"Who was the man in the motorboat?" he demanded suddenly.

When he saw the hesitation in the other's face, he raised his pistol and commanded, "Speak while you still can."

"I don't know. I never seen his face. He keeps that cover over it," the young man blurted out, evidently referring to the speedster's helmet and goggles. "He comes to get the pearls," the fellow added.

Although Charlie had given up any hope of finding Lew in the river, he kept the boat headed downstream, and as they flew along he questioned the prisoner further. "What's your name?"

"Sid Thompson."

"Was Smead in either boat?" Charlie demanded.

"No," Sid denied. "Smead wasn't with us. But two of his best boys were in the other boat."

"Well, I suppose you know I'm taking you in for illegal pearling. And for murder!"

Sid shivered at that. "I don't know what happened to your partner," he finally said. "But I never done nothin' but rake clams."

"Where does the speedboat dock?"

"I don't know," came a hesitating reply.

"You lie!" Charlie accused in an ominous tone and raised the pistol. But all the other would add were protests of ignorance. Charlie saw he could force no information concerning the mystery boat.

Charlie considered what he should do with Sid. He was evidently a worker, not a gang leader. Was it worthwhile putting him in jail? It would mean a trip to the county seat and lost time that could be devoted to finding Lew. Just where he would look for his partner he could not say yet, but he knew he must look.

"Sid, I'm going to turn you loose," he decided. "You've broken the law, and it's more serious business than you may realize. I know your face and I can find you again if I want. But I'm going to send you home, instead. Stay away from the river and Smead."

As he steered to the bank, Sid thanked him profusely. "I tell you," he finished. "Your partner fell in the river, and with that current, if he couldn't swim, he's a goner."

Was Lew alive or dead?

Would Charlie ever know what had happened?

Chapter 5 – Mysterious Enemies

"Where the deuce am I?" Lew wondered as he slowly regained consciousness. He could hear the steady throb of a motor and the sound of waves splashing against wood by his head. He was on his face, knees doubled up under his chin.

Putting everything together, his dazed senses gradually realized that he must be lying in the bottom of a boat.

His head ached terribly, and there was a suggestion of nausea in his stomach. Slowly he pieced together his last remembered thoughts. The mysterious speedboat had charged them just as he stepped over to the pearlers' boat. It had struck them a glancing blow. He had lost his balance and fallen. Then, a blow to the head must have knocked him out. His fingers explored the side of his head. Yes, there was a bump as big as a chicken's egg.

Charlie must have dragged him out of the water. He had a vague memory of bullets flying and wood splintering. Charlie must have had a busy time shooting it out with the pearl poachers and dragging him in at the same time. But where were they going now?

Lew suddenly realized that his clothing was dry. Anybody who had been fished out of the river would be soaked. He raised his head with a jerk. This wasn't their river skiff. Their motor didn't purr with that steady hum.

Then Lew realized that he lay on the bottom of the speedboat that had attacked them out on the lake. He must have fallen over into the enemy's boat. His heartbeat quickened. Wriggling about, he tested arms and legs to see how badly he was hurt.

One arm felt numb, but as he gently rolled over he discovered that he was lying on it. That could easily account for a lack of feeling. Lew raised the arm as strength returned to the muscles. Something was between his fingers. He thrilled with excitement as they closed over the butt of his pistol. Through his fall and then unconsciousness, somehow he had kept a grip on the gun.

Things were not so bad, now, and he thankfully remembered how he had restrained the first impulse to call out to Charlie. Why, this unknown pilot probably didn't even know he had fallen aboard. Otherwise, he wouldn't have left the gun in his hand. He was up at the wheel steering, unaware he had a passenger.

Lew grinned at that, raised his head and caught sight of the helmeted head bending forward at the helm, crouching to miss the spray from the cutting prow. This was going to be easy. There was only one man to deal with, and the advantage of surprise was all his.

Lew decided to take his time. He must take no chance of bungling this opportunity. He must wait for circulation and feeling to return to his arms and legs. He looked at the pistol, cautiously pulled the slide back and saw a load in the chamber.

Slowly and with steady caution, Lew got up on his knees. Thrusting the gun ahead, he crept toward the goggled figure that gazed unsuspecting ahead. The roar of the motor drowned out the creaks and clicks as he crawled over the 10 feet of boat that separated them. The pilot's seat had a rather high back; in fact, it formed the partition between two cockpits. Lew could just see the man's head over its edge.

This was just too good. Lew saw the whole mystery solved and the case closed in a minute more. He would order the boat turned landwards. Then, as they drifted into the riverbank, he would strip off that black leather disguise and see the face of the unknown who had attempted murder to protect the pearl poachers of Wayne Lake.

Lew leaned forward, leveled the pistol—and the boat motor missed with a popping sound. Lew hesitated, and as he waited the engine died. The boat slowed until they were coasting with little momentum. As he crouched, hesitating, Lew realized that one of Charlie's pistol bullets might have pierced the gas tank and allowed the fuel to leak away.

With a sharp exclamation, the hooded figure turned with astonishing quickness, and goggled eyes stared straight into Lew's.

For a second, Lew thought with odd distraction how much it resembled a diver's helmet. Then, realizing he must act quickly, he jerked back the hammer of the gun. But with surprising agility, the big man dove headfirst for the bottom of the boat, and before Lew could react to this unexpected maneuver, a heavy kick struck the pistol and sent it flying over his shoulder into the boat's stern.

Lew was taken utterly by surprise, and before he could recover, two strong hands were wrapped around his throat. As he twisted and tugged to free himself, Lew realized he was fighting a strength greater than his own. These were bands of steel, throttling the life out of him. Never had he closed with such muscle.

Grunting, they rolled across the boat's bottom. Lew's feet came together, braced on the edge of the raised floor, and with quick decision, he straightened his legs, pushing with all of his strength.

This would probably be his only chance, and he propelled his body straight over the side of the boat. His adversary tried to pull him back in the boat, but Lew had the leverage now, and with his full body weight in motion, the masked pilot could either go overboard with him or release his grip and stay in the boat.

He chose the latter, and Lew landed alone in the water.

His mind was working overtime as he dove deep with a powerful kick and stroke. He stayed under until his bursting lungs demanded air and then shot to the surface. As his head cleared the water, three quick shots flashed from the drifting boat.

He dove and propelled his body deeper underwater. The next time he appeared, he knew he must be many yards downstream of the boat. It was merely drifting with the current, he was both drifting and swimming, and he felt sure he would make it.

When his head cleared the surface no bullets struck the water. He could hear the man working on the motor, and with long, powerful strokes, Lew made for the bank. Three minutes later, he crawled out on land and turned panting to look for the boat. The motor was running now, and he saw the craft flash by downriver, disappearing from sight.

Lew wrung the water from his clothes, silently cursing himself for being a fool. He had the man completely at his mercy and had let him escape with his boat.

Wouldn't Charlie be disappointed? And foe the first time Lew wondered where Charlie might be. How had he come out in the battle while he lay stunned in the speedster?

The drone of a boat motor filtered through the night air, and for a moment he wondered if his enemy was turning back to search for him. No, this boat was coming downstream. Then he realized that it might be his partner and stepped closer to the river's edge, watching through the night. When he recognized the familiar lines of the boat he hailed.

Charlie's voice rang back over the water. "Lew? Thank Heaven!"

After he pulled the boat up to the bank, Lew stepped aboard, grinning sourly.

"I had almost given up ever seeing you again," Charlie said soberly. "What happened?"

He rapidly told Charlie of his failed attempt to capture the pilot of the speedster.

"That was some adventure!" was all Charlie exclaimed. "I'm so glad to find you alive I can't even bawl you out. But you did have him right at your fingertips, perhaps a solution to this entire business."

"We'll get the bird," Lew replied quietly. "He doesn't know that we know where he holes up the boat and changes over to a car. I say we run down to the moonshiner's cabin and grab his boat."

Charlie shook his head. "No, we don't want the just the boat. We want the pilot, too, and we want to catch him red-handed with pearls. We haven't any evidence that he is even involved with the poaching, don't even know who he is. No, that wouldn't do."

"Then we might as well return to Wayne Lake," Lew replied, "and camp on the bank until we get another chance to catch the pearlers."

"I can't think of anything better," Charlie admitted. "But tonight was our best chance. They may not work again for weeks. It will be a long wait, I'm afraid.

"I suppose we might as well move in at the village and forget about hiding. We can patrol the lake as game wardens. But that's about all we can do now."

"I need a new gun," Lew reminded him. "On second thought, a blackjack might be better. I wouldn't hesitate to use that."

"We'll order another gun," Charlie assured him. "And the next time you get a shot at that fellow, take it. Shoot him in the shoulder and then talk matters over, but wing him first. He's one tough customer."

They landed at the dock directly below the settlement, and Charlie looked at his watch. "About morning. Seems like we never get a chance to sleep nights. But let's rest a couple of hours in the boat."

Creaking wood and shouts awoke them. Wagonloads of railroad ties and cordwood were arriving at the village. They climbed the riverbank and knocked on the door of the station agent's home.

"What are the chances of breakfast?" Lew asked when the astonished face of Boggs appeared.

"I declare! I thought you boys had cleared out. Then I heard a right smart lot of shootin' on the lake last night. Maybe you know something about that?"

"There isn't much to tell," answered Charlie. "We got off to a good start and then muddled things up at the finish. We had them on the run for a while, though."

"What now?" Boggs asked.

"We're going to stay in the village. There isn't any chance left to surprise anyone. So we'll patrol the lake and enforce the law like regular game wardens."

"You may stop the pearling," Boggs allowed. "But you can't catch Bill that way. He's too smart."

"I would sure like to get a better look at Smead in the daylight," Charlie replied.

"You won't have any trouble. Smead hangs around the station every day at train time. Guess he's watchin' for more game wardens."

"Wayne Lake doesn't need more," Lew assured him quietly. "We will handle Bill Smead."

Maybe it was just the rising sun, but Lew could have sworn he saw a fresh glint in Boggs's eyes at that.

Charlie and Lew stayed in the village all day, strolling from store to store, at times trying to engage the locals. But with the single exception of Ben Scribbens, they had scant success. Everybody was civil enough, but then they edged away. Everyone seemed to know their purpose in Wayne Lake, and Charlie wondered how many of the men lounging about were members of Smead's pearl-poaching gang.

Ben was the lone exception, as friendly and affable as his uncle Asa back at the county seat.

As Charlie and Lew stood beside the station watching the crooked roadbed for the evening train, a powerful man of exceeding height rode into town. Thin to gauntness, there was no way to miss the bone and muscle. He rode in recklessly over the rough streets and halted his lathered horse before Scribbens' store.

Boggs nudged Charlie. "That's Bill Smead."

They watched with mounting curiosity as the man dismounted with an easy swing and then walked into the store. A minute later he came back outside and strode straight to where they stood beside the station. Boggs grunted and retired to his ticket office.

With rolling gait, Smead approached. His cool, insolent eyes surveyed them. A bare pace off, he finally halted.

"Waal," his half-sneering voice spoke. "So these aire the new game wardens? Heard you had a mite bad luck last night, boys."

Charlie felt the blood flush his face, but he stared mildly back into Smead's eyes. The man's face was big and broad, and if the nose had not been high and long and the chin truculently pointed, he would have sworn there was Indian blood in the man.

"Somebody said you wuz lookin' fer me," Smead continued smugly. "Here I be."

"Mighty glad to meet you, Mr. Smead," Lew replied evenly. "The air seems a little heavy. I think it might rain tonight."

Smead glared at him, searching for a sign Lew was poking fun at him. But Lew's eyes remained innocently polite.

Then the man sneered without any attempt to conceal his scorn. "If you're lookin' fer me tonight, I'll tell you where to come. I'm goin' ter be on the river in my skiff boat! Anytime after the moon rises, you'll find me thar!"

He spat contemptuously, whirled and strode back to the store.

"Could Smead be the man who piloted the boat last night?" Charlie asked as soon as he was out of earshot.

"No," Lew replied. "Smead is half a foot taller."

"Well," mused Charlie. "I see another sleepless night ahead. We must get an early supper and then start for the lake. It won't do to disappoint Bill Smead."

Night approached as Charlie fueled their motor's tank. They were still tied off in the village, waiting for the moon to light the river. This time, Lew carried a big-game rifle over his arm.

As they waited they could see dim, shadowy forms milling about the village. Smead's challenge had been overheard, perhaps deliberately broadcast, and now the locals were waiting to see if the new wardens would take him up on it.

Charlie wasn't afraid but slightly uneasy; he felt as though there was a trick in all of this, one they hadn't grasped. It was hardly reasonable for Smead to defy them like this unless he had a plan. But he knew they dared not back down or they would forever lose the respect and any possible support of the local people, something a game warden needs if he hopes to do the job right.

When the time arrived, a deft jerk of the starter rope set their boat motor spinning. They circled out from the bank, headed for Wayne Lake. The moon was up, and a strip of silver lit the center of the river, a strip that widened as they cruised along.

The lake soon spread out before them, and as they entered its lower end Lew pointed with the rifle barrel. "There they are!"

Two boats were lying close to shore. A man stood erect in each, working at something that was partly hidden in the bank shadows.

"They're pearling right in front of us," Lew growled. "Put me aboard that first craft; I'll get them to shore in a hurry."

Charlie ran up close to the skiff, surprised to see Smead himself aboard. Lew spoke first. "Don't move. I've got you covered. You're all under arrest!"

Smead laughed, loud and long. "Don't start anything you can't finish," he finally said. Charlie recognized an intentional effort to anger them. Lew rose to step over into the other boat. Then he realized the trick and drew back.

"Ha! Ha! Ha!" roared Bill. "Takes a mighty smart game warden to catch poor mountain folk runnin' catfish set lines."

And at that, the man in the stern of the boat began pulling up, hand over hand, a heavy trot line hung with baited fishhooks.

With an angry snap of his jaw, Lew pushed their boat away from the other, and Charlie opened the motor, heading back towards the village. Boisterous shouts of mirth floated across the water from the two other boats.

Charlie had not spoken. He saw there was nothing to be gained, and the less said the better. Smead had lured them out on the lake to make a joke of them, and he had succeeded.

"The son-of-a-gun!" snorted Lew.

"Clever, too," Charlie agreed. "I haven't any doubt but they will start to pearling again as soon as we are out of sight. But I won't go back tonight. I don't want Smead telling everyone how he kept us up all night watching them bait catfish hooks."

They returned to the village and tied up the boat. Then, after detaching the motor, they carried it up to Boggs' home.

The old fellow listened to their tale of woe.

"Right smart of Smead," he agreed. "Wants to make you the joke of the village. Then everybody will be on his side. He's tryin' to run you out that way."

It appeared to be working, because snickers greeted them at every turn the next morning. When Lew nearly lost his temper, Charlie decided it would be better to get his hot-headed friend out of the village for the day. They spent several hours exploring the mountains behind the settlement and did not return until evening.

Boggs handed them a package when they returned—a small, heavy bundle which they opened curiously. Inside the wadded paper lay a blue-black pistol.

"Mine as sure as you're born," Lew whistled. Charlie examined the outside wrapping. No return address as is generally demanded by express agents. Their names neatly printed—that was all. Somebody who knew them and their business had returned the gun—and that could only be one man.

Charlie tested the action. It seemed to be in working order.

"That beats me," Lew admitted.

"And me," Charlie agreed. "Just the same, we better test this pistol before you carry it."

After sitting up talking with Boggs a few hours they turned in to sleep. "This is the first full night's rest we've had in a week," Lew said.

The next morning, they walked out into the woods to test Lew's returned gun. Charlie stuck up a small target and emptied the magazine with slow, deliberate fire. After he examined the group of bullet holes he said, "The sights now throw shots a foot to the left. Smead knew you could get a new gun easy enough, so he doctored up this one and returned it thinking there was a chance you would carry it without trying it first. If you didn't, he was losing nothing but a handgun in the bargain. That's clever."

"Shows we're bucking a brain," Lew agreed.

They turned back to the settlement. And as they walked through the timber Lew kept an eye out. "Must be some game up here," he said. "We were sent up here to be game wardens, after all."

The pine and oak trees were close with brush hickory and persimmons. Lew's eyes were searching the branches for a squirrel when he stumbled over an exposed root and fell forward. And, just as he fell, a shotgun roared and a load of pellets peppered the tree trunk where his head had been before he tripped.

Charlie ducked behind a tree, pulling his gun. He peered around as Lew crawled back of another trunk. Then, as they watched, a shadow lit out through the trees.

Charlie dashed out, circling to the right. Lew followed, circling wide the opposite direction. They ran at top speed, and then, as the forest opened a little, turned back to each other. Their pincer movement trapped the man, who waited behind a thick oak trunk.

Chapter 6 – Cave Secrets

Charlie was beside the fellow before he could turn. Lew simultaneously gripped a shoulder on the other side. The shotgun lying across his arm must be the weapon that had sent the charge of lead directly for Lew's head. They stared, astonished, into the face of Ben Scribbens.

Lew was shaking with anger and also the shock of the close call. His tripping at that exact moment had been a miraculous stroke of luck.

"We've got you now!" he cried.

Ben looked into their stern faces, his own blank. Eyes blinking, he turned from one to the other. "What do you mean?" he finally asked. "A fellow shooting at a squirrel ain't agin the law, is it?"

Lew glared at him. "Bad things happen when someone sends a load of shot my way!"

"I didn't shoot at you," Ben protested. "I was aiming at a fox squirrel that ran up the side of a tree." He pointed to an oak halfway between where they were standing now and the place where Lew had almost been shot.

Ben's jaw dropped as Lew explained how narrow his escape had been. Standing quietly to one side, Charlie studied the man's face. If he was not telling the truth, he was indeed a good actor. His voice broke as he declared his relief that things had turned out so luckily.

"Well, for Heaven's sake," Lew finally said. "Next time make sure there isn't a man standing behind the squirrel you're shooting at. He's liable to shoot back. I know I'm going to next time," he warned.

Ben swore by everything he could call to mind that he would never take a shot again without first checking the backdrop. Then he invited them to walk with him on his morning squirrel hunt.

"One close shave is all I can stand in a day," Lew replied with a crooked grin. Ben's smile was strained, too, as he left them.

"Did he just lie to us?" Lew asked after Ben was out of hearing.

"I think so," Charlie said. "And I think this is how poor old Burt Lee got his."

"He couldn't shoot two of us and claim it was accidental," Lew said thoughtfully

"I don't know how he was going to work it," Charlie replied. "But I don't think that load of heavy shot was meant for a squirrel."

"Well, at least we know another member of the gang. The man from Hocks City, Bill Smead, the boy you dropped up on the riverbank, and now Ben Scribbens," Lew tallied up the score.

"I'm getting tired of hanging around here waiting for someone to pot us. Can't we start something ourselves?"

"Maybe," Charlie told him. "But first, we must examine the cliff where we saw the speedboat disappear. I think that's where we may find some answers to all of this."

Back at the village they stopped at Boggs' home where Lew straightened out the sights of the pistol. Then they picked up their motor, clamped it on the boat and started upriver.

"Deploy your fishing rod," Charlie suggested. "Act like you're trolling. It will slow us, but it will also make us difficult to tail."

After a long, slow boat ride, Lew finally said, "I remember those three trees on top of the cliff. Throttle down and ease in close."

Their boat hugged the base of the tall cliff. It was straight and blank, save for an occasional cedar which, oddly enough, appeared to grow out from solid stone. Streaks of gray and red marked varying strata of rock.

Charlie felt sure a discovery awaited them. A fair-sized boat could not just disappear before their very eyes. There had to be some logical explanation.

"Right about here," Lew said. "This is the place."

Yard by yard they eased upstream, barely moving against the current. Sharp as their eyes were, well trained by years of outdoor life, neither would have discovered the secret lair of the speedboat had not a faint trace of oil on the water caught Lew's keen gaze.

He pointed to the rainbow hue that flowed out from behind a bent and broken cedar, a thickly branched tree that drooped down the cliff almost sweeping the water. Charlie pointed their skiff right into it. When Lew grabbed the treetop, it swayed to one side disclosing a narrow channel back into the cliff.

It was a tight squeeze, but they soon found themselves under an arched roof of stone. Twenty feet farther in, a patch of blue sky showed where the arch broke opened into a narrow bay some 40 feet across.

It was a hiding place only revealed by that random streak of oil, and their eyes were riveted on a black speedboat with hooded cowl moored tight against the cliff. Charlie reached for his pistol as Lew silently propelled their skiff by pushing against the stone wall.

The boat was 20 feet long, narrow in beam with every line suggesting speed. Lew stared with unadulterated admiration at the gleaming 6-cylinder power plant.

"I knew it was powerful," he whispered, "but we haven't seen half. This baby could pull an airplane. She was never more than half open when we trailed her upriver."

They searched the boat thoroughly but found nothing except cans of fuel and tools, nothing that might identify the owner.

"A wonderful hiding place," Charlie finally said. "But to disappear under our eyes that way he had to have help moving the cedar tree. I would say two men were here. And the oil indicates the boat probably came back this morning."

They climbed back into their own skiff and shoved it to the end of the little bay. At the rear there was a strip of bank separating water from perpendicular cliff. On this bank were huge piles of mussel shells.

Without a doubt, this was headquarters for the pearl-poaching gang of Bill Smead. And then they saw something more. Setting back into the cliff 6 feet above the water was an opening, a cave with entrance blocked by a stout door of oak planks.

"That looks interesting," was all Lew said.

They landed, both now with guns in hand, and proceeded to the door. It was bolted and secured with a heavy padlock. Charlie laid his ear against it, but no sounds were audible. They returned to their boat.

"We've learned everything we can without breaking that door, and I don't want to do that, not yet. So far we have just a hidden bay and a speedster, both perfectly lawful. When we catch someone using them illegally, then we act."

"I see plenty of mussel shells," Lew observed, "but we couldn't prove how they got here."

"I figure this speedboat may be ready for another trip tonight," said Charlie. "Therefore, I think you and I should return right at dark."

"Think we can catch it loaded with pearls?" asked Lew.

"Pearls—or something else," answered Charlie.

Despite Lew's insistent questioning, he refused to add anything more. Whatever his suspicion, he kept it to himself.

They drifted back downriver and landed at the village, ostensibly fishing as they went. Lew even landed two nice bass.

They spent the afternoon in the station with Boggs. Not a word was said of their discovery, but Charlie encouraged the old man to talk, and he led the conversation back to Bill Smead whenever he could.

"Did Bill always live here?" he asked.

Boggs denied this vigorously.

"Smead came to the mountains from Oklahoma, about fifteen years ago, and he's been makin' trouble ever since."

"Smead is not his real name, I suppose?"

"Reckon not. I remember one time right after he arrived a package came and Bill saw it on my truck. It was a different name, but Bill took it sayin' it was for a friend that stayed at his house. I think it was his real name, but I can't remember just what it was."

"If ever do, tell me," was all Charlie said.

A letter from Sanderson arrived on the evening train. Charlie tore it open eagerly. After a glance at the contents he handed it to Lew.

Lew read it and then remarked, "Short and sweet. He admits things are not right, and he puts it on us to straighten them out."

"I like working for a man like that," confided Charlie. "He may lay the responsibility on our shoulders, but he'll back us to the limit. We will get paid back for the boat and motor, but don't look for any reinforcements from the capital."

"We won't need any," Lew answered. "Say, look there! An old friend came up on the train." A minute later they were shaking hands with Asa Wright. His greeting was hearty and cordial.

"Glad to see you, boys," he cried. "Doin' any good?"

"About fifty-fifty," Lew admitted.

"Boggs told me you were havin' a little trouble," Asa continued. "But don't get discouraged. These mountaineers may be a little rough, but they ain't criminal like Smead. Just keep hammerin' away."

"We intend to," Charlie replied. "Did you come up for a visit?"

"Not exactly. Ben's collectin' a note for me, and I thought he might need a little help. I got a few hundred dollars out with Wayne folks, you know."

He turned towards the Scribbens store. "Well, see you later."

As night fell Lew grew excited. "This time is going to be different," he kept repeating.

Charlie explained the plan. "We run our boat upriver and tie it up on the bank. Then we walk back down to the cave. I don't want the noise of a motor warning them."

"How are we going to get down from the top of the cliff?" Lew asked. "The wall was straight up and down."

"I've got a coil of rope for that."

"Won't someone see it hanging there?"

"No, because as soon as I climb down into the bay, you're going to pull the rope back up," explained Charlie.

"Like thunder!" Lew exploded. "I'm going down in with you."

But Charlie stuck to the plan, and at last, Lew agreed to stay up on the cliff. "If things go wrong, I can jump in the water and swim," Charlie explained. "You can cover me from the top with the rifle and be more help than if you were down there with me. I'll count on you holding them back in the cave."

"And I'll do it," Lew assured him.

After tying off the boat as planned, and hiding it again with cut cane, they followed the riverbank downstream. After a steep climb to the top of the cliff, they paused to rest. Then they pressed on, keeping a watch for any signs of habitation. They had left the village unnoticed and hoped nothing would warn Smead of their approach.

From this side it was not difficult to find the rend in the cliff with the little bay at its bottom. Charlie tied his rope securely to a tree and tossed it down.

Swinging over the edge, he lowered himself hand over hand. Lew was crouching beside the tree with night glasses in one hand and rifle in the other. They had heard nothing and believed the cave was empty, but Lew was taking no chances guarding his partner as he swung down exposed on the rope.

As his feet crunched in mussel shells, Charlie glanced quickly at the cave door. It remained shut. The speedboat was still in its place. He gave the rope a sharp tug and Lew drew it up.

Then the thrill of adventure seized him. He was alone in the lair of Smead and his gang. There was no escape save through the narrow channel that led out to the river.

Charlie decided to hide and watch from a pile of shells up against the cliff. He scooped out a trough and crawled into the pile, settling his back to the rock. Then he arranged handfuls of shells about his face so he could peer out without being seen.

The shells were damp and cold, and he was glad for the heavy clothing he wore. But in spite of this he began to shiver before he had been hidden half an hour. He wondered what Lew was doing up on the cliff. It must be a long wait for him, too.

Charlie believed they were close to solving the mystery that plagued the lake. He suspected something bigger than pearl poaching, though he had no idea what that might be. The murder of one game warden might be explained by a hot-headed moment, but not two.

Charlie also could not reconcile that expensive speedboat with such an operation. Cheap river skiffs made sense for gathering mussels, and he could not see where a powerful speedboat fit. Handfuls of smuggled river pearls, while valuable, would not call for secret night voyages in a speedboat. Charlie believed the gang was poaching pearls, might even be paying their expenses that way, but the ruthlessness of Smead and his men indicated something else was going on here, too.

Then he heard them coming, announced by paddles scraping on boat sides and the low buzz of voices. He flexed his limbs to restore circulation and clutched his pistol. From the sounds there must be two boats. The voices grew louder and he realized they had stopped at the mouth of the channel. As he peeked out from his heaped screen of shells, he saw the prow of a skiff poke into the bay. Four men sat in it.

The craft pushed by the moored speedster and landed at the cave, less than 20 feet from where he lay. Bill Smead was one of the men; there was no mistaking his height and broad shoulders. A smaller, broader man jumped from the boat beside Smead, and as he turned Charlie recognized Ben Scribbens.

Waiting tensely, Charlie wondered if one of the others might be the speedster pilot. If so, luck was playing this hand for him. But both were hill men, youths with drooping shoulders and lean, rangy limbs.

Smead was climbing up to the cave door. "Come on!" he growled back over his shoulder. "Time you wuz gettin' on the lake to work. We wasted enough time already."

He slid a key into the heavy padlock. Then with a wrench he pulled back the iron hasp and swung open the cave door.

"Git in thar and pick up yore tools," Smead commanded. The entrance was low. Smead had to stoop to squeeze his giant frame through. The other two followed like puppies at his heels.

Less than a minute had elapsed from the time Smead's boat landed, but in that brief interval Charlie had thought of and discarded half a dozen plans. If Smead entered the cave and locked the door after him, he would miss what he wanted most. His most earnest desire was to see what was going on inside that cavern. He felt that the secret back of everything was hidden in those rock walls.

A daring thought swept through his mind. Even before he had taken the time to consider what were its chances of success, Charlie crawled swiftly yet quietly out from behind his screen of mussel shells. He stood, brushed off his clothes with a quick sweep of his hands, and climbed nimbly up behind the men.

Dusk hung over the little bay, and Charlie knew the interior of the cave must be pitch black. He hoped to slip in behind the men, unseen and unheard. Once inside, he would have a few seconds to hide before Smead could light a lantern.

Charlie fell in at the rear and slipped through the door with the rest. Once inside, he lay back against a wall, out of line with the door where his silhouette would be outlined.

Everything was dark as he had hoped. He could hear Smead fumbling about, and he guessed the man was searching for a lantern. Charlie wanted to press in farther but dared not.

"Help me," Smead growled, and there was a general movement forward, everyone eager to jump at his command. This was Charlie's chance, and he walked swiftly after them until his feet trod on loose mussel shells. He stopped and thrust out his hands. There was a large pile of shells heaped against the side of the cave. Without looking further, he crawled on his hands and knees over them.

The manner in which they were piled gave only a shallow space to squeeze in, but he wriggled down, trusting that Smead's light would be feeble and that he would lie undetected. But as he settled down, loose shells on the very top of the pile came clattering down to the cave floor. Charlie's heart skipped a beat. It was another bad break just when things looked hopeful.

"What's that?" Smead's hoarse voice demanded. There was a scraping sound, a metallic click, and light flared up in the cave. Smead straightened up with lantern in hand and turned towards the pile of shells. Charlie clutched the automatic pistol in his hand.

Chapter 7 – Unmasked

With Smead turning a lantern on him, Charlie could not expect to escape discovery as he lay partially concealed in a pile of mussel shells. And then one of the younger men spoke, "Reckon I musta knocked them loose."

"Kain't you be a little careful?" Smead demanded. "Now git ahold of them tools and git busy."

Charlie watched the two mountaineers gather up rakes and what resembled long tongs, fashioned no doubt by a local blacksmith expressly for scraping mussels off the rocks on the river bottom. The two men turned toward the door with their load. As the last one stooped at the entrance he turned to ask, "What we goin' to do if them wardens come snoopin' about?"

"You needn't worry about them," Smead assured with a dangerous chuckle. "They won't be on the lake. Them two smarties are pokin' about this bank of the river lookin' fer me. Their boat is tied up two miles downriver. I seen them leave it. Now git ter work."

Charlie's scalp prickled at that. So he had seen them tie up the skiff. Did he also know Lew was up on the cliff?

Ben Scribbens spoke next. "You think they found the cave, Bill?"

"Naw," Smead returned. "Them boys couldn't find nothin.' Anyway, I told Hank and Lem to look about the top of the cliff after a bit. If they find anybody up thar, they got orders to pitch 'em in the river."

Charlie was deeply regretting his decision to leave Lew alone up on the cliff. He had learned nothing so far and had managed to get himself as good as trapped. Then, just as he was debating whether it might be wise to dash for the door, Smead's next words assured him it had been the right move.

"Come on, Ben. Let's git busy, too," he said. "The boys will stay out pearlin' until midnight. That will give us time enough fer what we really came here to do."

Smead walked to the entrance, looked out about the little bay, and then slammed the door shut. Charlie heard a bolt go home. Smead was locking it from the inside, against interruption.

Smead walked past where Charlie lay, following Ben into the depths of the cave. The lantern threw grotesque shadows of their swinging legs as it bobbed along. Then that also disappeared except for a faint glow, as they had turned a corner.

Charlie crouched behind the shells, waiting anxiously. He wanted to follow, but he needed to be sure neither of the men would start back and meet him halfway. There might not be a hiding place so handily located farther back in the rock tunnel.

But he also was fearful that if he waited too long, he might miss the secret work that was about to start. He desperately wanted to know what these characters really were up to. After five minutes had passed with no sign of a returning lantern, Charlie decided to risk it. He crawled cautiously from his hiding place and then noiselessly felt his way along the cave wall. Remembering the loose clam shells, he moved with pronounced care.

The cave was pitch black, but the glow that marked Smead's lantern was growing brighter. Charlie estimated he was 100 feet in from the entrance, and it appeared the roof opened into a higher vaulted ceiling, although he had no way of actually seeing that far up.

He reached the corner and crouched close to the floor where he knew his head would be less conspicuous at knee level. Then he peeked around the rock. Bill and Ben were working in the bright light of two pressure lanterns, heads together over a bench of rough planking. They faced back toward the passage, and if either showed a sign of raising his head, Charlie must duck hastily or be seen.

Smead's shoulders straightened, and Charlie slipped back into the safety of the shadowed passage. He heard Smead walk to the rear of the room, and then there were sounds as if he was washing something under water. "This stuff he brings gets worse every trip," Smead complained. "It's got to get better, or I quit!"

Charlie started to edge his face forward for another look when a sound back at the mouth of the cave sent his heart racing. Someone was hammering on the plank door. Smead exclaimed impatiently as he stepped forward. Charlie missed the words but was much more interested in concealment just then. He was sandwiched between two enemies, and there was no place to hide.

The light from the lantern in Smead's hand flashed into the passage and then fell across his face. A yard more, and Smead would be confronting him. Again he drew his automatic.

But then Fate intervened to save him again. As the shadow of Smead's feet projected out into the passage behind Charlie, Ben called. "I have to have that light, Bill. I can't see well enough with only one."

And with an impatient exclamation, Smead turned back, set down the lantern and came stumbling out into the dark. Charlie shrank close to the wall as the outlaw passed with scant inches of space between them. Charlie breathed a little more freely and set his hat firmly down on his head.

Smead reached the cave entrance, slid the bolt, and as the door swung open, Charlie saw the bay was bathed in moonlight. Whoever was out there began conversing earnestly with Smead. Charlie wondered if anything had happened to Lew. Was this man reporting the discovery of his partner?

Charlie decided this was as good a chance as he would get. When Smead and the newcomer passed on their way back to where Ben worked, he would slip out the door, shut it and lock it on the outside— trapping them inside. Then he would find Lew and take care of the rest of the gang.

Charlie waited for them to come back. But then a wild cry rang out from the cliff above. Charlie's first thought was of Lew, and he sprang to his feet, determined to rush out. He'd taken three steps when the cave door slammed shut. Before it sealed the frame, he heard a loud splash, the sound of a man hitting water.

Charlie stopped. The door was shut now, probably locked. Between it and him was Smead, armed without a doubt and desperate. He shrank back against the rock thinking hard. And then the distinct sound of the speedboat motor throbbed faintly through the heavy door.

The man talking to Smead at the entrance had been the pilot. He had taken alarm and was escaping.

Charlie groaned. Lew was in danger, perhaps already floating in the river. The mystery pilot, the key to the whole puzzle, was escaping in a motorboat. Everything had gone blooey.

Ben called, "What's goin' on, Bill?"

"Some kind of a fracas up on the cliff. I reckon the boys found one of them game wardens and pitched him in the river."

"Where's the boss?"

"He went outside to look around. Said he would stay until he saw what had happened."

"Did he take off?"

"Jest lookin' about on the river. He'll be back in time to take the stuff back with him."

Charlie was deciding what to do next when a crash exploded in the cave, smiting his eardrums as the air vibrated in waves. A bullet hummed past his head, so close he felt the wave of heat on his cheek. He fell flat on his face, gun out and ready for action.

"Thar's somebody in here, Ben!" Smead yelled. "I saw his shadow. Bring the lantern, quick!"

Light flashed out. Ben was bringing the lantern, and Smead would shoot the instant he could see a target. Charlie felt trapped as surely as a coyote in a No. 4 Newhouse. He crouched as close to the floor as he could, facing the man who approached. He would shoot either Ben or the lantern. And he knew he must act fast before Smead had a chance to use his own gun. It was going to take split-second timing.

Charlie was hoping Ben held the lantern at his side. But as he lay waiting with poised pistol, the glaring lens was thrust suddenly into his very face. Ben had pushed it out ahead of him, flooding the cave with light while keeping his own body screened behind a rock wall.

Charlie shot with rapid aim then rolled swiftly over to the center of the cave. If he had moved a fraction of a second later, the two quick shots that Smead sent crashing into the floor would have found a fatal mark. His own aim also had been true. With a jingle of glass the light went out, and he lay enveloped in darkness again.

A volley of oaths came from the cave door. "Get the other light, you dern fool! And don't hold it out for him to shoot!"

Charlie heard Ben run back for the second lantern.

In a desperate effort to gain time, Charlie picked up a heavy rock and pitched it towards Smead. It hit the floor with a crunch. Smead shot, as Charlie had expected. Charlie felt for another stone. He might not be able to work the same trick again, but he could throw it the other way and maybe delay Ben. He tossed the stone, and as it fell Ben stopped, listening and waiting.

"Come on!" Smead yelled. "He's just heavin' rocks. Now show that light!"

The showdown was coming fast. Charlie knew he would have to shoot or be shot. He rolled back and forth over the cave floor, desperately searching for some cover that would at least partly conceal him. But he found nothing, and the advancing lantern was swinging back and forth, throwing darting arrows of light.

"Maybe we better ditch the stuff, Bill."

Bill swore violently at that. "You're a fool! We'll have him in a half-minute if you just do something to help me."

The lantern flashed into view. Charlie shot and missed. Close on the heels of his shot Smead fired. But Charlie had rolled away, and the swinging shadows from the light also impaired his enemy's aim.

Charlie noted that Ben was swinging the light with regular moves. Just so far up and then so far down. Training his pistol as target shooters aim at a swinging bull's-eye, Charlie waited for the upswing and shot again.

It was a clean miss.

Smead fired twice in rapid succession, and again Charlie felt the sting of flying lead. Only the darting shadows had again saved Charlie from Smead's gun.

Just as he lined his sights for another desperate try, he heard a sharp click and then a suppressed oath from Smead. His gun was empty! The hammer had clicked on an empty chamber.

With a bold spring, Charlie was on his feet. He dashed at Ben, and as he caught sight of the fellow's form he shot from the hip.

Ben fell, dropping the lantern. Ben was groaning, but Charlie knew he had aimed low and the fellow could only be suffering from a broken leg, at worst. The pungent odor of gasoline filled the cave.

Then he turned back towards Smead, and softly as a cat, Charlie crept forward. As he advanced, the conviction grew in Charlie's mind that Smead was getting ready to dash. If he did, he would get one shot as the wide shoulders were outlined by the moonlit portal.

A smashing sound from the rear halted him. Then he realized Ben had dragged himself back and was destroying the evidence of their crime. Charlie could not let this happen, and as he half-turned, the cave door flew open and the tall form of Smead leaped out and away. It happened so quickly there was no time to fire.

A short cry sounded out in the bay, and then another splash.

"Where are you, Charlie?" Lew cried into the darkness.

With a glad shout, Charlie answered. "I'm in here. Smead just ran out. Take care of him."

"I already have. I tripped Smead into the water. I'm waiting for him to come up for air, now. Then I may just plug him."

Charlie ran back to where Ben Scribbens was working. He pulled a tiny flashlight from his pocket and threw the slender beam around the corner. Ben was propped up against the workbench pounding something with a hammer.

Charlie thrust his gun in Ben's nose. "Drop it!" he ordered. "Now turn and crawl out the cave door."

Ben whined, crying that his leg was shot and he couldn't walk. But Charlie was firm. He saw the leg had merely suffered a painful wound in the fleshy part of the thigh. He was losing blood, though, and undoubtedly growing weak. Charlie decided that would just make him easier to handle.

When they finally reached the outside, Lew was standing beside the water. "Smead never came up. He must have swam underwater all the way out to the river."

"That makes two out of three to get away," Charlie replied ruefully. "You nearly had your hands on the speedster pilot. And now Smead slips out, too."

"Not so fast," Lew replied. "I haven't been watching the moon all evening. I got that pilot tied up like a Christmas turkey."

Charlie grinned at that. "Watch Ben; he's winged but not dying. I'm going back to bring out the evidence that will lay these fellows in cold storage for twenty years. Maybe more.

"Better tie up Ben," he added. "Then go back and stand over that pilot. Don't let him get away again!"

"Never fear," Lew grinned. "He's still batty from the jolt over the head I gave him."

Charlie ran back inside, gathered up what he needed, and as he came out of the cave, looked down in time to see the dark prow of the speedboat loom in sight. Lew was pushing it up to the bank.

"Where's the prisoner?" Charlie called anxiously.

"I'm sitting on him," replied Lew. "Goggles and all. I thought I'd leave the unveiling until the audience was larger."

Charlie carefully deposited his load in the boat.

"What is all that stuff?" Lew demanded. "I'm dying to know what this has really been about."

"It looks to me like a counterfeiting operation," Charlie answered. "I don't know much about that game, but here are a few samples of their work. If you search our mysterious friend, I believe you will find a wad of bogus bills on him, too. We've got enough to convict the gang—no doubt. And now we take a peek at him," continued Charlie. "Although I've already got a pretty good idea who it is."

Lew turned to him in surprise.

"Strip off the goggles and helmet," ordered Charlie. "See if it isn't an old friend we've only met twice."

Lew obeyed and then stared into the face of Asa Wright.

"Well, I'll be a son-of-a-gun!" breathed Lew.

"As soon as I discovered Ben was mixed up in this business," Charlie explained, "I picked Asa as the boat runner. He gave such an impression of indolence when we first saw him. It was the best kind of a disguise. He's actually a pretty stout fellow—as you found out."

Lew grinned ruefully at that. "Go on. Spill the rest."

"There isn't much," said Charlie. "Smead must be the old-timer in the game. Take my word for it. When his record is looked up, he has done time for counterfeiting. Wright planted him here in the mountains to run the production end. The pearls were just a blind. They paid expenses and enough to the locals to keep them more or less in sympathy with the gang. Poaching river mussels isn't considered much of a crime in the mountains."

"I guess you knew a lot you never told," Lew said.

"Nothing for sure," Charlie assured him. "Just suspicions. Even Smead's gang didn't know what went on in the back of that cave."

"I wish we had Smead," Lew mourned. "That would make the party complete."

"We'll get him," Charlie predicted confidently. "He will be a much wanted man as soon as I get in touch with the federal men at the Capitol. They may not take much interest in poaching river pearls, but counterfeiting U.S. currency is a whole 'nother matter."

The End

Silver Blacks of Folly Farm

Chapter 1 – The Unlocked Door

Black pines towered menacingly over the ribbon of concrete road. Low-flying storm clouds marched across the sky like waves of infantry, hurling bursts of sleet against the car's windshield. It was early fall in the Northwoods, barely 50 miles south of the gale-lashed shores of Lake Superior. Night was falling fast, and Lew leaned nearer the steering wheel to peer out through the wet windshield glass.

"B-r-r-r!" he shivered. "Guess we stayed too long down South. Either that or my blood must be getting thin. We need a heater in this sedan if we plan to do much winter driving."

Charlie yawned. "We're almost there. I'd say ten miles more and we'll land at the farm. Thank Heaven they have good roads up here, even if the towns are mighty thin."

After a moment of silence in the car, Lew permitted himself the luxury of self-congratulations. "Quite a clever idea of mine, if I do say so," he began. "For ten years we've puttered around in the woods trying to make money trapping fur. Lived on sourdough biscuits or no biscuits at all. Now we're going to be the big shots of the fur game. We're going to raise our fur and sell it right on schedule."

"I admit this looks good," Charlie replied. "A nice, quiet winter with silver black foxes right in our dooryard ready to skin at the peak of prime. But don't go cashing any checks just yet."

Two headlights suddenly burst around a curve in the road. The powerful glare dazzled Lew's eyes through the rain-streaked windshield, and he swung the wheel just in time to miss a large car that roared past, slightly left of center.

"That son-of-a-gun," Lew growled. "He just held to the center and let her rip."

"Look out!" Charlie warned. "Here comes another!"

Again lights bore down upon them through the black night. Again, Lew swung the car over until the wheels were just off the pavement. This time a towering shape swept by.

"They sure travel up here," Charlie observed. "I never saw such

56

bright headlights, either. It's like they don't know what a dimmer switch is for."

They drove on in silence for another 10 minutes before Charlie spoke again, "Watch out for the farm gate. The house sits back a from the road, and we won't see it in the dark. So go a little slower. We were only out here once."

When Lew saw a man walking the road berm with a lantern, head and shoulders hunched forward into the rain, he announced, "I'm going to ask him where we are."

After carefully pulling over to avoid splashing the man, Lew rolled down his window and called, "Howdy! We anywhere near the Patton Fur Farm?"

The man approached the car, reluctantly it seemed, and peered in with distrustful eyes. "Patton Fur Farm?" he repeated. "I never heard of—wait a minute. You mean the Folly Farm. Frenchman's Folly, they call it here. I heard a couple of strangers bought it last week from Patton. You know them?"

"We're the babies," Lew declared, a trifle importantly.

The other glanced at him quickly. "You got a bit of road to travel yet. 'Bout five miles. What you aimin' to do? Raise foxes?"

"That's the program," Charlie spoke up.

"I knew Patton was sellin' out," the man replied. For some reason he seemed willing to talk now, despite the rain.

"He's been tryin' to sell for over a year," the man continued. "I hope you boys didn't pay too much. Patton is a pretty slick boy. He came here from Chicago and worked a few smooth ones on the locals before they found him out."

"What's the matter?" asked Lew. "Things looked all right to us last week. Land is level, lots of good timber. House is sort of rundown but roomy, and we can fix her up. Patton threw in ten pair of dandy breeders, nice silver blacks that are worth some dough themselves."

"I don't reckon Patton told you he didn't raise a single pup last year?" was the reply. "Or the year before? Well, I wouldn't neither if I wanted to sell as bad as he did."

"No, he didn't," cried Lew. "He told us that he raised over a hundred young foxes."

"Well, he didn't do no such thing," chuckled the man. "I've lived here all my life, and I know. The mothers got to bitin' the pups and nary a one pulled through. That stock is inbred, if you ask me. The best you can do is pelt 'em all out and start over. That's what I'd do."

Lew's face was lengthening rapidly.

"Yes," went on the native, "if you paid Patton four thousand for the place, you didn't do so bad. The land and house are worth half of that, and the animals might bring the rest for the pelts. They're big ones, bein' so old."

The gloom inside the sedan grew so dense the dreary evening outside seemed to brighten by contrast. They had given Patton exactly twice that—eight thousand dollars, every cent they had except a couple of hundred laid aside to buy winter supplies and grub.

"Where did the farm get that name—Frenchman's Folly?" Charlie asked in an effort to turn the conversation. If they had been swindled, there wasn't any use to let everyone know about it. That would only brand them as easy marks for every sharper in the county.

"A queer duck of a Frenchie came over from the Canada side and built the place," the man answered. "That was about 30 years ago. Everybody thought he was crazy to build so big a house. Most of us live in cabins, you know. There's a dozen big rooms in that shake-down, a regular hotel. So we got to callin' it Frenchman's Folly."

He started to walk away, then turned and said, "Frenchie got hisself bumped off one October night 'bout ten years ago, such a night as this. And folks say he comes back to the old house with a lantern lookin' fer something he hid there."

Then he grinned and splashed off down the road.

Lew slid the car into gear, stepped on the gas pedal and growled, "I never thought of myself as a babe in the woods."

"Go easy on yourself," advised Charlie. "That fellow may have been stringing us, trying to discourage us like folks do when a newcomer buys in the neighborhood. He may know nothing about foxes. Anybody could see Patton was a slacker. It takes hard work to run a profitable fur farm, and you know we can cut that. Things may be perfectly jake. Cheer up!"

"I hope you're right," Lew replied in a more cheerful tone. "And it won't be long until we know. We'll get the straight scoop from the man who still lives on the place taking care of the foxes. He'll know."

"I was thinking of him," began Charlie. "We can't afford to pay a hand, regardless. I say we keep him on for a week or two until we get the hang of things and then let him go. I didn't fall any too hard for him last week. Looked like he might be a little daft."

"My thoughts, too," Lew agreed. "There! That looks like the gate. I think we're there."

He turned off the road and drove in past an open gate of sagging boards. The grass-grown drive looked solid enough, but Lew drove slowly. After an all-day rain the ground might be soft enough to mire them. A rambling board structure sprang up ahead, gradually taking form in the car's lights. Lew parked, got out and headed for the front door. "Look!" he cried out in surprise. "A light inside."

Charlie followed his pointing finger. Was a light fading away from a front upper window? Or was it just the reflection of their car's dying headlamps? Charlie shivered, recalling what the man back on the road had said about the dead Frenchman's nighttime returns.

"Looked more like glare from the car lamps," he said.

"Or a lantern," Lew spoke in a low voice.

Charlie slapped him on the back. "Snap out of it! I'm ashamed of you falling for a ghost story."

"Well, we'll find out soon enough," Lew answered. But he stepped slowly up on the sagging porch before rapping loudly on the door. No answer came from within.

"Try again," Charlie advised, and again, Lew hammered vigorously on the wood. It stayed as silent as a tomb inside.

"If I had only ..." Lew began. Then a faint crash echoed from the rear. "That was a door slamming!" whispered Lew.

"Could have been the wind slamming a loose screen door," Charlie offered uncertainly.

"I'm going to look," Lew said. "Somebody was in this house with a lamp when we drove up, and now he's slammed a door on his way out the back. Come on!"

He pulled his service pistol, snapping back the bolt to load a chamber under the protection of his coat. Then he strode around the building with long, noiseless strides. Charlie swung in beside him. "Did you pull the car key?" he whispered. "We don't want anybody running off with the car while we're around back."

"Of course," Lew nodded assent.

They turned the corner and found a small yard overgrown with brush. Hugging close to the house, they crept shoulder to shoulder down the long side. Back a hundred feet were more trees, pines that sang a mournful dirge as the wind howled through their needles.

When a door loomed beside them, Lew halted before it and listened. Then he grasped the knob and pushed. The panel swung noiselessly open, and they peered in through the frame. Pitch-black silence oozed out with the mustiness of a prison's poison breath. Their flesh began to crawl in spite of the habitual firm grip they kept on their nerves. Lew thrust the pistol out from under his coat, and Charlie shot the concentrated beam of a flashlight over the threshold.

Inside the room well back from the threshold they saw plainly the imprint of a wet shoe mark on the dry pine floor. "Guess it wasn't the wind," was all Charlie said as he closed the door softly. They turned and half-ran back around to the front where their car stood.

"Well," remarked Lew. "I suppose you want to go inside and sleep where the ghosts can poke their bony fingers in your eyes. No, thanks. I'll spread my blanket over the car seat and catch what few winks I can out here."

"Don't tell me you're afraid of an empty house!" Charlie demanded in surprise.

"Course not!" Lew snapped. "It's the ones that aren't empty I don't like."

"Let's go inside and look around," Charlie insisted. "A car seat is no better than a park bench for sleeping. The house will be warmer, and I think ten hours of solid slumber will do us both a heap of good."

"If the goblins run off with us like they did Orphan Annie," Lew growled, "don't blame me!"

They piled the sleeping bags on the porch and Charlie used the old-fashioned skeleton door key Patton had turned over to them. As they stepped inside, they played their pocket lamps over a wide, deep entry hall. Three doors opened from it into adjoining rooms, one on each side and one at the rear. A narrow, steep stairway led up to the second floor. The ceiling was high, giving the room an eerie sense of space. As Lew said later, it was like walking into a deserted cathedral.

Their steps echoed off floor boards that did not give or squeak, indicating the building had been strongly constructed.

Lew motioned to the stairs. Charlie pulled back on his arm. "Take the lower rooms first," he whispered. For some reason, neither cared to speak louder than absolutely necessary.

Lew opened the door to the right, and Charlie played the beam of his light swiftly over the walls and ceiling. It was empty. In swift succession they checked the other rooms and found not even a stick of furniture. Just worn pine floorboards and the musty odor that fills a deserted house.

They passed into the rear wing. Here was the door they had found unlocked and had opened from outside. Three wet shoe marks were fading slowly on the dry wood. The footprints led inside from the door towards the center of the room and then stopped.

"Where did he go from here?" asked Lew.

"I suppose his shoes dried when he got that far," explained Charlie. "He made these when he entered. When he ran out, of course, his feet were dry and left no mark."

"Maybe we're all worked up over nothing," Lew began. "It may have been a hobo looking for a place to sleep. And we scared him off when we drove up."

Charlie agreed with a nod and then added, "Can we lock this rear door, anyway? I'll sleep better if it's fastened."

The lock was a cast-iron affair with a rusty broken bolt. The key would not turn it. "Find a stick and wedge the door shut," suggested Lew. Charlie stepped out in the dark yard and returned with a broken board. Lew swiftly whittled it into a long wedge and used that to block the door at the bottom.

"We'll get a real lock as soon as we can," Charlie said. "Now, for the upstairs."

They retraced their steps to the front hall and then went up stairs that creaked ever so little under their weight. The wide hall upstairs was almost a duplicate of the one below. They found six large rooms, all bedrooms with high ceilings and tall, narrow windows. As they stepped into the last room, Lew whispered, "This is where I saw the light—in that window."

He stepped across the threshold and stumbled over a slender, square-edged pole. He kicked it to one side and passed on inside the room, but Charlie paused and picked up the pole. He saw narrow marks cut into the surface and realized he held an 8-foot pole graduated in feet, such a measure as loggers use when checking rough timber. One end was graduated in inches for a short distance.

"Funny we find this here when every other room has been bare," Charlie observed.

"We'll use it when we cut firewood this winter," Lew replied, dismissing the pole from his thoughts. "Well, we've looked in every room. So I suppose we can go down and spread the beds. Or would you rather sleep up here?"

"Hardly," Charlie answered with a grin. "We'll camp out close to the front door and the car."

They spread sleeping bags in the front room by the window that faced their automobile. Beneath the rolled up coats that served as pillows they stashed pistols and flashlights.

Charlie sank into slumber first. But then he awoke with a start, ears ringing from a loud crash that overwhelmed the rattle of the storm outside. He grabbed his lamp and turned the light towards Lew. But the other sleeping bag was empty. As he played the light about the room trying to find his partner, Charlie realized what had brought him so sharply out of sleep. It had been the report of a gun. The smell of burned powder filled the room.

Chapter 2 – Invisible Feet

Clutching pistol and electric torch, Charlie ran to the door and shot his light shot out into the hall. Then he heard footsteps, switched off the light and stepped back from the doorway before calling, "Lew!"

"Okay!" Lew answered and then stepped into the room. "I woke up when a board creaked. You know how good my ears are. Someone was going up the stairs in the hall. I got my gun and light and slipped over to the door. I was going to trap him upstairs. But he heard me, I guess, because just as my light went on, I saw someone jump down three or four steps and then light out for the back room."

"What did you shoot for?" asked Charlie.

"I had the safety catch off the gun, and when a shadow jumped down the steps my finger tightened instinctively and the pistol went off," Lew replied sheepishly. "He went out the back."

Lew led the way into the rear room. The door was open, and the wedge they had used to hold it lay in the center of the room.

"See those tracks?" Lew pointed. "Some coming in and some going out? He may be hiding out in the brush. It's such a pleasant thought that I'm going to sit up until morning."

As they turned back towards the sleeping bags, Charlie turned his light on his watch. "Well, it's after four o'clock. No use either of us trying to sleep now."

"Morning can't come any too soon," Lew agreed. "There's a lot of things to check out. But first, I want to speak with the man who is taking care of the foxes."

"His name is Anton Blierut," Charlie offered.

"Whatever his name is," Lew replied, "I want to know if he was snooping around the house last night—and why."

"Better go easy," advised Charlie. "If he was in here he won't admit it. And if he wasn't, he'll resent the suspicion."

Dawn broke cold and clear with fleecy clouds racing over the trees. Lew and Charlie both climbed out of their sleeping bags to watch the first glow of morning fill the sky. But then each dropped off for a short nap. Now they were stiff and cramped.

Lew went out to the car and returned with their folding camp stove and a bundle of food. As he pumped up the gas tank, he remarked,

"This place looks twice as big as it did last night. What'll we do? Rent out apartments or something?"

"We might invite our mysterious visitor to move in where we can keep an eye on him," grinned Charlie. "No, we'll shut eleven rooms and live in one. I say we fill the back rooms with dry firewood and hang the pelts upstairs."

Charlie finished preparing breakfast and they began eating.

"Last week when we were here," Charlie began again, "I saw a tumble-down shed back of the house. Most of the boards looked sound. I suggest we pull it down and spend the day making rough furniture. A table and benches. Then a few cupboards."

"Good idea," Lew agreed. "But first, I'm going upstairs to look around for sign of the fellow who sneaked in last night."

Charlie stayed downstairs, listening to Lew walk swiftly from room to room, once pausing for a minute, and then coming back down. Charlie looked up from his plate. "Find anything?"

"Nothing," Lew replied with a puzzled look. "But the measuring pole I stumbled over last night is gone!"

"Gone?" Charlie repeated. "Then your visitor made it upstairs after all. I thought you caught him on the way up."

"I thought so, too," Lew replied thoughtfully. "Why do you suppose anybody would take such a chance to retrieve a homemade measuring pole?"

"Beats me," Charlie finally said. "I could make a pole like that in a few minutes. Anyway, we must lock all of the doors so they'll stay locked. I don't want to be disturbed again tonight."

"That makes several jobs on the schedule," Lew replied. "Build furniture, bolt up the doors, and interview Anton. Which comes first?"

"After the dishes are done, let's walk down to Anton's cabin."

"That won't be necessary," Lew announced, looking out the window. "Unless I'm mistaken, Anton is stepping up on the porch."

In answer to a firm rap on the door, Charlie called out to enter. The door swung open, and Anton Blierut stood on the threshold, peering in at them with bright black eyes. He was unmistakably French, undeniably dirty, and square of shoulder with enormous depth of chest, a man with a torso like a barrel. Charlie correctly guessed that prodigious strength lurked in the thick arms and shoulders.

Long rolls of black hair curled out from under the coonskin cap on his head, and a pair of curling mustaches framed his mouth like the horns of a Texas steer. A three-day stubble bristled over chin and cheeks, but the eyes were alive with energy and good spirits.

"Good day, M'sieurs! Good day!" Anton's face broke into a wide grin. "When I feed foxes I see strange car in yard and say to myself, 'Anton, thees be new owners.' Am I right? Yes?"

"Correct," Charlie said. "We're the new owners, and we're glad to see you." He gripped Anton's hand firmly. "Foxes well?"

"Everything ees good. Nothing bad but dee weather. You eat so soon? Too bad. Anton tell wife to feex breakfast for you."

"Ask again about noon and we'll come running!" Lew replied.

"She will be honored," the man replied. "And now, M'sieurs, you wish to see things? I show you pens and foxes. Timber and fields. I show you everything. If you ees ready, we begin."

Anton led them around the house and through the timbered yard behind. A clearing of about 5 acres lay beyond, with long, narrow pens of woven wire. Back of these fox pens and on each side were more strips of timber.

A well-worn path led through tangled grass and briars to a shed serving as feed and store room. Charlie was examining everything with a cold, calculating gaze, wondering how he could have missed so many indications of decay, which now seemed apparent.

Anton paused before a padlocked gate into the enclosures. Lew looked eagerly at the long black shapes that jumped from the low roofs of the kennels and disappeared inside.

"M'sieurs must be careful," Anton explained. "After dees fox know you, then you go inside. Now, you better keep back."

"How many young fox did Patton raise this year?" Lew asked.

Anton shot a quick glance at him. "M'sieur Patton not buy right feed. Foxes fight and all dee young die. Not a one live. Everything she go bad."

Lew looked grimly over at his partner.

Anton shrugged his bear-like shoulders. "M'sieur Patton he tell you different. I know, I hear. But what can Anton do? He still work for M'sieur Patton."

"I don't blame you," Charlie broke in. "But there isn't hardly anything right with this layout. I started reading up on fur farming as soon as we bought the place, and I can see a good many things that are just not right."

He turned to Anton and asked, "Do the old foxes fight through the fence wire?"

"Of a certainty, M'sieur. They bleed all over the snow, and

M'sieur Patton, he do nothing."

"They fight like that when there is only a single fence between pens," Charlie replied, turning more toward Lew. "The first thing we must do is build double partitions everywhere with at least two feet between. A double partition will also help prevent disease from spreading through the animals."

"I'm not wild about these kennels, either," Lew observed. "They sit right on the ground. I'll bet they are damp and hard to clean. This ranch needs a thorough overhauling. We'll be busy boys for a couple of months."

They walked around the pens. Charlie was anxious to count the stock and make sure 20 animals were in the kennels. But he took Anton's advice. It might not be wise for strangers to enter the pens and agitate the stock. They turned back to the house.

"We'll unpack our stuff," Charlie informed Anton. "But then we'll be down to your cabin for lunch. And until we get better acquainted with the foxes, you can keep on feeding and caring for them. Got enough feed on hand?"

"Plenty oats and corn," Anton shook his head sadly. "But no meat, M'sieur. Dee meat, she been gone over a month."

"We must get some fresh meat," Charlie agreed. "Any neighbor maybe got an old horse they will sell cheap?"

Anton shook his head no. "We buy up all dees old animals last year. None left."

Charlie shrugged his shoulders.

"This doesn't seem to be such a swell fox ranch after all, Lew. But the climate is OK, cold enough with plenty of humidity, both necessary to produce first-class fox pelts. We'll have to work out the problems as best we can."

As Anton returned to his cabin on the other side of the pens, they caught sight of his roof behind the pine trees. Back at the big house, Charlie opened their tool kit and laid out saws, a plane and two hammers then turned to his partner.

"Suppose you drive back to Bundy Flat—that's the closest town—and pick up some of the things we need. Get a strong bolt for each of the outside doors. In fact, get a pair of them for the outside doors and one bolt for the inside ones, too. We're going to bolt this old castle up so no more ghosts disturb our sleep. And we need a lot of nails, two rolls of roofing to patch up the feed shed and hinges for the cupboards we will make. Believe me, we're going to fix up this place so it looks like the money we spent on it. If you can't find the right sort of woven wire for pens at the store, have them order some. Let's measure up what we need now."

After Charlie had made a list of the things they needed, Lew took it and drove to Bundy Flats, 12 miles down the road. He was pleased to make it in under 20 minutes but then looked rather ruefully at a general store that, along with a boxcar shack of a railroad station, comprised the entire business district. He did find some strong door bolts in the hardware stock of the combined general store and post office. The proprietor looked at him curiously as he laid out the large number.

"Goin' to build a jail?" he grinned.

Lew grinned back. "No, we're going to keep stray varmints out of our new home. We bought the Patton fur farm—you know, Frenchman's Folly as it's called around here."

"Well, from what the neighbors say, you'll need more than bolts," the man answered with a sober face.

"What do they say?" Lew asked curiously.

The storekeeper hesitated a moment and then rushed in. "Some say the place is haunted. The Frenchman that built it, Old Henri Ducross, was found dead one night. He had been hit over the temple with a strange sort of weapon—a log measuring pole."

"Who did it?" Lew inquired, trying his best to sound only casually interested.

"They never found out," the storekeeper resumed. "There isn't much law about here, and after a week or so the inquiry was just dropped. Some of us suspected a son he had run off four or five years before came back and did it. The old man had let it slip that he had money hid somewhere about the place."

Lew pondered this as he checked his list one more time.

"That be all for you?" the storekeeper asked.

Lew ordered the woven wire, as the store had only common farm fencing in stock.

A short Cree Indian in dirty overalls had been standing in the store watching. Now he sidled over and said, "You buy horse, mebbe? I got goot one. Him haul wood, plow corn."

"Why, I don't know," Lew replied. "We might buy one—if we can get him cheap enough."

"Me sell cheap," was the response. "Come look."

Lew followed him out to the side of the store. The Cree paused beside a most decrepit animal, all skin and hips, as lean as a rail.

"Big, strong fellow," asserted the Cree as he pointed to the wreck leaning against the hitching bar. "Him do plenty hard work."

"How much, John?" Lew asked.

"Me give away—hundred dollar!"

"I'll tell you what," Lew replied. "You bring him over to the farm tonight, and I'll give you three dollars cash, good hard coin."

"All right," the Cree agreed with such alacrity that Lew wondered if he had offered too much. "I come."

Lew drove back to the farm. As he entered the yard he heard a crash from behind the house. Running around the wing, he saw Charlie standing over the ruins of the old board shed with a satisfied look on his face. He had knocked the sides off, cut down the posts and let the roof cave in.

"Plenty of good lumber," he announced as Lew approached. "Enough to make the furniture we need. Some left for kindling, too."

"And I've solved the question of fox meat for a few days," Lew answered and then told Charlie about the horse.

Charlie applauded his business acumen.

"Wait until you see the animal before you pat me on the back," interposed Lew. "The more I think of it, the more I wish I'd offered a dollar ninety-eight instead of three."

It was noon, so Charlie laid down his hammer. After washing, they started walking over to Anton's cabin. It was a square log cabin roofed with corrugated iron. As they approached they noticed something lacking. There were neither children nor dogs. Anton waved them inside from the doorway.

"Dees is wife," he pronounced. A bronze-faced woman straightened up from the kitchen stove and smiled shyly at them. She was younger than Anton and equally vigorous; the appetizing aromas in the room proclaimed her prowess as a cook. Stewed squirrel, potatoes and cabbage were on the table beside corn bread and strong black coffee.

They sat down at another inviting wave from Anton. The food tasted every bit as good as it smelled, and Lew ate with visible appreciation. Anton's wife stood beside her stove, watching to make sure they lacked nothing.

Finally, they pushed back chairs and Anton led them out to the front of the cabin. It had no porch but he placed chairs for them on a bare spot under a pine.

"Patton told us he paid you forty dollars a month," Charlie began. "Is that right?"

Anton nodded. "Forty dollars, a cabin to live, wood to burn, and some ground for potatoes."

Charlie nodded and then got right to the point. "I don't know how we're coming out on all of this, Anton. We want you to stay with us for now. Later, maybe we won't need a man. We paid about all of our money to Patton, and we haven't enough left to pay you very long, anyway. I'm telling you now so I don't have to lay you off suddenly in the middle of the winter."

Anton only grinned. "I trap fur and hunt when you no pay me. If I no work for you, let me live in cabin, anyway? Until spring?"

"Yes," Charlie assured him. "I just want you to know the score. We'll keep you busy for a while; there're lots of posts to cut. Then, if Lew and I find out we can do it all, you can start trapping fur."

"Ees a bargin, M'sieur," agreed Anton.

"Speaking of chopping," Charlie said, "I forgot to have you get another axe at the store, Lew."

"I have extra," Anton spoke up. "You welcome, M'sieurs."

They gladly accepted and followed Anton inside to thank his wife for the excellent meal. In a corner stood a crosscut saw, two axes and a maul. As Anton picked up one of the axes, Lew nudged his partner. Charlie glanced up at the cabin ceiling. Lying across the rafters was a long, square-edged pole with knife-cut graduations.

They took the double-bit chopping axe from Anton and were halfway back to their house before Lew spoke. "That measuring pole looked rather familiar to me."

"Me, too," agreed Charlie. "But everyone up here probably has one, and it seems like Anton would have had plenty of time to prowl around the house during the day without coming in at night."

"I'm still voting him as our nocturnal visitor," Lew announced firmly. "Did you notice how light he walks for so heavy a man? He has a step like a cat's. He would be an ugly customer to mix with."

They worked hard all afternoon, sawing and nailing boards salvaged from the shed. The lumber was weathered but solid, and they fashioned sturdy cupboards, a table with a smoothly planed top and two benches. As they worked they could hear the steady ring of Anton's axe out in the timber back of his cabin, chopping posts for new partition fences in the fox pens.

Night closed in, and they reluctantly set down their tools. Charlie brought out the gasoline pressure lantern and lit it to prepare supper.

"We'll also have to build some sort of shelter for the car," Lew declared. "We can't just leave it out all winter."

"We might cut a wide door in this back room and use that for a garage," Charlie suggested, half in jest.

"Why not?" Lew asked. "The car will be inside where it's warm; we've certainly got plenty of room. I'll get some big hinges and a garage door lock next time I go to town."

Charlie's fingers grasped his shoulder with a sudden grip of steel. "Listen!" he whispered tensely in his ear.

Footsteps were echoing down the stairway, someone walking easily, the steps of a man sure of his surroundings.

Lew's mouth gaped in surprise, and then they both ran swiftly into the front hall. Charlie had picked up the pressure lantern and Lew had seized a billet of wood from the floor to use as a club. The pistols were in their coats, hanging in the room they had used as combination sleeping room and kitchen.

Charlie flashed his light up the stairs, feeling first bewilderment and then a shiver of fear. The stairway was empty. Every door but the one they had opened was shut. Charlie held the lantern above his head to throw its brilliant rays into the hall above. But the door leading from the stairs also was shut. The bolt Lew had screwed on its lower panel was still shot home. No one could have entered the room and then locked the door from the outside.

And then, as they stood watching, steps rang out in the room. One, two, three footfalls rang out from a perfectly empty stairway. They turned and looked at each other with fearful amazement.

Chapter 3 – A Real Estate Boom

Charlie stood listening intently. Lew stood poised with heavy club raised. Finally, Charlie lowered the lantern he had been holding at arm's length above his head and they turned away from the stairway. But as they moved a new sound froze them—a soft rustling like ghostly clothing brushing against a wall.

Then a long-drawn sigh chilled their blood.

Lew turned and walked straight for the rear door. After one last glance about the empty room, Charlie followed and reached his side just as he stepped outdoors.

"Where are you going?"

"Out to sleep with the foxes," Lew said. "I'd rather bunk under the pines on the ground than listen to that all night!"

"Come back inside and get a grip on yourself," Charlie commanded sternly. "If it is a ghost, which I doubt, it never hurt Patton. He lived here a couple of years, remember?"

"My idea right now is to set fire to this ghost haven and let her burn," Lew replied. "We can sleep in a tent."

But he followed Charlie back into the front room, where his partner started the stove and eventually laid food out for supper. They ate hastily, eyeing the stairway through the open door with furtive glances. Then they stepped outside on the porch for a breath of fresh air filled with the tang of autumn, a crispness that reminded them of the frost to come. That put an end to Lew's talk of living in a tent.

But his nerves were about shot, and when a man on horseback suddenly loomed up before them, he almost jumped. The visitor's approach had been silent. Then, as the figure dismounted and came closer leading his mount on foot, Lew recognized the Cree.

"That's our new livestock," he told Charlie with a nervous chuckle. Lew paid the promised three dollars and invited the man inside, but he shook his head vigorously. "I walk back," was all the Cree said before turning towards the gate.

"Suppose he's afraid of ghosts?" Lew asked. Then he took the animal by its mane and led it around the house.

Charlie followed and remarked, "We'd better let it eat a week or two and put some meat on those bones before we turn it into fox feed."

"That's a good idea," Lew replied. "And this overgrown backyard ought to keep old Nebuchadnezzar until the snow flies. About all he's good for right now is soup. Well, shall we go back inside and try to get some sleep?"

"I'm half asleep now," Charlie assured him.

They entered the house, glancing at the stairway as they passed. But there was no sound save the faint roar of the pressure lantern and the wind rattling the loose window sashes.

They went carefully over the entire house, locking the four outside doors with double bolts and fastening the one at the head of the stairs. After locking the door of their sleeping room, Charlie examined the windows, locking all but one he opened for ventilation. He laid his sleeping bag close to it. Nobody could enter without stepping on him.

"Want to leave the lantern burn?" Charlie asked.

Lew grinned at that. "I'm OK. But those footfalls had me going. I was about ready to walk out on you. If some husky bozo of a burglar had come down the steps, I could have swatted him over the head with my club, and that would have been that. But ghostly footsteps, something you hear but don't see—what's the answer, Charlie?"

"Your guess is as good as mine," Charlie replied. "Maybe this is my first ghost. Maybe the old Frenchman is prowling the old homestead at night. But I never before ran across a real live ghost, and I say it is highly improbable. I'm going to sleep sound. No live man can get in tonight without waking us, and I've never heard of a ghost actually hurting anyone."

"We must tighten up these loose sashes to stop them rattling," Lew suggested. "They may prevent me hearing other sounds."

"We have weeks of work ahead of us," Charlie agreed. "Just as soon as we get the fox pens in the condition they should be, I want to examine this castle real close. There are just too many places for ghosts to hide."

"Funny there isn't a cellar," Lew remarked. "Seems like one would have been dug to store potatoes in winter."

Charlie awoke to daylight filling the room. He glanced over at his partner and was relieved to find Lew snoring like a sawmill. Charlie tossed a shoe at him. "Wake up—time to get to work."

Lew grumbled sleepily. Then he sat up and shook his head vigorously. "Boy, I haven't slept so good in weeks. I guess the ghost didn't walk. I heard nothing all night."

"I doubt if you could have heard anything over your own snoring," Charlie retorted as he lit the camp stove.

Lew grabbed the water pail and started through the house for the pump in the backyard. "Wonder how old Nebuchadnezzar made it last night?" he muttered to himself. "He should have put on fifty pounds in that long grass."

As Charlie reached for the coffeepot he heard Lew's step halt abruptly, then a low whistle of surprise from the rear room and Lew's voice calling, "Come here, Charlie! Quick!"

Charlie came on the double, speaking as he ran. "What's up, Lew? What is…" his voice trailed off in amazed surprise as his eyes took in the scene before them.

There was sand and mud on the clean pine floor, a double line of boot tracks that led from the middle of the floor to a tall window overlooking the yard. A trap door was raised a crack, a door that had been craftily hidden in the joints of the pine flooring.

Charlie bent over for a closer look. Instead of a ring or handle to lift it, he saw a small knothole had been shoved through. He pressed down with his foot and the trap closed with a light scraping sound.

He straightened up, and Lew, catching his eye, pointed to the window. Charlie remembered they had taken particular care to lock every sash, and his eyes narrowed again as he saw how the intruder had gained entrance. A pane of glass above the window lock had been neatly removed where a hand could reach in and undo the catch.

"What's under here?" Lew asked.

"The cellar you were wondering about last night, I suppose," Charlie said. He bent over, inserted two fingers in the knothole and pulled the door all the way up, swinging it over to one side.

"Get the lantern, Lew, and your gun."

First, they tied a cord to the lantern and lowered that slowly into the cellar. It was empty, a square excavation with rough, fieldstone sides. Charlie next swung down after the light and dropped to the bottom. The floor was soft sand, and he landed with scarcely a sound.

There was no other door, just the trap in the floor above, nearly 7 feet off the sand floor.

Charlie stooped over. Something queer about the sand had caught his eye. Pock marks, hundreds of tiny holes scarcely half an inch across had been bored in the sand. The entire floor was covered with them, spaced some four or five inches apart. Footprints were mingled with the queer craters.

"Get me a long splinter of wood," he called up to Lew, who soon handed down a thin stick over a foot long. Charlie poked it down one of the puzzling holes.

In a flash he understood the meaning of it all. Someone had entered the cellar in the night and searched the sand floor with a sharp probe, probably a thin iron rod. Every square foot had been tested—a painstaking search—for what?

Charlie reached up, caught a grip on the floor and pulled himself up. Then he reported his discovery to Lew.

"Somebody's looking for something in this house," Lew agreed. "If we figure out who and what they are looking for, I suspect all of the mystery will be solved. We do know this much," Lew continued. "They didn't find what they were looking for. If they had, the floor would have been dug up. So we can expect them back."

"Exactly," answered Charlie, pushing the trap door back in place. Then he walked over and looked at the window. The pane of glass that had been removed sat unbroken against the side of the house.

"We may have to put iron bars over every window," Lew said. "Then I suppose one of our invisible friends will play Santa Claus and come down the chimney But for now, we might as well just finish breakfast and then get to work."

Lew sat eyeing the pile of flapjacks on his plate. He tipped the syrup can and let a golden stream cascade over the tower of hotcakes.

"I got an idea," he blurted. "Maybe Anton was in the house last night. Suppose I watch his cabin tonight. If he starts out to prowl around, I can follow and maybe find out what it's all about. I reckon Anton might get more confiding if I shoved a pistol in his ribs."

"I doubt it," returned Charlie. "I think he would close up like a clam. And don't make such a mistake as to shove a gun in his ribs. Stand back four feet and cover him if he starts anything. I'll bet he's got a grip like steel and is quick as a panther."

"I guess you're right," Lew admitted. "But what do you think of my idea of watching his cabin?"

"That, I agree with."

They went outside and Charlie laid out the plans he had drawn up for the new kennels. Then he started cutting boards for the first set of panel, planning to use them as patterns. The lumber was dry and well-seasoned, and in a couple of hours one kennel was up and they had a set of pattern boards from which to mark off the others.

The occasional car whizzed past on the road in front of the house, and both were hammering so lustily they did not notice when one pulled up and stopped. Lew sensed the stranger's presence, and looking up, saw a man thin of build with a waxy face watching them work.

The stranger was clad in a brown check suit; a diamond pin gleamed on his tie. "Morning," he volunteered.

Lew returned the greeting as Charlie came up from the dismantled shed with a fresh armful of boards.

The stranger smiled, a superior, cynical sort of smirk that somehow rankled Lew instantly. "Lots of work to do here," he spoke. "Place looks pretty run-down."

"Not so bad," Lew answered evenly. "We'll have everything in shape in a week. Why don't you come around then and look."

The other laughed. "No offense meant," he offered. "As it happens, I'm in the real estate business. I sell quite a number of these farms to city people from Chicago and Milwaukee. I was driving by and stopped to see if this one might be on the market."

He handed Lew a card that read: *George J. Davidson, Real Estate and Investments, Chicago, Ill.*

"Everything's for sale," Lew countered, "at a price."

"That's the way," came the quick response. "I'm sure you would be just as well off letting me sell this to some Chicago slicker who could spend his own wad fixing it up. That's what they like. And then in a couple of years you can come back and buy it back for half of what you sold it to him for."

Lew bent back over his nailed panel.

"What do you have to have for the place?" the man asked.

"What can you get us?" Lew parried.

"Well, let's see," began George J. Davidson. "I'd say about eight thousand for the entire layout, the way she stands now."

Lew nearly lost his grip on his hammer, but he made no outward show of surprise. He shot a glance at Charlie and read disapproval in the set face of his partner. Lew looked back at Davidson.

"I guess we'll keep it," he said shortly. "We haven't anything lined else up, and this fox business looks like it might pay. After we spend a month or so fixing up things, we can get more, maybe make a profit on our labor."

"That's where you are mistaken," shot back the real estate dealer. "Fox ranching is risky. I've got a half-dozen fox farms on my list right now, farther south, and I can't move a one of them. I could move this because it's in summer resort country. Businessmen like to come up here to hunt and fish. I'm bringing a buyer out next Monday, and I think I could unload this on him."

"If we were selling," Charlie spoke for the first time.

Davidson's face flushed at that and then the color faded, leaving the pallor that covered his features like a mask.

"Tell you what," he finally said, and although his voice was calm and collected, they both suspected it cost him an effort to keep it that way. They had each noticed the sudden flush of anger of a man unaccustomed to not getting his way. "I'll do a little better. I'll make the price ten thousand—cash. I'll hand over the money and take my chance of unloading it for more. That's too good of an offer to refuse. You better think sharp!"

Lew's heart jumped to see such an easy way out of a bad investment. They had undoubtedly paid Patton too much, but here they could get all of it back and a profit of two thousand dollars. He turned eagerly to Charlie and felt a pang of disappointment as he read refusal in Charlie's eyes. He had been ready to blurt out that they would take it, but instead he said, "I guess we better think it over."

Again Davidson flushed. "What the devil do you want, anyway?" he burst out impatiently. "I'm offering you a good profit. You should have enough sense to take it!"

Lew knew Davidson was right. What was the matter with Charlie, anyway? But he stuck by his partner.

"No sale," was all he said, and with an assumption of boredom that he was far from feeling bent back to his work.

Davidson took a step forward, his manner so threatening Lew's hand dropped instinctively to the hammer by his side.

"You better take my offer," Davidson warned angrily. "This is your last chance, a big chance, too. Take it or leave it. I'll give you ten minutes. Think it over."

Lew stared into a pair of ugly eyes. Davidson's mouth was drawn in a hard, tense line, and his right hand had strayed back a little to the side of his leg.

Charlie caught the hand movement, too, and his own hand doubled back towards his hip. He returned the fellow's gaze without expression. The change in Davidson was instant. His face relaxed, and his hand fell to his side, empty.

"How about it?" he asked. "Ten minutes is nearly up."

"We're not selling," Charlie said shortly.

With a grunt, Davidson turned and strode back around the house. A minute later they heard a car door slam, a motor start, and then the roar as it tore off down the country road.

"Tough customer," Lew commented. "But gosh, I wanted to sell. What the devil was eating you?"

"No legitimate offer for real estate would only be good for ten minutes," answered Charlie. "Something's rotten here. There were a number of things I noticed while you talked with him. In the first place, he knew the value of the place as well or better than we do. He never asked how many acres or anything else about it. Just strolled up and made an offer for more than it's worth."

"That's why I wanted to close with him," mourned Lew.

"Second thing," Charlie went on, "the first offer was exactly what we had paid Patton. Didn't that strike you as strange?"

"Darned if it doesn't now," Lew said wonderingly.

"Yes, he shot us an offer that would let us get out clean. Then, as soon as he saw we weren't taking, what did he do? Did he raise it five hundred? No, he came across with another two thousand. Just sweet enough for a pair of young fellows to jump and not ask any questions as to why a run-down fur farm might be so valuable."

"I see your point," Lew agreed. "He wants this place too bad. Something is putrid in Patagonia."

"Exactly," answered Charlie. "And when somebody wants something I own that badly, I don't sell until I know why."

"We are throwing away a chance to make easy money, though," Lew returned.

"Did you notice his hand when we refused to sell?" Charlie came back with the clincher. "He reached back to his hip and then held the pose of a gunman. I doubt a legitimate real estate broker would be packing a hip holster. And did you see him back down as soon as I returned the gesture? I'm not heeled, but I'm sure he believed I was. No, we've somehow acquired a valuable piece of property—valuable to Mr. Davidson. The question now is: why?"

Lew pondered that with puzzled brow. "Maybe it's the same thing somebody was looking for in our cellar last night."

"My idea, too," Charlie agreed. "And he gave me a pretty fair idea of what this unknown asset is worth. A man like George would try to at least double his money. Then he would have to share something with the fellow he hired to search in the cellar. I put a rough guess that whatever is hidden in this old shack is capable of being turned into in excess of twenty thousand cash."

Lew whistled at that. "I hope you're right, even if I don't believe it. Are some of those foxes wearing pearl necklaces? But I do have an idea. Why don't we tear the old house down and build a smaller bungalow with the lumber. Then we may find whatever is hidden."

"About once every twenty years you get a really good idea, Lew," Charlie replied thoughtfully. "Well, you can rest your brain for twenty more now, because you've come through. That idea is a peach! And when George J. Davidson comes back, as I'm sure he will, I'm going to spring it on him. When I do, watch his face."

"You think he's coming back?" asked Lew.

"Sure," Charlie said. "He's no fool, even if he did lose his temper. His better business sense will come back before he's driven ten miles. Then he'll come back as meek as Mary's lamb with something new to persuade us into letting loose of this old fox farm."

"Listen," Lew cried. "I hear a car now."

"And it's stopping out front," grinned Charlie. "Maybe we're about to get an offer that will really stagger us."

"And if we do, you better grab it," Lew warned. "Don't miss ten thousand in hand for a hazy twenty grand in the bush. Get me?"

They were both busily nailing boards when George J. Davidson strode around the house. He was smiling affably this time when they both looked up in well-simulated surprise.

"I guess I got upset when I thought I wasn't going to make my commission," the man began. "You see, I already got a fellow who wants just such a place. I could sell this to him in a minute, and stuff is moving so slow this fall it about broke me to discover that I couldn't pull this easy one."

"Oh, that's all right," said Lew, grinning cheerfully. "I don't blame a fellow for wanting to make a little money."

"That's what we live for," beamed George J. "Now, you boys could have a nice little time on that ten thousand I offered."

"We were talking the matter over when you left," Lew began. "We had been planning to fix this old house up, you know. But the more we looked at it, the more we saw it as a hopeless job."

"You're right," George J. replied, beaming wider than ever. "Yes, this old place would cost more to fix up than it's worth. And then, after you were done, you'd still have a dump."

"That's why we sort of changed our plans," said Lew.

"So you're going to sell? Good. Let me…"

"No," broke in Charlie. "We're going to tear the old place down to the last board and brick and then use the material to build a modern bungalow that a city slicker would really appreciate."

Davidson handled it well. But Lew could see the blow striking below the belt. The man stiffened, and the friendly manner vanished. He barely held his temper in check, but he managed.

"I think that's unwise," he spoke the words clearly and carefully. "I'm going to make you boys a real offer. Listen and don't say anything until you've heard me out. I'll pay you eleven thousand cash for this farm, lock, stock and barrel. Come down with me to the county seat right now and get the money. But you move out tonight."

At his last words Lew and Charlie both stiffened. The man obviously wanted immediate possession, badly. But why?

Chapter 4 – Lew Makes a Discovery

George J. Davidson stood watching their faces with narrowed eyes, waiting for a sign that Charlie would accept his offer of eleven thousand dollars for the farm. He already had determined that Charlie was the one who would make the call.

Charlie was thinking rapidly. Common sense told him to take the money and clear away from this house of mystery. There might be only trouble in store if they hung on. Why risk disaster to get involved in something shady that concerned them not?

Charlie had almost decided to say yes, to take a profit of three thousand dollars and leave. But then a glance at Davidson's face swung him the other way. The man looked crooked clear through. Whatever was in the house that was so valuable, he knew Davidson had no legal right to it. He could not bring himself to sell to such a person. If it had been almost anybody else, he might have sold.

"Sorry," he said quietly. "But we're not selling."

Davidson merely shrugged at that, and without another word, turned and walked back to his car. But as he wheeled by Charlie caught a glimpse of his face. The eyes held as ugly a light as he had ever seen.

Once more, the car roared away.

"And we haven't seen the last of that fellow," prophesied Charlie. "If it had been anybody else, I would have accepted, but whatever is hidden in this old shack does not belong to Davidson. I know that, and I just couldn't hand the place over to him. Now, we must be even more cautious. He tried to buy us out fairly, and unless I'm a poor judge of human nature, he'll try to get the place by other means."

Lew groaned. "We came up North for a quiet winter. I expected to watch foxes grow fat while we sat around a hot stove. And look what we got instead. Cutthroats and ghosts! I'll have to sleep with an eye open, a gun in one hand and a flashlight in the other."

Then he continued briskly. "Well, let's get busy. From the way Davidson talked, he wanted us to move out right away. I suppose the fireworks will start soon, and I hope so. I'm getting tired of driving nails and pushing a saw. I'm going in now to oil up the old automatic. And since I'm going to prowl around friend Anton's cabin tonight, guess I'll sleep a bit after dinner."

"That's okay with me," Charlie agreed.

After the meal, Lew lay down to rest and Charlie walked out to the fox pens where Anton had started to dig post holes for the new partitions. In the morning, they would start setting the posts. Anton had promised to get a neighbor with a team to haul them in from the timber. Charlie doubted if Nebuchadnezzar could drag in more than one post at a time, and they could carry them faster than that.

When Charlie returned to the house, he called in the door to Lew, "I'm going to the store. I think I can fix up this house so nobody can break into it without warning us. If I can get the stuff I need, I'll have the rear burglarproofed before nightfall."

Lew grunted sleepily in answer. Then, just before four o'clock, he awoke to find Charlie working in the backyard with coils of small copper wire, tiny pulleys, coiled springs and a sheet of brass.

"What's the big idea?" Lew asked.

"This is my burglar alarm," Charlie answered. "I was lucky the store had the things I needed. Here's an electric bell like they connect up with door buttons. I got four dry cells, too, and we'll string this copper wire close to the ground across the back wing since that seems to be the favorite approach for prowlers. I think I can rig this up so when a trip wire is touched, it will start the bell going by my pillow."

"That's great," Lew cried. "You can meet visitors at the door and let them in. They needn't go to the trouble of taking out a windowpane. Give them a hearty welcome, Charlie."

Charlie smiled at that. "Leave it to me," he said simply.

First, he fastened the bell to a block of wood and set that close to the sleeping bags. Then he led wires out along the wall to the rear door. For nearly an hour, Charlie worked on the switching device before he had it working satisfactorily. It was a simple trip, much like a gun lock. The hammer was held back by a notched trigger, both cut from the sheet of brass. A coil spring was hitched back of the hammer to force it forward when the trigger released, and the hammer struck against another piece of brass to complete the electric circuit. The trip wire was fastened to the trigger then run through the house walls in small gimlet holes and out into the yard.

Now came the tricky part. He still had to string the trip wire close to the ground where it would be invisible in the dark, and in such fashion it would slide easily and trip the hammer when pushed.

Charlie drove stakes every 15 feet, concealing them in clumps of tall grass. He threaded the trip wire through tiny pulleys nailed on their tops. When it was finished, Lew tested at several different places, striking the wire an easy blow with his feet. After some adjustment, he was rewarded at each trial with a faint click of the tripped hammer followed by the steady music of the bell.

"All we want is warning of approach, we don't want to scare them off until we get a look," said Charlie. "If a prowler hears the bell ringing, he'll know the game is up and vanish. I'll set the bell close to my head and cover it with a coat. That should muffle the sound but not enough so I won't hear it."

Lew promised to stay out of the rear yard while he ran his own errand that night. "I'm liable to be all over the rest of the farm, though. When I come back to the house, I'll signal you with six knocks on the front door so you'll now it's me."

He started to demonstrate. But then the faint, steady ring of the alarm bell sounded from beside Charlie's sleeping bag.

For a moment they just looked at each other. Then they leaped together for the rear door. They flung open the door, and there beside the trip wire stood Nebuchadnezzar, calmly chewing a mouthful of the long grass that covered the yard.

Lew could not contain his laughter.

So you're the ghost this time, you old skeleton. I'm going to pen you up. We can't be bothered with you; our trap is set for dangerous game. Come on," and he led the animal out to the fox pens where he strung up two lengths of barbed wire to form a makeshift pen.

Charlie looked up from a cup of coffee as Lew entered the house. "As a cook, Lew, you make a good carpenter. Have you forgotten how to make coffee?"

"Mine's all right," Lew replied. "If you didn't put so much sugar in yours, maybe you would be able to taste the java, too."

"I guess I'd better make the next pot," Charlie replied. "I can stand your bum biscuits, but I want a real cup of coffee."

After supper they lit the gasoline lantern and sat talking until nine o'clock. Then Charlie turned the light low and settled in his sleeping bag. Lew dressed for night patrol. They had decided to simulate as nearly as possible their usual program of turning in, in case someone might be listening from the back yard. Charlie dropped his boots twice on the floor and then continued conversation as Lew noiselessly opened a side door and stepped out into the front yard. As Lew closed the door quietly, Charlie continued talking in casual tones.

Lew had dressed warmly with two flannel shirts, a wool cap, and soft-soled moccasins for stealth.

"I'll run down to Anton's first," he thought as he swung out around the burglar alarm in the yard. "I think our French friend knows more than he admits. After an honest laborer has dug post holes all day, he will be ready for sleep by nine o'clock. So, if I find Anton waiting up, I'll know there's mischief afoot."

Lew walked past the fox pens and into the timber. With no dog at the Frenchman's home, it should be possible to creep quite close and maybe even look through a window into the house.

The dim outline of the structure was before him, and the windows all looked dark. Lew decided things looked alright. Anton and his wife were doubtless in bed, fast asleep, and he could go back and rejoin Charlie where they would wait together for whatever else might be coming. Lew still felt certain some mysterious action would come in the night, for Davidson had been insistent they accept his offer and give over possession of the house that very day.

Just to make sure, Lew crept up to one of the front windows. He remembered that this sash set just before the little wood heater in the front of the cabin, and his heart skipped a beat when he saw a dim glow, a point of light like a live coal less than a yard from his eyes. It could not be the stove—that he distinctly remembered as a low, squat affair hugging the floor.

As he stood wondering what it might be, the glint moved with the slow motion of a man turning his head, and Lew realized that he was looking at a lighted pipe glowing in the pitch black interior of the cabin. Lew fancied that he could catch the odor of burning tobacco and backed noiselessly away from the window.

So, Anton was up and waiting. But waiting for what?

Lew backed farther away until he was covered by the branches of a low spruce. He crouched with his back against the trunk and waited. Two could play this game. He pulled his heavy wool garments closer and settled in to await developments.

A sound like a car stopping out on the road brought him sharply alert. Maybe he was posted at the wrong spot. It might have been best to wait in their own front yard.

He glanced at the cabin window. The glow of the Frenchman's pipe had disappeared. Now he heard a low creaking and shrank back still farther under the covering spruce, for he knew Anton had pushed the cabin door open. Movement caught his eye, and Lew smelled the burning pipe clearly this time. Had Anton, too, heard the faint noise back on the road? If so, his ears were also keen.

Footsteps were coming towards the cabin from behind Lew. Steps that plainly betrayed the walker as a poor woodsman treading awkwardly over rough trail. A form passed close by Lew, and when he next looked at the porch, he could see the outline of two figures.

Low voices mingled with the moan of the wind in the pines. Lew could scarcely restrain the impulse to move nearer and overhear the words, but he knew the folly of such action. His own ears were keen, and he had barely picked up the sound of that stopping car. Anton had evidently heard it through the walls of the cabin. Lew decided the wisest course was to stay put where he was well hidden.

The men were talking fast, and finally a voice lifted loud enough for Lew to hear. Unless he was badly mistaken, it was George J. Davidson. Lew could scarcely restrain a chuckle.

Light was breaking over the mystery, and as Davidson was making no effort to keep his voice down, he hoped to soon hold the solution of everything strange that had happened.

"You get it before tomorrow," Davidson was saying. "You had chance enough the day before they came."

Anton's voice rumbled in reply. "I try, M'sieur. I measure dees rooms as we did together. I sound dees walls. But I find—nothing!"

"Well, get busy tonight!" Davidson ordered. "They told me they're going to tear the house down. Probably start in the morning. You go over there and really look this time."

"You come, too?" asked Anton. "Maybe we have better luck?"

"No, no," hastily cut in Davidson, and Lew thought he could detect a trace of fear in his voice. "I'm busy tonight. Remember, I'll pay double for results right now."

"I do my best, M'sieur," was Anton's reply.

Davidson then turned away from the edge of the porch, and Lew shrank back into the cover of the spreading spruce.

But a warning "Shhh!" in Anton's deep voice brought Davidson up. Lew clutched the pistol under his arm. Had Anton heard him, or just sensed his presence? Then he relaxed as the Frenchman whispered, "I hear car stop on road."

To Lew's surprise, Davidson cursed softly yet with bitter vehemence. "I wonder if it can be..."

Then Davidson snapped into silence, and turning, ran straight past where Lew was hiding. Back along the trail that led to the road the man ran, and forgetting for a moment the listening Anton at the edge of the porch, Lew followed him.

What Anton heard or what he thought, Lew did not stop to ponder. Something was about to happen back at the road, and Lew wanted to be in on it. He already had made one important discovery. Anton was searching their house for something hidden within its walls, and he was searching at the bidding of Davidson. With that much to guide them, they could deal with the Frenchman later.

The trail wound in curves through the timber, and as he ran he realized it was farther than he thought. Davidson had gotten such a start he could not catch sight of him in the dim light that framed the spot where trail and highway met.

At the road he slackened his pace, stopping at the timberline in covering shadows. The moon had started to break through the heavy pall of clouds, and in its dim light Lew could see a truck parked just off the pavement with the motor running. It was a fleet monster such as had crowded them off the road on their drive out to Folly Farm.

Lew stepped up for a better view when a stifled exclamation caught his ear. Two men were fighting in the center of the road. As he watched, one broke loose and then a pistol exploded. One of the figures leaped down the trail like a frightened deer, and Lew thought he detected something familiar in the outline.

Another man came running past, and Lew saw a pistol glinting in an outstretched hand. Then the starter whirred, gears clashed, and a car shot out into the road, whining shrilly in second gear as it disappeared.

The pursuing figure stopped, half-leveled gun still gripped in tense fingers. Then the man stepped straight towards Lew.

"That you, Patton?" a harsh voice rasped. "What the heck is goin' on here tonight? Who was that bird I chased off? I thought you had all the country dicks fixed. I'm gettin' nervous. Something's goin' to crack wide open pretty soon."

He halted directly in front of Lew, peering at his face. Lew, staring back with a gaze just as keen, saw the man was short but wiry. He could feel dangerous eyes boring straight into his own.

"Speak up!" the man growled with just a trace of a Chicago accent. "I got the stuff. Let's put it away."

Lew could not think of anything to say. Then the flare of a suddenly lit match blinded his eyes.

"You ain't Patton! Tryin' to hijack me, was ya?" A sharp click informed Lew the safety on the pistol had been released.

With a gun leveled at his heart, Lew suddenly found the words that had escaped him a moment ago..

"No, I'm not Patton. He left a number of days ago. Who the deuce are you, and what do you want? Don't get reckless with that gun, either, until you are wise to the way things are now."

"Patton gone?" The other's voice carried surprise and doubt. "Did he leave you in charge? Speak up, man. Get your tongue goin' before it's too late."

"Patton sold out to us," Lew spoke quickly. "Never said a word about you or anyone else. We bought the farm, and that's all I know about any of this."

"Us?" echoed the other softly. "How many more are there?"

The gun pressed dangerously close, and Lew drew back instinctively, deeper into the shadows. Lew was poised on the balls of his feet, ready to spring in and try to avert the deadly muzzle. Then a hand reached out of the gloom beside him and closed about the gun. Lew saw a lean thumb press swiftly down in front of the pistol's cocked hammer, and he knew it had been rendered momentarily harmless.

"There's just one more—me," Charlie's quiet voice spoke as he rose up from the crouch he had assumed as he had crept up beside them. "Get behind him, Lew, and shove your gun into his back while I draw this snake's teeth."

"Good boy!" Lew praised as he whipped about the man and jammed the muzzle of his own weapon against a shoulder blade.

Charlie twisted the gun from limp fingers.

"Now," he said, "it's your turn to talk. Who are you? Where are you going, what's in that truck, and why did you stop here?"

The fellow stared at them for thirty seconds. Then he smiled crookedly, having made up his mind.

"That's a truckload of Canadian whiskey," he began. "I'm on my way to Chi, and I'm one of the best drivers the Big Boss has. I loaded up at the border early this morning.

"Patton was in with the Boss. We used the house here to hide a load whenever things got hot. An' they was hot about noon. I was chased over thirty miles, and the boys trailin' behind me had a regular dogfight on their hands. I stopped, expectin' to find Patton here, ready to hide the stuff."

"Who chased you?" Lew asked.

"Hijackers," the man said shortly. "Red Blusco's gang. They been layin' for us ever since we lifted two loads off of them. The boys was still shootin' it out as I pulled away. So I thought I better lay low until things cooled off."

As Charlie and Lew continued eyeing him in silence, he spoke impatiently. "Well? You goin' to let me unload? The Boss'll make it okay with you. Patton got good pay for helpin' out. What do you say?"

"Things are already too exciting around here," Lew said dryly. "Better get in that truck and take it on the lam."

The fellow glared at him. Then his features changed as his pose became one of listening. Lew heard it, too—the steady hum of a speeding car. And as two dazzling headlamps shot into view, he remembered what the man had said about "the boys trailin' behind." The armed guards protecting his cargo were coming, and it looked like a tight pinch for Charlie and himself if the gangsters wanted to play tough.

Instinctively, he stepped back beside Charlie and watched the car slide to a quick stop. Then the truck driver stepped out into the glaring beams and waved his arms.

"What's up, Blinky?" a voice came from the car.

"These two guys bought out Patton. They told me to head on down the road. An' they got fresh and frisked my gun. We'll see about that, won't we?"

A chorus of assent filled the air as all four doors of the long, low-hung car burst open. With belligerent shouts, a host of armed men poured out onto the moonlit road.

Chapter 5 – Lew Takes a Ride

The gangsters crowded close about the truck driver and someone asked, "Where are they?" Hands waved menacingly, and in each fist a pistol glinted in the swelling moonlight.

The man they had hailed as Blinky pointed into the shadows where Lew and Charlie were just starting to edge stealthily back under cover of the timber. "Get them before they scatter!"

Lew snapped back the bolt of his pistol to check the loaded shell in the chamber. "Run for it!" he whispered. "I've got a plan."

Then, before Charlie could protest or even answer, Lew turned and darted swiftly along the edge of the road, crouching until his head was below the tops of the weeds. He ran straight for the big truck parked in front of the sedan that had just arrived.

The men in the road did not see him. Instead, they moved forward in grim silence, spreading out in a picket line. The end man just missed running into Lew, running crouched low to the earth.

Lew knew Charlie could take care of himself in the woods, and he had heard his partner already running as they separated. He also was confident that his plan soon would draw the armed wolves off of Charlie's trail.

He straightened up and ran for the road as the line of men reached the black timber. One might turn about for a look now, but he doubted it. When he reached the black sedan, he pressed his pistol close to a front tire and pulled the trigger. The double report of gun and burst tire brought a startled yell from the trees. The door of the big truck was open, just as Blinky had left it, and Lew jumped in and took the wheel,. Thankfully, the powerful motor was idling smoothly.

Lew didn't stop to close the cab door. He seized the gear lever and felt through the notched slots for low gear. He had to guess at the right mesh, and if he guessed wrong, the motor would stall. More shouts were echoing from the trees as Lew snapped the gear lever home and tramped down on the gas pedal.

The motor roared, and as he slipped back the clutch, the big tires bit into the soft gravel shoulder of the highway. With a shower of flying stones, the truck climbed onto pavement and took off down the road— straight at the gangsters who were running towards it.

Faces in which anger and astonishment curiously mingled appeared in the glare of the truck lights. With startled shouts, they dodged back just in time to escape the juggernaut as Lew held straight in the center, shifting rapidly into a higher gear.

As he roared past one of the man sprang for the running board of the cab, grabbed the edge of the door, and swung up. A dark face with close-clipped mustache appeared before Lew's eyes, and he saw a pistol rising. Lew crashed his fist into the sallow face just as the gun roared. Something ripped past his cheek like a hot whiplash.

The face reeled back as Lew struck again, and then Lew thrust out his foot and kicked the struggling man. He heard a sharp cry as the truck swerved off the road. The man let go as Lew straightened the front wheels back on the road. He felt the heavy load sway dangerously but kept the gas pedal flat against the floor as he struggled with the steering wheel, trying to right the truck.

Lew had about given up hope when he felt the truck lift on the opposite side, and that slid the load back into balance. He breathed a sigh of relief. The back wheel must have driven over a log. Whatever it was, it saved him from crashing into the trees.

Now he was roaring down the center of the highway, picking up speed even faster than he had hoped. He knew he could not outrun the car behind, but he also knew they could not drive it with a blown tire, and it would take several minutes to make the change. By that time he expected to be far enough away that when they did follow, Charlie would have had ample time to escape.

But it would only be a matter of minutes before the sedan came hurtling through the night. Lew considered not stopping when they caught up with him but discarded the idea immediately. They would simply shoot him through the flimsy cab walls.

No, the safest play would be to pull off the road before the sedan caught up and then run for the trees. Night timber was an old friend to Lew. Give him 50 yards start, and he was as good as gone.

Lew glanced in the rearview mirror. A patch of light, faint but unmistakable, was breaking through a timbered bend. They were coming, and Lew instinctively pressed down on the accelerator. He was surprised to feel a surge and realize he had not yet reached the motor's limit. He glanced at the speedometer. The big truck was making 55 miles an hour and picking up to 60. There was quite a powerplant engine under the hood.

As he approached another curve, Lew decided this would be the place to jump. If he could keep a strip of timber between him and the lights coming behind, the gangsters would have no clue which way he went. If they decided to pursue, they would be forced to split up into parties and search both sides of the road.

At first Lew thought of setting the brake and jumping before the truck rumbled to a stop. Then he decided this would be unwise. If the truck turned over, the gangsters would seek revenge. If they found everything in good order, they might just wheel on into Chicago.

Lew started around the curve. Another glance in the side mirror showed two gleaming lights bearing swiftly down.

Holding the wheel to follow the road, Lew glanced rearwards once more. This time timber screened the lights of the sedan, and his foot shot down on the air brake. The truck slid across the pavement, all four wheels locked. Lew switched off the lights, waiting for the truck to stop. Then he released the air brake, jammed on the emergency brake, and jumped. When his feet touched the ground he was already running desperately for the timber before the sedan's headlamps shot around the curve and picked up his fleeing form. He took a chance running across the road, figuring his pursuers would naturally assume he had ducked into the cover nearest at hand.

A beam of light flashed down the roadbed as he sprang for the pines. Lew wondered if they had seen him but kept running deeper into the trees. He heard a squeal of applied brakes and then car doors opening and closing. They did not start to comb the timber for him, and perhaps they wouldn't. Lew paused to catch his breath. Then he grinned, picturing them crowding about the empty truck cab, baffled.

Curiosity got the upper hand on caution, and Lew crept back through the second-growth to the edge he had been so eager to escape a moment before. When he reached the last of the thick shadows, he saw one of the men climbing down from the truck.

"Everything's okay," the fellow called. "An' it's mighty lucky for you, Blinky. If this load had got smashed up, you'd never get a chance to leave another truck standin' along the road with the engine going."

Lew watched a man shove himself through the knot of men that crowded about the speaker. Then Blinky's voice rasped angrily. "What are we standin' around here for? Let's get goin' after them fellows. They'll get away if we wait."

"Cool down, Blinky," a calm voice answered. "The best thing we can do now is just wheel on into town. You got out of this lucky. The truck might have been smashed up. That would give the game away, and that would make the Big Boss really mad."

Silence fell over the group, and then the same voice continued, "Get on up in the truck, Blinky. And better lock yourself in 'fore one of these local hicks steals your pants and shirt."

The rest laughed loudly at that. Then Lew heard the cab slam. The motor of the big truck roared, and with a whine of gears, it started racing down the road.

"Now what?" a voice asked.

"Get in the car," came the answer. "We can't waste any more time up here. These guys that bought out Patton can wait. When we come along next time, they get their lesson in manners."

A door closed on these words, and the sedan roared off.

Lew crouched beside the road for a full 20 minutes until he was sure the entire gang had gone. It would have been an old trick to leave a couple of guys waiting.

When the sound of truck and car had long since died in the distance, gun in hand, he stepped out into the center of the pavement, turned and began walking back to the fur farm. He had no idea just how far he had driven the big truck, and he was surprised when the better part of an hour passed before he saw the dim outline of "The Frenchman's Folly" standing out against the night sky ahead.

What had become of Charlie? The thought kept turning over in his mind. Lew paused before the gloomy yard in front of the house. Everything was dark. Charlie was either waiting in that darkness or else he was still in the timber.

Lew decided Charlie might be waiting for him where they had parted. He slid noiselessly along the edge of the road, eyes keenly searching the shadowy trees. He felt sure all of the gangsters had followed in the car. The truck and its valuable load had been uppermost in their minds. Still, one or two might have stayed behind.

Lew had decided to call out to Charlie when a short, hollow scream froze him like a statue, alertly listening. Then Lew relaxed and grinned. His nerves were so on edge that an owl, and a small one at that, had given him a thrill. Then he remembered that the cry of the little tuft-eared beings who patrol the night-cloaked forest carries a message of foreboding to the woodsman. And while he wouldn't admit it, Lew shared this superstitious belief.

When a twig snapped, Lew wheeled about, fingers tightly gripping the butt of his pistol. He called softly, "Charlie!"

No answering sound reached his ears, only the wind moaning

through the pines. He felt strangely safe as he stood there. But then an unnamed fear for his partner froze Lew in his tracks. Charlie and he had been so closely associated these many years it was only natural that a bond now linked them, and he sensed danger still afoot.

Pistol in hand, Lew began running with long, swift strides towards the house. He did not pause to unlatch the gate but vaulted over and ran up on the porch. Then he slowed and his soft-soled moccasins trod noiselessly over the worn boards. When he tiptoed to the big door a fresh thrill confronted him. The heavy panel stood open. Lew pushed his way in, gun in hand.

Charlie surely would have bolted the door, Lew thought as he stepped swiftly to one side so he would not be silhouetted against the opening. Pressing his back against a wall, he listened to a strange sound that caused him to lean forward in startled amazement.

It was rather a mix of sounds, feet shuffling on bare boards the sucking hiss of sharp breaths drawn fast and short. And then Lew knew what was before him in the pitch blackness. Men were fighting silently but with desperate fury. He reached swiftly to his hip for his flash but found the pocket empty. The lamp must have fallen out as he dashed through the timber. His gun was useless unless he could see who was fighting who in the black room. He must know which one was Charlie before he could shoot. Then he heard a short, muffled cry and sprang forward, determined to clinch with one of the struggling forms and trust to luck that it would be the right one.

Someone collided with him, and he seized him.

"Charlie! Where are you?" he called quickly.

"Let go of me!" The voice of his partner spoke in his ear. "Quick! Before he gets away!"

Then Lew heard someone running down the hall, but in what direction he could not tell. Charlie switched on his light, and the beam flashed across an empty room. They ran to the next room.

It was empty, too.

Then they swiftly checked all of the rooms on the lower floor but found nothing. The door at the top of the stairs they could see was still bolted on the outside.

"He must have got out the front door!" Lew cried.

Then soft sounds brought them about—first a faint creak like feet ascending a stairway and then a low-pitched murmur as though some-one had sighed. Charlie played his beam of light up the steps. They were not surprised to find them empty this time.

Lew brought the gasoline lantern, and its brilliant flame flooded the room. Charlie had sat down on a bench, breathing heavily.

Lew could see marks on his partner's face, and his woolen shirt was torn from both shoulders. "What happened?" Lew asked.

Charlie answered slowly, sounding completely washed out.

"After you went wheeling down the road in the truck, I ran for it. That was a remarkable plan, Lew. I heard you shoot the tire, and it drew them away from me and the house. Otherwise, I suppose we would have had a running gun battle in the trees.

"I never knew a tire could be changed as quickly as they shifted that one. Nobody spoke a word, only one fellow gave a short order then they piled into the sedan and were hot-footing it on your tail. I suspected you would ditch the truck and run for the woods. If you had shot out two tires, you could have gotten clean away."

"But I didn't want the truck," Lew replied. "And that would have brought the gang back here."

"Of course," Charlie answered with an admiring nod. "I returned and waited beside the road for nearly an hour. But everything was silent, so I went back to the house. I don't know why I did it, but I walked around the building before I went in. Even as I stepped inside the door I thought I should wait for you. Now I wish I had.

"I unlocked the door and stepped in, and just as I started to close the door, I heard something in the hall. I made my second mistake then. I should have taken out my light, but instead, I crept ahead trying to get closer. I don't know why, but I just wasn't thinking clear."

"Gosh," Lew said. "I never thought you did anything foolish."

"It was a bad slip," Charlie admitted. "And I knew it the minute I clinched with the prowler. We fought for what seemed hours. He was strong. I landed several stiff blows, but my arms just didn't seem to have their usual punch.

"I couldn't reach my gun; it was in my coat pocket and he stayed pressed close up against me. And then I heard you open the door. At least I thought it was you. The other heard it, too, and tried to break loose. Although I held on as hard as I could, he broke my grip and slipped away. I should have called out to you, but I was panting so hard, I guess I couldn't find my voice. Then I tried to follow and bumped into you. You know the rest."

"I don't see how he passed without my knowing it, but he had to use the front door for his getaway," Lew said.

"What about those spooky footsteps on the stairs?" Charlie asked quietly.

"We'll know in time," Lew answered. "In fact, I learned a lot tonight. My trip down to Anton's cabin was quite fruitful."

Charlie leaned forward. "Tell me," he said simply.

"I know who has been snooping through the house."

"Spill it," Charlie spoke impatiently.

"Our friend, Anton!"

"You think so?" Charlie asked.

"I know it. And I'm sure Anton was the guy you grappled with tonight. Wait until I look over the barrel of my pistol at our French friend. Boy, won't that be good?"

Lew then told Charlie the details from his watch at Anton's cabin. After he had finished, Charlie replied, "I know it wasn't Anton I fought with tonight."

"How do you know?" Lew said. "You couldn't see in the dark. You said the fellow was strong, and Anton is powerfully built."

"When you saw Anton at the cabin tonight," Charlie asked, "had he shaved off the stubble on his face?"

"No," Lew said slowly. "And I could see well enough to know he hadn't. But what's that got to do with it?"

"Plenty," answered Charlie. "Tonight, while I was fighting with the unknown prowler, my hands found his face several times. And his cheeks were as clean-shaven as yours."

Chapter 6 – An Insidious Menace

Lew sat up at Charlie's assurance than Anton was not the intruder with whom he had grappled in the dark. "Sure of that?" he asked.

"Absolutely," replied Charlie. "Anton has a regular bush growing over his mug, and the intruder was clean-shaven. Anyway, we can see in the morning, whiskers or not, because whoever I fought is going to have a few bruises about his eyes."

"Anton might have shaved last night after I left him," Lew mused, "but I don't see why he would. So, that makes three bad actors: Anton, Davidson, and a new bird of mystery. Not to mention Blinky and the gangsters—who will come back to even the score."

"We can pull out," Charlie suggested. "Davidson may come around in the morning to renew his offer. We can take it and go."

"I'm sitting tight," Lew replied defiantly, "until I find out what all of this monkey business means. And I'm going to nail some hides to the wall when I do. And after that, maybe this will be a peaceful place for a couple of worn out trappers to spend a winter raising fur."

"I sure feel worn out," Charlie agreed. "How about you make us something to eat?"

"Sounds good," Lew replied. "But you make the coffee since mine hasn't suited you lately."

Lew started the stove then set bread, jam, and cold beef on the table. Lew ate ravenously, but Charlie merely played with his fork and knife. "Your coffee any better?" Lew finally stopped chewing to ask.

"Not a whole lot," Charlie admitted. "Funny, I thought I was real hungry, but I don't want anything."

Lew scanned his partner's face anxiously. "You're worn out, old-timer, and we haven't had a good night's sleep since we got here. Sure this ghost business isn't getting on your nerves?"

"Don't talk silly," Charlie retorted.

"Tomorrow is going to be a big day," Lew asserted as he refilled his own coffee cup.

"In what way?" Charlie wanted to know.

"We are going to begin a job that should have been done as soon as we moved in. We're going to give the old house a thorough going over. I'm not satisfied with several things."

"And they are?" Charlie suggested.

"For one thing, footsteps made by someone we can't see. I don't believe in ghosts any more than you do. Then we have intruders that seem to appear and disappear right inside the house. There is a lot of room between the upstairs ceilings and the peak of the roof. Yet we haven't found a trap or scuttle hole to enter an attic."

Charlie straightened up at that. "You're right. There must be an attic of some kind over the upper rooms."

"I'm going to get up there if I have to saw a hole in the ceiling," Lew assured him. "And that isn't all. There are four big chimneys, great wide affairs. And they all seem to be plastered over. There aren't even flue holes in a couple of them."

"I noticed that, too," Charlie said. "But they might have all been used at one time. A house as big as this one this far north needs a stove in several rooms if it is to be kept warm in winter."

"And," resumed Lew, ticking the items off on his fingers, "there is evidently some sort of space under that stairway. When folks build such a space-eating affair, they usually put a closet under it or else stairs leading to a cellar underneath. Well, there isn't any closet, and while we've found a sort of cellar, there aren't any stairs to it."

"I believe you're on to something," Charlie agreed. "What else?"

"That's all for now. But tomorrow I give this shack a real going over. Anton already has had a go at it, but something is still hidden in this house, and I'm going to find it."

Charlie pushed back his plate. He had scarcely touched any of the food. "I'm ready to turn in," he declared.

"Me too," Lew agreed, unlacing his moccasins. "On the whole, I'm satisfied with my day's work."

They slid down into warm sleeping bags, and Charlie dozed off immediately. As Lew reached for the lantern to turn it out, he noticed his partner's sleep looked more like a stupor. Charlie was not well, and Lew leaned over his partner to listen to breaths coming shallow and short. Ordinarily, Charlie was a deep breather. This seemed decidedly bad. He resolved to get a doctor out to the house if Charlie was no better in the morning.

Lew lay awake for nearly an hour, thinking of the night's events but mostly of the malady that had seized his partner. It is always the unknown that frightens us most, and Lew had to admit he was scared by the way Charlie lay breathing so faintly.

He must have fallen asleep himself, for he found himself awake with a start, quivering with a sensation that he and Charlie were not alone in the big house. And this feeling was so real Lew grasped his pistol and reached under his head for the flashlight.

Then, remembering he had lost his electric torch, he stretched out a hand and fumbled under the other bed for Charlie's. His fingers closed around the tubular body of the lamp, but then he lay quietly, wondering if he should shoot a beam of light around the room.

Finally the suspense became unbearable and he snapped the switch on the light. The room was empty.

Now fully awake with gun in hand, Lew crawled from the sleeping bag and stepped quickly into the hall. Then he walked to the rear room. All was silent, but as he turned back towards his bed he could not help imagining that eyes watched his every move. It was not a comfortable sensation, and Lew felt oddly relieved as he crawled in between the layers of blanket with his back against a wall. Then he lay alertly awake for some time, listening and staring out towards the hall and the mysterious staircase.

Lew finally decided they should get a watchdog and keep him in the house with them at night. The more he considered the idea, the better it sounded. Finally, he drifted away in sleep.

When Lew's eyes opened next, the sun was lighting up the sky. Charlie's eyes opened more slowly. Then he stared vacantly into Lew's face for a long moment before those eyes regained their customary gleam of alert intelligence.

"How do you feel, old-timer?" Lew asked.

"Rotten," Charlie replied thickly. "My head aches, and there's a terrible taste in my mouth."

"Take a drink of water," Lew offered the cup.

"I don't know what's the matter with me, Lew. I never felt like this before. I had bad dreams all night, and my chest is awfully heavy."

"You're to stay in bed today," Lew announced. "You've got to get on your feet again, and the quickest way will be to get some rest. I'll have food cooked in a few minutes. You can have breakfast in bed—how's that for luxury? Almost too good for a bum trapper."

Charlie grinned at that, but Lew could see little real mirth in the forced smile. In a few minutes he brought over to the bed a plate of crisp bacon and two eggs, sunny side up the way Charlie liked them. He had arranged the eggs attractively over browned toast. Charlie seized the coffee cup and drained that first.

"Fill her up again," he ordered, hoping the java would clear his head. But he only ate one of the eggs and a single strip of bacon. Lew breakfasted in his customary hearty manner.

Then Charlie lay back on his bed while Lew washed the dishes.

As he worked, Lew also talked.

"Just as soon as I get these plates put away, I'm going to rip a hole in every wall that looks too wide. First, I'll kick a hole under the staircase. Think you'll be able to help a bit by noon? You can just hold one end of the tape while we measure some of the rooms."

He waited for Charlie's answer, but none came. He wheeled about and saw Charlie was back on his blankets with eyes closed.

Lew hurried to his side. Charlie was breathing in the same shallow manner as last night, chest barely rising and falling. He seized Charlie by the arm and called to him sharply, but the still form did not respond. Lew shook him. His partner's head rolled from side to side, but the eyes did not open.

And that was when Lew really got frightened. Charlie was in a stupor, and he had never seen anything like it before, not in a man as vigorous as his partner. He bathed Charlie's face with cold water, rubbed his hands, which seemed to be growing colder, and worked his arms much in the manner of bringing a drowned man to life. His heart chilled with the thought his partner might be dying.

Wetting one end of a towel in cold water, he stood up and gently flicked Charlie's cheeks with the damp cloth. This brought results, and Lew almost cried aloud when he saw an eyelid flutter open.

"What the devil made you pass out?" Lew demanded.

"Didn't know I did," Charlie slurred. "Let me sleep."

"Sure, sleep," Lew replied casually, a tone that belied his jumping heart. To himself he muttered, "He must have a doctor. I'll go down and see if Anton can help me find one."

As he walked out of the back room Lew locked the door, put the key in his pocket and ran swiftly to Anton's cabin. He had decided Charlie must not be left alone. He would ask Anton to sit with him. He didn't relish the thought, but there was no other way.

The cabin door swung open at Lew's knock and a fresh surprise confronted him. It was Anton—whiskers all gone. His cheeks were shaved as smoothly as Lew's, leaving a white expanse of skin that contrasted oddly with the tanned forehead. Lew's astonishment must have shown in his eyes, for Anton grinned.

"My face—she surprise, eh? The wife say I must get rid of dee bush on my face. So I get the old razor out and do it dees morning."

Lew found his tongue with difficulty and tried to grin as he answered. "You look ten years younger. I doubt the foxes will recognize you." His eyes searched the other's face as he spoke. The features were regular and strong. Before, the heavy mustache and beard had blotted out the greater portion of Anton's face.

"Where's the nearest doctor?" he asked, remembering his errand.

"Who seek?" Anton inquired. "There is a good doctor at the Flat. The only one I know."

"It's Charlie. I don't know what's wrong, but he's not well. I want you to come down to the house and stay while I get the doctor."

Anton was already grabbing his hat and coat. "Of a certainty," he cried. "And dees wife—she go, too. She know better than I what to do with seekness."

He called to the woman in the kitchen. "Come at once! One of dees young men seek. We go down to help while M'sieur Lew brings Doctor Bardeaux."

Lew was already passing out the door. "Follow as soon as you can," he called back over his shoulder.

He ran back to the house, and as he swung along through the sparse timber he was thinking hard. It must have been Anton who had struggled with Charlie in the night, Anton with cleanly shaved cheeks. Did he dare leave Charlie in the care of the man and his wife? He winced at the thought of what they might do if they were so minded. They might end any chance Charlie had to ever recover.

But he could think of no better plan. Anton apparently did not drive, and if he sent him on foot to town, it might be mid-afternoon before a doctor came. Lew did not want to wait that long. He would have to go and risk leaving Charlie in Anton's care.

He started the car and left it warming up. Charlie was asleep when he entered the room. His breathing was the same as before—faint and short. Lew wondered if he should try to awaken him. Perhaps it would be best to let the doctor examine him in this condition. Anton and his wife were knocking at the door, and he hurried to admit them.

Lew scrutinized their faces, particularly Anton's as they approached the bed. Unless the Frenchman was a superb actor, Lew decided that the sympathy in the man's eyes was genuine. The face of his wife was less expressive—that could be accounted for by her Indian blood—but her touch as she leaned over to feel of the sick man's cheek and forehead was gentle.

Anton followed him out to the porch. "We do our best, M'sieur."

Lew paused and then turned around. "Did you hear a lot of noise on the road last night?"

Following a barely perceptible pause, Anton answered, "Of a certainty, M'sieur. Who could help?" His voice was low but calm. "M'sieur Patton sometime have visitors in the night. But he say to Anton, 'Mind of your own business.'"

Lew started to reply and then changed his mind.

He drove at a fast clip to town and pulled up before the general store with a squeal of brakes that stampeded the flock of hens scratching about the doorway. Lew dashed up the steps and inside. The storekeeper hailed him from behind the counter, where he stood watching a solitary customer try on a pair of leather gloves.

"What can I do for you?" he asked genially.

"I need the doctor. Where does he live?"

The customer turned about slowly. Lew saw a thin man of perhaps sixty years, stooped of shoulder with eyes gleaming behind thick glasses. "I'm Doctor Bardeaux," he said in a slow drawl. "What's the trouble, young man?"

"My partner's very sick, but darned if I know how. He just lays in bed like he's in a stupor, and he won't eat. Weak, too—something unusual for him. I got my car out front. Let's go!"

"I reckon we should," the man answered. "Charge this pair of gloves to me, Jim."

Lew had seized him by the arm and was pulling him along.

"Don't hurry me, young man," the doctor said kindly but firmly. "I don't like to rush off for anything except maybe a birthing. But this seems to be an emergency. So let's go."

They climbed in the car and Lew told more of Charlie's sickness as he drove. Doctor Bardeaux listened attentively but did not comment on what might be the trouble. And while he still talked, Lew drew up to the gate, slowed enough to make the turn and then drove up close to the front door. He dashed inside to Charlie's side.

Anton and his wife sat beside the sleeping man, and the Frenchman whispered, "He not wake up since you go."

As Lew watched Bardeaux check Charlie's pulse, he wondered if he should get a specialist up from the city. Bardeaux was doubtless a good country doctor, fit to dress wounds and treat the fevers that prevailed in such places. But Lew felt this strange sickness of Charlie's needed special skill.

Bardeaux reached over, grasped the edge of an eyelid and rolled it back. Then he spoke sideways to Lew.

"Has he been taking any kind of medicine?"

"No," Lew answered shortly.

"What did he have for breakfast?"

"Not much: an egg, one strip of bacon and coffee."

Doctor Bardeaux removed a hypodermic from his leather case and a phial of tablets. Calling for water, he dissolved one of the pellets and then drew it up in the hypodermic. His skilled fingers pushed up Charlie's sleeve and pressed the needle deep into the arm.

"Now get him on his feet and walk him around the room," he ordered. "Open a couple of windows to keep the air fresh and cool."

Lew and Anton seized Charlie and pulled him erect. It was a difficult job, but they managed to support hi. Then, half-carrying, half-leading the unresisting form, they began to pace around the room. Doctor Bardeaux watched, eyes gleaming behind the thick glasses.

Finally, the stimulant he had administered and the forced exercise showed results. Charlie's muscles stiffened, and he began to walk on his own. His eyes fluttered open though they fell shut again.

Bardeaux stopped them, checked the sick man's pulse and listened to his heart once more.

"That will do," he ordered. "Lay him down. He'll sleep for an hour or two, but he should be all right when he wakes. Now take me back to town," he finished, turning to Lew, "And go slower this time."

Lew followed him silently to the car. When they were on the road Lew finally asked, "What's the matter with him?"

Bardeaux answered the question with his own question.

"Does your friend take drugs of any kind?"

Lew's eyes opened wide at that.

"Heck no!" he exploded. "Why do you ask that?"

"Because he shows every symptom of having suffered an overdose of an opiate or narcotic."

"That's impossible," Lew asserted. "I've lived too close with Charlie the past five years to be mistaken."

Bardeaux shrugged. "That is my medical opinion, and I'll stick to it until something changes my mind. The man is drugged. He's not ill. Where he got the narcotic, I don't know. But if I had a friend in his condition, I'd watch him pretty close."

Lew was thinking hard. Clearly Bardeaux was not keen enough to discover the real reason of Charlie's condition, and he resolved to get that second opinion

"I'll look in on him tomorrow," the doctor said as Lew dropped him back at the store. "Don't leave him alone until you find where the drug is coming from. Some of the patent medicines are overloaded with opium and morphine. He may have taken an accidental overdose."

Lew was angry as he wheeled the car around and started for home. The idea of his partner having a supply hidden away and indulging secretly in the stuff was utter rot. And then something clicked in Lew's brain, a thought that flashed like lightning across his mind and left him trembling. He lifted his foot from the gas and let the car roll forward with diminishing speed

It was all so confoundedly simple. He raised a hand and smote the wheel a resounding blow, impatient with his own stupidity.

Then his foot jammed down on the throttle, and he tore for home with every bit of power he could pull from the capable engine. He must not lose a second getting back—it was a matter of life or death!

Chapter 7 – The False Wall

He had seen the reason in the words of Doctor Bardeaux, that the diagnosis was sound if the explanation not.

What Lew had recalled was that Charlie's mysterious trance-like sleep had struck twice, and each time it had been after eating. If an enemy was somehow mixing a drug with their food or water, Charlie could be taking it without even knowing it.

They had plenty of enemies, too. They seemed to have acquired quite a line-up of them during their brief stay at the fox farm. And, as he reviewed them, Lew picked the Frenchman, Anton, as the one most likely back of this dastardly act. And if he was right, Lew had given the man a splendid chance to finish off Charlie.

The car shot over the road like a frightened rabbit, and Lew still gritted his teeth impatiently. It seemed to him as though it took hours to make the short drive back to their house.

Lew slowed as the gate appeared, but not enough to prevent lifting up on two wheels as he turned into the drive. A moment later he slid the brake-locked wheels up beside the porch and dashed inside the house, eyes darting swiftly about the room. Charlie still slept, and Anton and his passive wife sat beside him. Lew tried to speak casually; he did not want to warn Anton of what he suspected.

"You can go now," Lew said. "I'm sure obliged for your trouble. The Doc said Charlie just needs rest."

Anton nodded and followed his wife to the door. "If we can help—you send for us," he said and stepped out.

"Work on the pen fences today," Lew called after him through the still-open door.

The Frenchman mumbled assent and closed the door. Lew stepped over and snapped the bolt shut.

Then he glanced about, wondering where to begin. And while he was deciding, a thought knocked his enthusiasm into a state of collapse. He had been eating the same food as Charlie—why hadn't the drug affected him, as well?

His eyes wandered about the kitchen before settling on the coffeepot. Charlie had complained about the coffee tasting rotten. It was not in Charlie's nature to complain about such things; therefore, there had been something decidedly unpleasant about what was in his cup. But Lew had not noticed any unusual flavor, and Lew drank as much coffee as Charlie. But he did not add sugar like Charlie, loading each cup with a couple of spoonfuls.

That had to be it.

Lew opened the sugar sack and poured some out on a plate. Then he carried it to the window and began spreading the grains carefully. It was rather coarse beet sugar, and as he stirred the stuff, his breath drew in sharply. Among the coarse grains were scattered flakes of a substance looking much like quinine. He opened his pocketknife and used the point of the blade to separate the flakes over to one side.

After much patient effort, he had a small heap. Lew raised a flake on the point of the knife to his tongue. There was just a suggestion of an acrid taste, and then the tip of his tongue went numb. He knew it was a powerful opiate, and Charlie had taken an especially heavy dose when he drank two cups of heavily sugared coffee that morning.

He stepped to the door with the sack in his hands, to throw the deadly stuff out into the yard. But then he decided it would be wise to save it. Charlie would want to see it, and Doctor Bardeaux might learn something by examination.

Looking down on Charlie's sleeping face, Lew spoke softly. "They came pretty near slipping a fast one past us, old-timer. If I liked sugar in my coffee the way you do, we might both be lying there with a good chance of never waking up."

Lew was no longer alarmed by the slow, quiet breathing of his partner. He was confident Charlie would be fine when this last dose of drug wore off. And Lew knew it would be the last dose.

It was nearly noon before Charlie's eyes finally opened. He blinked for a moment and then sat up. "Have I been sleeping all day? What time is it?" he asked groggily.

"You've only slept half a day," Lew replied cheerfully. "How do you feel?"

"Not so good," Charlie said, rubbing his eyes. "I'm hungry, for one thing."

Lew hurried out to the kitchen. He had decided to wait until after dinner before telling Charlie of the events of the morning. He could tell that his partner had no memory of the doctor's visit. As they seated themselves to eat, Charlie glanced about. "No sugar, Lew?"

Lew looked at him grimly. "There isn't going to be any more sugar for a while, Charlie—not until we get a fresh supply. That sack of sugar…"

A brisk knock at the door interrupted Lew. He sprang nimbly to a window and peered out. Anton was standing before the door, something in his hand. Lew stepped noiselessly back beside Charlie.

"It's Anton. I'm going to ask him in. Don't use a grain of that sugar until we speak alone!"

Charlie stared at him with blank amazement, but Lew had returned to the door and was swinging it open. Anton grinned widely.

"Dees wife, she send dees for seek man," he said. "Squirrel soup—I shoot heem dees morning."

He thrust a small covered kettle in Lew's hands.

"Come in," Lew said, his tone a demand rather than an invitation. Anton stood by the door, twisting his cap in grimy fingers. "Sit down and have a cup of coffee," Lew ordered.

Anton declined with a confused shake of his head. "I eat already," he said. But Lew insisted, and the Frenchman finally accepted a cup of steaming liquid—there was scarcely anything else he could do. Charlie was watching Lew with apparent disapproval. But Lew was offering the sugar sack and a small tin of milk to Anton.

"I drink heem black," Anton said.

The lines around Lew's mouth tightened. Anton finished his coffee, affixed the cap back on his head, and departed.

"What the devil has got into you, Lew?" Charlie asked irritably. "You darned near poured a cup of coffee down the man's throat."

Lew was watching Anton walk around the wing of the house.

"There goes a dandy target for my pistol," he muttered, and Charlie stared at him in surprise. "And," Lew continued, "He's too big to miss."

"Okay. What's up?" Charlie demanded.

"Everything," Lew growled. "For one thing, did you notice Anton's face?"

"Of course," Charlie retorted. "His whiskers are gone."

"Which, by the way, means I was right," Lew snapped. "Anton was the clean-shaven intruder with who you grappled in the dark."

"Hold on," Charlie interrupted. "Don't put the handcuffs on him just yet. Anton's face has that blue-white look you only find on fresh-shaven skin. A couple of small cuts about his chin looked very fresh. I'd bet he shaved this morning. And that isn't all. The fellow I fought with in the dark took some pretty good shots around the eyes and is wearing some dandy bruises—did you see any of that on Anton?"

"No," Lew admitted. "And I remember now that this morning when I went down to the cabin, those cuts on Anton's chin were bleeding—which means they were fresh. But I've got enough on Anton without any of that. And it's serious, Charlie—the worst thing we've run up against yet."

"Shoot your yarn," Charlie commented. "But first slip me some sugar for this coffee."

Lew's fingers tightened about his partner's wrist as Charlie reached for the sack. "It's loaded with a deadly drug!"

Charlie straightened in amazement. "The sugar drugged? What kind of mystery story are you weaving, Lew?"

"None," Lew retorted. "There's plenty of real mystery going on right here in this house. I know you don't remember much of what happened this morning. But right after you drank a second cup of coffee at breakfast, with a lot of sugar in each one, you drifted off in a stupor that scared me stiff. Last night you did the same thing, but I thought then it was because you were dog-tired. This time I went for a doctor."

Charlie was listening, his face intent.

"Well, a Doctor Bardeaux came out and examined you. He said the only thing he could think of was that you'd been taking drugs. I thought he was a half-baked country bumpkin. So I drove him back to town and decided to get a specialist from the city to look you over. But then, as I was driving back home, something clicked in my brain and I saw that he might be right."

Lew reached over for the sugar sack. "I knew you would never take drugs on purpose, but suppose our midnight prowler had mixed some with our food, to put us to sleep so he could prowl without concern? I hadn't been affected by it, so that meant it could only be in the sugar. I seldom touch the stuff, you know. I drink my coffee straight and pour syrup on my flapjacks."

He began to spread out a little of the stuff on a plate with his knife point. Working out the tiny flakes, he pointed to them. "Touch a little to your tongue."

Charlie obeyed. Then he spat vigorously.

"You're right, and you think Anton put it here?"

"Who else?" Lew wanted to know. "It would give him the best chance to search the house at night. If I used sugar like you do, Davidson would be buying the farm from our heirs inside of a few days. That was why I tried Anton with a cup of coffee."

"He may not like sugar," Charlie speculated thoughtfully. "Can you remember if he used it when we ate dinner at the cabin?"

"No, I can't," Lew admitted. "But see that pot of squirrel stew? How much drug do you think is in it? Maybe Anton wanted us to have a double dose—in our coffee and with the soup."

"Perhaps," Charlie admitted.

"Well, he's going to get sadly fooled," Lew spoke through gritted teeth. "We're both going to be wide awake, and I suggest we shoot first and ask questions later."

Lew walked to the door and dumped the squirrel soup on the ground. "It smells good," he admitted, "but I'm afraid to touch it. I think the sugar was doped yesterday evening, after supper, for you didn't pass out until we had our late snack about midnight."

"But I complained about the coffee tasting queer before that," Charlie replied thoughtfully. "Remember?"

"Sure," Lew said. "That was probably the first time he doped it, and he didn't get enough in, so he came back last night and poured a lot in. He had just finished when you caught him in the dark."

"Wait a minute," Charlie remonstrated. "I thought we had decided that I didn't catch Anton here last night—that it was somebody else who is wearing a pair of black eyes right now."

Again Lew's face fell with disappointment.

"And if that wasn't Anton, when could he have doped our sugar yesterday?" Charlie asked. "We worked close to the house all day, and I can remember his ax going steady. At noon we were in here. Afternoon we were outside but so was Anton, down in the timber. He couldn't have got inside without our knowing it. Neither the man who put drugs in the sugar nor the man I fought was Anton. But they were the same—I'll bet on that."

"Then," Lew said slowly, "there is an unknown stranger in the mix. He got inside the house yesterday when we were working in the backyard—and I kept the front door locked all the time!"

"That's right—and it means the fellow can get inside whenever he wants, no matter if we lock the front and back."

Lew's eyes were glittering. "Or," he spoke slowly, "it means that he is already inside, and has been ever since we moved here!"

That brought Charlie up on his feet. "You're right, and that clears up much of this mystery! But where is he hiding?"

"In the attic," Lew cried promptly.

"But how does he get up and down? There aren't any stairs and we have seen no trapdoor."

"No, and we didn't see any trapdoor in the kitchen floor, either, not until somebody slipped and left it cracked open," Lew retorted. "I planned to give the old castle a real going over but didn't because you were sick. Suppose we begin that job right now?"

"There is one other job we must do first," Charlie protested. "We must lock up all of our food so nobody can drug it. We'll put a padlock on the cupboard—anybody could force it, but they would leave evidence that they had. If we don't, we will never dare eat anything in the house. Drugs could be mixed in anything—how would we tell?"

They went over the cupboard carefully, sinking every nailhead with a slender punch. This would reveal any attempt to pry up a panel or board. A padlock and hasp secured the doors, the latter so constructed that it covered the holding screws. After a half-hour of painstaking labor, they stood up to survey the job.

"A kid could break into it with a butter knife," Lew declared. "But a professional burglar couldn't open it and not leave signs to warn us. Before every meal, we'll give the box the once-over. If it looks bad, we throw away every bit of food inside. But I think this drugging business will stop after we clean out the attic."

"And we need to do the job right," Charlie concurred. He found a large sheet of wrapping paper. Then he tacked it on the tabletop. Next, he procured his square and a sharp pencil. "Bring the tape line outside," he directed Lew.

They carefully measured each wing, and Charlie drew a plan of the building to scale, marking the exact exterior dimensions.

"Now," he announced, "we're ready for the inside."

With tape line and rule, they measured each room and drew it on the plan. Every wall was checked for thickness across the door jambs. Charlie examined the drawing minutely and finally said, "Everything on the ground floor checks out, except the chimney coming down behind the stairway. It seems to be larger than necessary. You wouldn't guess it was about four feet thick, would you?"

"Hardly," Lew replied. "But part of it is inside the partition wall."

"Of course," Charlie replied. "It would be. And there isn't any flue hole. Come upstairs and we'll finish."

The upper rooms were measured and drawn on the plan. When the last had been laid out to scale, Charlie examined the results while Lew fidgeted impatiently. "Let's get the ax and with just a few swings we'll know what is real or not," Lew muttered.

"Sure," Charlie grinned. "But we want to live in the house this winter and sell it when we're ready. It isn't necessary to destroy the place. In a half-minute, I'll know just where any secret stairway to the attic might be hidden."

He straightened up with a queer expression.

"Get the tape, Lew. I want to check the closets upstairs again."

"Something wrong?" Lew asked, but his partner did not reply as they ran up the steps. They remeasured the lengths of two closets separating a pair of large bedrooms. Lew tried to conceal his impatience as Charlie checked the figures against his plan.

"There's something funny about those closets," Charlie finally declared. "A space four feet deep was left for them. But while this space is twenty-six feet long, each closet is only eleven feet. That leaves at least three feet not accounted for."

"An ax would have discovered that faster," Lew retorted.

"What's more," continued Charlie, disregarding Lew's words, "the three feet of extra space is directly behind the big chimney!"

At that, Lew ran out to the yard.

A minute later, he entered carrying the ax.

"Come on," he invited. "Let's find those three missing feet."

But as he stepped on the lower tread of the staircase, a familiar sound caught his ear. "Listen," he said. "A car just stopped outside."

Charlie stepped to a front window. "It's Davidson."

Lew dropped the ax with an impatient gesture. Although he was curious about what had brought the real estate man back, he was more impatient to chop into the concealed space and see what lay beyond.

Davidson climbed leisurely out of his powerful roadster and approached. Lew and Charlie sat casually on the benches. Fingers rapped loudly on the panel. Charlie arose and swung it open.

"Ah," he said in well-simulated surprise. "Come in!"

Davidson smiled, but his face was set with businesslike purpose. They could see that he was about to make his final offer for the farm. If they didn't sell now, he would not return to make another.

"Thought I'd drop in on my way back to the city," he began. "You might have changed your minds since yesterday. I have, in fact, changed mine. My offer of eleven thousand dollars is withdrawn."

Lew shot a meaningful glance at Charlie.

"I'm glad you didn't take me up. If you want to sell today, my offer is eight thousand. And I don't much care if you take it."

"Real estate around here must have taken a terrible slump," Lew replied. "Surprised we didn't see anything in the morning paper."

Davidson smiled at that. "Things have changed—things that don't appear in a newspaper," he retorted. "I heard that it was a bootleggers' hideout when Patton lived here. That is going to make trouble for whoever buys the place."

He seemed to concentrate all of the cold light in his eyes upon Lew and then said, "Somebody is going to be in bad when that bunch of killers comes this way again."

Lew's eyes opened with wide innocence. "Bootleggers?"

"You know what I mean, all right," Davidson's short laugh was ugly. "So this is your last chance to get out with your hides and your bankroll intact. What do you say—and this time, make it snappy!"

"The answer is still no," Charlie replied quietly.

"I thought it would be," Davidson said. "Well, you can't blame me for whatever happens next. So long."

They watched him cross the yard, vault the fence and climb into his car. They followed out onto the porch, and a lesser sound blended in with the roar of Davidson's exhaust. They glanced back in the direction from which the real estate man had come and saw a motorcycle slowing. The leather-jacketed man on the seat was waving, beckoning them out to the fence.

"Who the devil is that?" Lew asked.

"The best way to find out is see what he wants," Charlie offered.

Their visitor was a rather young fellow clad in khaki breeches and battered puttees. His face was freckled, nose flat. But what caught their gaze and held it were two colorless eyes that bored into their own. The man was almost albino, scarcely a shred of color tinted the irises of his eyes or the brows and lashes that outlined them. His gaze—a cool, deadly look—left them somewhat disconcerted.

"Who was that bird who just pulled away from here?" the stranger asked curtly. There was no request in his voice. He was not asking for a reply, he was demanding it.

"That?" Lew drawled. "Why, that was the Prince of Wales. He left us an order for fox skins."

"Ain't you funny," the man on the motorcycle sneered. "See this?" a hand deftly whipped back the lapel of his jacket to reveal a nickel star, the badge of a highway policeman.

"Spit it out! An' quick!"

Chapter 8 – The Secret of the Attic

The humor faded from Lew's face at the crisp command of the man before him. But before he could answer, Charlie spoke up.

"That was George J. Davidson, a real estate dealer from Chicago. He has been trying to buy this farm from us."

"That's better." The stranger grinned. "So he calls himself a real estate dealer now, does he? The last time I saw him, it was in the big house at Joliet, behind steel bars." The colorless eyes were searching their faces with persistence. "And you didn't sell?"

"No, but darned if I don't wish we had," Lew mourned.

"Why? Some of Patton's old friends drop in on you?"

They looked at him with startled surprise. Was this stranger actually a policeman? He knew about the bootlegging gang that had used the farm as a hideout when Patton owned the land. Blinky, the driver of the big truck, had said something about Patton "fixing" all of the local law—they wondered if this was one of them. But the cold eyes saw their doubt, and the freckled face—Charlie wondered that freckles could be on a visage so devoid of other color—softened in a grin.

"You boys needn't worry about me. Name's Johnny Bass, State Highway Police. I've had a line on Patton and his game for some time, but he cleared out before I could round him up."

When neither Lew nor Charlie spoke, he continued.

"So, you bought the place? Well, I'm going to spill some things for you. Patton was mixing in with an ugly bunch. I got a hint, too, that something was pulled off along the road last night. How about it? You boys better tell me. Part of my job's to protect the innocent, and believe me, if you fouled that Chicago outfit, you're going to need it."

Charlie must have decided to trust the man because he rapidly told of their run-in with the gangsters. But not a word did he say about the tricks that had taken place in the house. Johnny Bass watched sharply, the colorless eyes growing more frosty with each sentence.

"Too bad I was out of the county last night," was all he said. Then, "You boys keep your eyes open. That gang will be back, maybe tonight. Better take to the woods when they come.

"That was clever," he added, turning to Lew, "the way you ran their truck down the road and led them away. I hope your luck holds up next time. I'll be in the locality tonight, and if something should get started, you can count on me to break in on it. So long—and don't talk to anybody else about any of this!"

Johnny Bass kicked the starting pedal of his motorcycle, and with a roar the machine carried him away down the road.

"That fellow would be useful in a jam," Lew remarked, "But a queer name—Johnny Bass. Bad pair of eyes, too."

"Not bad—just dangerous," Charlie corrected. "I hope he's wrong about that gang starting back in with us tonight. We are going to have plenty on our hands without that."

"I agree," Lew replied. "One thing at a time is my motto from now on, and there's plenty to do up in the attic. Come, we must finish the job."

Then Lew fairly ran back inside the house, and as he picked up the ax he declared, "Nothing is going to delay me any longer."

He turned impatiently to Charlie, but his partner was staring at the kitchen table. "Look," Charlie half-whispered.

Lew looked down at a bare tabletop. Then he realized Charlie's carefully drawn plans of the house had disappeared. Charlie had fastened the corners with four tacks. And the tacks were still in place, holding fragments of paper. The plan had been quickly torn away. Bewilderment gripped them both. Lew shook it off first and up the stairway he went, two steps at a jump. Charlie was close on his heels.

"Stand back," Lew warned, and stepping to the rear wall of a closet, he swung the ax into the partition. Two quick blows, and the keen blade crashed through into an open space.

Lew worked eagerly, enlarging the hole. When the opening was wide enough to squeeze through, he slipped inside.

"About three feet—just as you estimated," he announced. "And there's a ladder going straight up into the attic."

Pushing out from the inside, Lew quickly smoothed the rough edges of busted lath and plaster. "Get a flashlight," he directed. "The attic will be dark as pitch."

Charlie ran back downstairs and snatched up an electric flash. He hesitated a second, then crossed the room and slipped the pistol from under his pillow into his pocket. He had climbed halfway up the staircase when a queer sound glued his feet to the treads.

A strange bumping noise sounded right under his feet. It ended with a dull thud, and the stairs on which he stood seemed to shake at the impact. He called, "You all right, Lew?"

There was no response. He leaped up the remaining steps and dashed into the narrow closet. The space was empty.

"Lew!" Charlie called, throwing the light about. As Lew had said, a stepladder led up into the attic. It had wide rungs and was nailed to the front wall studs. When Charlie looked to the back ,he saw a wide space exactly where the wall of a chimney should be.

The chimney clearly was a false structure. Charlie stepped close to the opening and flashed the light down. A steep stairs with treads like a ship's ladder led straight down. Clearly this was the secret passage from the attic. You climbed down the ladder from the attic then used the stairs inside the chimney to reach the lower floor. Charlie wondered if the shaft extended all of the way down into the cellar.

Then the light of understanding burst over him. Here was the explanation of the mysterious footsteps that seemed to sound from an empty stairway. When a man climbed up through the false chimney, his footfalls could be plainly heard, creating an illusion of invisible feet on the stairs.

Charlie shot his lamp down through the shaft. Something lay at the bottom, a tumbled heap. Focusing the beam into a narrow ray, Charlie saw a white hand stretched up, and with a sharp cry he realized that he was staring down at Lew.

Charlie looked for the ax on the closet floor—he needed that ax, for there was a quicker way to reach Lew that didn't require the narrow passage down. When he didn't see it, Charlie turned to the ladder. It would be just like Lew to start up to the attic alone without a light. He climbed swiftly and then reached up and felt at the edge of the attic floor. The ax lay on the floor close to the ladder top, as he expected.

Had Lew fallen from up there? If so, it had been a long tumble. As he dropped back to the floor, Charlie wondered at the queerness of it all. Lew was not one to slip—he was remarkably sure of foot and hand.

Charlie raced down the visible staircase and then sent the ax crashing into the base of the false chimney shaft. The blade burst through a board wall and then he worked more carefully, cutting high to miss his partner lying close against the wall inside. He ripped at the boards with his hands, and finally a square panel swung out on concealed hinges. He had found the secret door into the false chimney.

As he worked, Charlie noticed how the joint and edges of the door had been skillfully concealed with the old wallpaper. Then he dragged Lew out into the room.

With intense relief he felt his partner's heart beating steadily. A swift examination showed no injury save a cut across one cheek and a fingernail torn from one hand. Legs and arms seemed to be intact.

But what had caused the tumble? Charlie splashed cold water over Lew's head, and his eyes opened then filled with swift understanding. "Hurry!" he said thickly. "He cracked me on the head just as I swung up to the attic. He's up there now—don't let him get away."

"He can't," Charlie soothed. "I've got my gun, and nobody is coming down either set of stairs without me seeing him. That's why I cut you out here in the doorway, so I could watch both stairways."

Lew sat up. "I should have waited for you, of course. But I was too anxious. I got up high enough to lay the ax on the floor and then when I started to swing myself up, bingo! I toppled over on the closet floor and that started me skidding down the chimney."

"It's a miracle you didn't break your neck," Charlie said. "Why, you must have slid headfirst."

"I did," Lew confirmed.

"We must get back up there as quick as we can," Charlie said. "Shall I go alone, or can you pull yourself together?"

"What do you think?" Lew retorted, "Get my gun, will you? But I don't think I had better go first this time. I'll cover you while you climb the ladder."

Armed with pistols and lights, they entered the little space between the closet ends. Charlie started up the ladder, pistol in one hand, climbing with the other. Lew stood below playing his light on the opening overhead, his gun already aimed for quick use.

"He's probably hiding behind the chimney," Lew advised.

Charlie went slowly until his head was almost level with the floor. Then, with a quick spring, he jumped up, clutched the top of the ladder and half-swung, half-rolled over and away from the opening. He pulled the light from his pocket and snapped it on.

Nothing but rafters, roof and the big chimney met his gaze. Charlie saw with surprise that it was red clay bricks up here. Someone had gone to a lot of trouble to hide that passageway.

Picking his way slowly over the rough floorboards, he directed his light into every possible hiding place but found nothing.

"I want you to come up now," he called down. "Watch the head of the ladder while I search back in the wings."

Lew's head slowly appeared in the opening, and drawing his legs up, he sat on the edge of the floor.

"Keep your light on me," Charlie ordered. "That will cover me better than if you were at my side."

The roof sloped back from the center, forming low spaces at the eaves where a man might creep on hands and knees. There were three wings to explore, and Charlie's had to creep along cautiously. Some places the floorboards did not meet, and that left just the plastered ceiling exposed underneath.

"If I get bumped off up here," Charlie called back, "jump down, set fire to this old castle, and then wait outside with your deer rifle to pot whoever runs out."

Although Charlie was joking, there was a grim quality in his voice, and Lew growled assent. He appreciated the deadly risk of his partner's job. But his own head was too unsteady to attempt to follow in the dark across an uneven attic floor. All he could do was hold his own gun and shine his light full on Charlie's back.

It was over the kitchen that Charlie made the next discovery. "Here's a half can of water and some pieces of dry bread. Now two empty cans. I see a bundle under the eaves. Steady with your light. I'll have it in a moment."

Following a long silence, Charlie spoke again. "Blankets, Lew. Two dandy wool ones. Somebody has been living in this attic."

"But where is he now?" Lew demanded.

"One more wing to search …"

Charlie turned into the peaked roof space and found it empty. "The bird has flown!" he called out.

"That can't be," Lew replied. "He batted me on the head just a few minutes ago, and nobody came down either stairway."

"Are you sure? You could have slipped and fallen," Charlie knew this conjecture was false, but he voiced the thought, anyway.

"I don't fall that easy," Lew snapped. "Say, do you suppose he's on the roof? Could a man crawl up through the top of the chimney?"

Charlie came hurrying back. "That's an idea. Let's check it out."

The brick chimney was solid up here, and they knew the only way to enter it would be from below. Charlie dropped down the ladder and ran to the bottom of the brickwork. He peered up. Yes, the flue was large enough for an athletic man to scramble up by simply digging his heels into the brick sides.

"He may be outside now, perched on a roof ridge," Charlie said and then leaped down the stairs to check

Lew heard the front door bang. Lew was hoping that he might also hear Charlie's pistol fire, but no such sound reached his ears. He hobbled down after his partner, getting stiffer every minute.

Charlie was standing in the yard looking at the rear roof gable.

Lew followed his gaze.

A large pine grew close to the house, and Charlie's attention was riveted upon it. Several thick branches actually rubbed against the wall, and one reached the roof. It would be easy for an athletic man to swing down from the roof, clutch a branch, work his way along it to the trunk of the tree, and then climb swiftly to the ground.

"He's got away," Lew groaned.

"We're too late," Charlie agreed. "We might as well go back inside. He could be a mile away by now."

"Charlie, I'm disgusted." Lew replied.

"Me, too, but we know much more now than we did before. We know where our mystery man has been hiding, and we can easily take care that he doesn't hide there again."

"I've got a better plan," Lew said. "Come on inside and listen."

When they were seated at the table, Lew explained. "We know this bird works in the dark and doesn't use a light because that would give him away."

"Sure," Charlie agreed.

"Well, I'm going to set three bear traps: one at the bottom of the chimney where the hidden panel opens into the room, and one in the little space upstairs. Then I'll put the third in the attic right at the head of the ladder. He'll either stick a hand in it when he climbs up, or he'll step in it on his way down. Either will be okay with me."

"Dandy," Charlie agreed heartily. "That crack on the bean seems to have started your brain working again. And since he's outside now, I believe we should alter our alarm so he can't climb the tree without tripping it. I'll string some of the wires among the branches so the bell will ring if he starts to climb. That will give us time to get ready."

As Lew brought out the three big traps, he wondered aloud, "Who is this fellow, anyway? And what does he want?"

Charlie shrugged his shoulders. "I guess he is after the same thing as Davidson and Anton. It must be something valuable, for all of them have taken some real risk to find it."

"I hope he comes back," Lew replied ruefully. "And the sooner the better."

"He'll come, all right," Charlie asserted. "None of the others has given up. Davidson is just running a bluff with that final offer."

"I'm going to name him 'X,' How's that?" Lew proclaimed.

"Then we can refer to 'Mr. X' when we talk about his prowling."

They pulled part of the wires of Charlie's burglar alarm and strung several strands in the tree, locating the fine strands so a climber would not touch the wires themselves but his weight on the lower branches would tighten them until they tripped the alarm and started the bell ringing. Then they set the big traps in the house and nailed the chains securely to the heavy floor joists.

Night was closing down on the northern forestland by the time they had finished and entered the kitchen to prepare supper. Lew agreed that it had been one of the busiest days of his life.

"But things finally seem to be moving right along," he declared with some satisfaction.

Charlie was looking the cupboard over with keen eyes. "Nothing disturbed," he decided. "We can eat without worry. And I'm glad, too, because I'm hungry."

Lew was heartened by that. But he also saw with a quick look that his partner's face was lined with fatigue. Although Lew himself was a bit shaky from his fall down the chimney stairs, he firmly announced, "You are going to lie down after supper and rest. I'll sit up and listen for the alarm. Then I'll wake you after a couple of hours. If we take shifts, one of us will be awake when Mr. X returns."

Charlie agreed this was sound. After he had eaten, he kicked off his shoes and lay down on his sleeping bag without undressing. Lew sat beside the table reading. An hour later, he turned off the lantern, laid pistol and flashlight within easy reach and sat in silence in the dark.

The moonless sky was black, the scene ideally set to trap a night prowler. Lew grinned as he remembered the surprises waiting for Mr. X should he attempt to climb up or down through the chimney. His only fear was that Mr. X might not appear.

Time dragged on until, hours later, the soft tinkle of the alarm bell jerked Lew's heavy eyes wide open. He sat clearing his head for a moment before springing over to shut off the bell.

Stooping over Charlie, he shook the sleeping form. "Wake up!" he whispered. "Someone's coming!"

Charlie was on his feet in an instant, and they crept noiselessly to the bottom of the stairway, feet in socks, pistols in hand.

A full minute passed. Had the alarm bell scared Mr. X away?

Lew gripped his partner's arm. His keen ears had detected a faint sound above. Now Charlie heard it, too, feet scraping over the roof or perhaps rubbing the chimney bricks as their owner climbed inside.

Lew took a step towards the stairs but Charlie drew him back. If the man avoided the big traps upstairs he might elude them by climbing on down to the first floor and then running out the door. They must stay and wait here, to cut him off.

Lew's head shot up, and this time a smile lit his face. His keen ears had caught a familiar metallic sound. Then a shrill yell split the night, and Lew was sure of the sound he had caught first. It had been the click of the big trap's jaws as they flashed up from the lock-notches below the pan. He snapped on his light and started up the stairs.

They rushed into the narrow closet. There was room for only one at a time, and Lew squeezed in first. Charlie pressed close behind. The trap chain rattled, and then everything was silent.

Lew saw him first, after thrusting gun and light around the corner of the shattered partition. But there was no need for such caution. In the glare of the light he saw a heavy man bent nearly double, hands pulling futilely at the jaws of the big bear trap that had neatly closed about both of his feet. The figure straightened slowly and stared at Lew.

Chapter 9 – A Shot from the Roof

Keen disappointment displaced Lew's elation as he stared into the eyes of Anton Blierut. He had set his trap for the mysterious Mr. X who had hidden in their attic and who they believed had been mixing drug with their sugar. But instead they had caught Anton—face twitching from the shock of the massive trap jaws snapped about his legs.

Charlie had insisted that they wrap the jaws with heavy strips of blanket, but the impact still had been intense.

"What the devil are you doing here?" Lew demanded.

"Take dees trap off my feet, an' I tell you," Anton replied. He spoke calmly; nothing in his voice indicated pain or the guilt of a trespasser caught in the act.

"Straighten up, and I'll clamp the jaws down," Lew agreed. "But it's taken us so long to catch you, I sort of hate to turn you loose."

"Catch me? M'sieur jokes! You know where to find Anton any time." His tone was mildly indignant.

"I mean to catch you prowling about in our house—especially after dark," Lew explained.

Anton drew a breath deep into his powerful chest. His posture straightened, and with a dignity that somehow impressed despite his awkward position, he spoke.

"I nevaire prowl in your house—nevaire but once," he added, correcting himself. "Today I find dees in your kitchen, and I take heem." He drew a folded paper from his coat and thrust it out.

Charlie's eyes opened with surprise as he unfolded the paper. It was the missing plan he had drawn of the house.

Lew scowled at the Frenchman. "We may be slow, but we're not dumb! We know you've been snooping around our house. Fact is, we caught you the night we moved in. You were upstairs with a lantern, and you ran out the back door when we knocked at the front."

"That was not what you call—prowling. It not yet your house then, any more than M'sieur Patton's. And I have not prowl since."

"You came back in the night, after we were asleep, to pick up the measuring pole you forgot. You know, the pole you used to measure the upstairs rooms. We know you and Davidson have been working together searching the house. I heard you talking about it night before last. Now laugh that off!"

Anton shrugged his shoulders, his face suddenly blanketed by an inscrutable mask. "If you tink dat—I say nothing."

"Oh, you'll say plenty when we get you in front of a judge for house-breaking," Lew responded grimly. His temper was beginning to overbalance his restraint.

"Wait, Lew. Let me do the talking," Charlie spoke up. "You get those trap springs locked down."

Charlie pushed closer into the narrow space before the chimney-like shaft. "You might as well tell us all about it, Anton. Who was the man you followed up on the roof a minute ago?"

The Frenchman's eyes blinked swiftly, and Lew lifted an astonished face. "What makes you think he followed another man?" Lew asked wonderingly.

"I thought that all along," Charlie replied. "You didn't jerk out the switch of our alarm bell when it rang. You merely wedged the striker mute with a fold of the blanket. And just before we started upstairs, I heard it vibrate, trying to sound again. You were listening for a sound up on the roof and didn't notice. But I suspected then that two men had climbed the tree—one close behind the other. And the last was Anton. How about it?"

"You ees right," Anton said. "I follow dees man when I see heem start up the tree. Then I know where he has hid. I follow to see if he do you harm—he a bad one."

"You know him—this fellow who hid in the attic?"

"Sure," Anton asserted. He gestured with eloquence, leaning back under the open flue of the chimney overhead in order to gain more space for his expressive hands.

"Who is he and what does he want?" Lew demanded.

"He ees..."

A pistol shot crashed from above. As they turned startled eyes upwards, Anton slumped with a groan, sentence unfinished. Stunned, they watched his big body crumple. A stream of blood trickled down one of the Frenchman's clean-shaven cheeks.

The sharp bite of smokeless powder stung their nostrils as Charlie seized Anton and dragged him away from the shaft. Anton had collapsed on the very edge of the steep stairway, and Charlie was afraid he would tumble headfirst.

"That shot came from above, Lew," Charlie whispered fiercely. "We've got him trapped if we work fast! Run down and head him off at the big pine. I'll see how badly Anton is hurt."

Lew already had leaped down the stairway before Charlie finished. But haste again proved his undoing. At the bottom step, Lew tripped and sprawled headlong across the floor. The pistol flew from his fingers and struck the baseboard of the wall.

Lew struggled to his feet and reached for the gun in the dark. It had slid farther than he expected, and his fingers groped empty floor. He jerked out a match and struck it viciously on the wall.

The head flew off.

Steadying his nerves, Lew drew a second match and rubbed it deliberately over the plaster. It flared and disclosed the pistol a yard away. Even as his fingers closed over the butt, Lew whirled towards the door, dashing out. Then he sped for the rear wing of the house.

He could barely see 10 feet in the shadows, and as he ran with disregard for the uneven footing, he thought desperately.

Did he dare use his pocket lamp? The man on the roof could shoot at the light beam.

As the thought tumbled swiftly in his mind, he hit upon the only safe way. Snapping on the light, Lew circled the tree, running about its base at a speed that would puzzle a marksman even in daylight. And as he ran, he threw the beam up towards the top of the house to where the big pine limb ran out and rubbed against the wall. If he caught the shape of a figure crouching, he intended to shoot.

But nothing except tree and a gray shingled roof met his eye. Running steps behind told him Charlie was coming. "Hurry!" Lew urged. "He must be on the other side. I haven't seen anything."

Shielding himself behind the tree, Charlie added the glow of his light to Lew's. One glance showed him that part of the roof was bare.

"Stay here, Lew, and watch the tree. Get back of it like I am. I'm going to circle the house. If he's hiding back of one of the other wings, I'll pick him out."

Charlie disappeared around the corner. In a minute he was back, circling from the opposite direction. "We're too late," he panted. "I've been clear around and seen the roof is empty. He must have slid down the tree before you made it out."

"How's Anton—dead?" Lew asked in a low voice.

"Knocked out. I left him on the floor. The bullet struck in front and above his right ear. It came at an angle down the chimney, and luckily Anton wasn't directly underneath. If he had been, chances are it would have killed him. The bullet may have nicked brick before glancing across his thick skull."

Lew slammed his flashlight to the ground.

"How the devil does this fellow get away?" he asked no one.

"Don't get hysterical," Charlie snapped. "And pick up that light. Now run down to the cabin and get Anton's wife. Then jump in the car and get the doctor. You can slam things around after we get Anton fixed up. If he dies, people may say we shot him. And what about the bear trap around his legs? We'd have a swell time explaining that."

Lew stifled his disappointment and started off through the trees. Charlie ran lightly back upstairs. He had left Anton on the floor of one of the large rooms, his head propped up with a coat. The head wound was bleeding freely, and Charlie changed the pack of gauze he kept pressing against it. That was all he could do until more skilled hands came to properly dress the gash.

Anton lay with closed eyes, his huge chest barely moving. His face was ghastly white, and Charlie began to grow afraid that he might die before Lew brought the physician.

The door downstairs banged and he heard his partner's voice. "Upstairs—go right up," Lew was saying. Then Anton's wife ran into the room. With a choked cry, she knelt beside the unconscious man.

Answering her mute look of inquiry, Charlie tried to explain. "He was shot in the head—by somebody up on the roof. He fell over and has been unconscious ever since."

Charlie decided it would be better not to say more. He heard Lew drive across the yard and out into the road at a terrific speed.

"Who would shoot your man?" he asked. "Anton knew—he had started to tell us when he was shot—and you do, too."

The woman shook her head in denial. But a veil of inscrutable caution had spread over her face, a mask similar to that which had covered the features of her husband a few minutes before he had been shot. Charlie saw that if she did know the man who had shot her husband, she would never say unless Anton gave her permission.

They stood silently waiting for the doctor. Charlie looked at his watch every few minutes, impatiently scanning its face, incredulous that more time had not elapsed. Then they heard the car far down the road, and from its sound Charlie guessed there was little if any free space between the throttle and the floor. Brakes squealed in the front yard. Then the door opened and men climbed the stairs.

Doctor Bardeaux knelt beside Anton with a professional air that instantly gave them confidence. Charlie noted that he asked no questions but started immediately to work cleaning and dressing the wound. Bardeaux glanced up once at Lew after he listened to Anton's heart.

"Haven't been giving him dope, too?"

Lew grinned back. "No, that ghost doesn't walk anymore. But you were right about Charlie. He was doped. I'll tell you about it as we drive back to town. How about Anton—badly hurt?"

"A glancing bullet won't hurt anybody with a skull as solid as Anton's. Especially when the bullet is a small one—I'd guess it to be a twenty-two. If it had struck him squarely, it could have killed him. But he'll come around in a few minutes. I've seen Anton cracked up worse than this—remember when he was caught under a falling tree three winters ago?" He glanced at the woman, who nodded assent.

Their eyes turned down as Anton groaned, moved his head and looked up at them with vacant eyes that gradually filled with understanding. He rolled his head feebly back and forth, closed his eyes and wrinkled his forehead. Anton was trying to place himself, understand where he lay and why.

"Who shot him?" Bardeaux asked.

"That's what we want to know," Charlie answered. "Anton knows, but he hasn't been able to tell us." Charlie explained rapidly what had happened, enlarging only slightly on what he had told Anton's wife.

Bardeaux walked back and examined the false chimney. They heard him mutter as he kicked the big trap. Then he reappeared with a serious face. "Rather complicated layout—that hidden stairway. I suppose that ends the ghost stories."

"Darned right!" Lew declared.

Anton again opened his eyes. Bardeaux leaned over him. "How does the head feel?"

"She ache—like dees devil," Anton muttered.

Bardeaux gathered up his leather case. "I'll come tomorrow and look at him again. It's nothing to worry over. Anton's tough."

He turned to the door. "You can take me back now, young fellow, and while I want to get all the sleep possible, I'd rather spend five minutes more making the trip back than we did coming here."

When they had gone, Anton sat up rather abruptly. "You get heem, M'sieur? Dees fellow who shoot me?"

Charlie admitted regretfully that they hadn't. Anton scowled.

"Dees fellow he smart. He hear me follow so he not climb down chimney. No, he hide over back of dees roof and watch me go down chimney like beeg fool. An' he sneak up to listen—poof! I should get shot in my head!"

"But who is he?" Charlie asked eagerly. "You started to tell us just before he shot—he must have fired to stop you. You must know him—what's his name?"

Anton stared silently for a moment. Then he said, "I not tell—now. Wait until M'sieur Lew come back. There is tings we must talk about—all of us. My head ache like the devil."

He got up and stood rather shakily. "I go home now. You come in dees morning. Then we talk."

The inscrutable expression was again covering his features, and Charlie saw there was no use whatsoever to challenge his decision. Aided by his wife, Anton clumped downstairs. Then they walked together across the dark yard.

Charlie closed the door thoughtfully and then sat down to wait for Lew. The mysterious events that had dogged their steps from the first night in the house seemed more enigmatic than ever. And yet Charlie felt that if he could put his finger on a single fact, he might unravel the whole puzzle. Before the shot, Anton had seemed about to talk, but the shot had changed that.

Lew swung the car up before the house, headlights flashing through the front window. He jumped out and rushed inside.

"Well, I got Doc home, but I can't say he takes kindly to my driving. I'd sure hate to be bleeding to death and waiting for him to arrive and save me. How's Anton? What'd he say while I was away?"

"Anton has gone home with his wife. And he said—nothing."

"Why didn't you worm it out of him?" Lew asked.

"I can't imagine anybody worming anything out of Anton that he didn't want to tell," Charlie responded with a grin. "But he asked us to come down to the cabin early in the morning. He said he wants to talk things over then, and I believe him."

Lew made a shrewd guess. "Anton must have a vital interest in what all of these birds have been searching for. Maybe that's why he won't talk, not until he discovers how we stand in the matter."

"That may be it," Charlie agreed. "But we better turn in if we expect to sleep at all tonight."

Lew was up at sunrise. "Come on," he urged his drowsy partner. "Remember our date with Anton."

After breakfast, as they walked to the Frenchman's cabin. Charlie said incredulously, "Do you realize we've only been here four days?

We haven't had time to give the foxes more than a glance."

Anton opened the door. His head was wrapped with wide bandages like a turban, but his eyes were bright and his cheeks full of color. "Come in, M'sieurs," he invited, and as they seated themselves he came to the point at once.

"Last night I prowl in your house — that ees true — but not for the reason I look before you come. Last night I scared for you — ees fellow on the roof shoot me — he might hurt you. Ees bad."

They acknowledged the obvious truth of that.

"After you come, I only go in house once. Dee time I take your paper from dees table."

"Why?" Charlie interrupted.

Anton looked somewhat ashamed. "I puzzle my head for days. But I not able to measure and draw like you. I not smart enough to measure dees closets inside."

He stopped to find words to continue. Anton was evidently not accustomed to long speeches in English. He was watching their faces with keen eyes. They felt as though a crucial decision was coming.

"When you buy dees farm from M'sieur Patton," he spoke slowly, "you buy land and buildings. Ees right?"

"Yes," Lew answered.

"Then eef there is something else in house, something you not buy, what then? The right owner get it?"

"Absolutely," Charlie assured him. "We won't keep anything that isn't ours — provided the rightful owner can prove his claim."

Anton nodded with evident relief. "Now I tell you. There ees money hid in heem. Money that belongs to me!"

"The devil!" Lew exclaimed. "Why does it belong to you?"

"Ees simple. Money ees my father's — an' he ees dead!"

"You mean your father was the old Frenchman who built the house — Henri Ducross?"

"I am Anton Ducross," the man replied formally. "I change last name when I find he ees dead and money gone."

And as they looked into his straightforward eyes, they could not do other than believe him.

"I have papers tell when and where I born," Anton continued. "My father come here from Canada, an' he leave my mother and me behind. He have another woman here, and have son by her. When my mother die, I start out to find heem. I come too late; my father ees dead. I know he bring money with heem — I know he make more money

125

here. He smuggle men across dees border into America, China men. That is why he feex up dees big chimney with stairs. He hide dees men and money here. But I tink then somebody rob heem."

Anton had to pause for breath and words.

"I find my father dead—no money—so I say nothing. Dees money is nevaire found. I forget about it until dees man Davidson come. He say dees money is still in house. Somebody that knows tell heem. If I help heem find it, he give me half. I say sure to heem, but to myself I say 'Anton, dees money is yours. When you find it, you keep it all.'

"At first dees Davidson help me, but then M'sieur Patton stick close in house. Then you come and Davidson still stay away. This look funny to me. Then I see someting."

"What did you see?" Lew asked.

"I use dees pole to measure rooms—you find pole that night. But I forget to take it home, an' next morning I see pole lying on ground back of fox pens. You throw heem there?"

"We didn't," Charlie said quietly.

"I tink not. Then I know somebody else in house. And Davidson he afraid of heem. I watch, and last night I see heem come to the pine. He pass close, and I know heem even in dees dark. Ees my father's son, my half-brother. I know he kill father but nevaire find money. Now he come back to steal eet from Anton."

His eyes were glowing with a cold rage.

"And Davidson was afraid of him? Why?"

"That I not know."

"I do," Lew exclaimed. "Johnny Bass said Davidson had been in prison. Probably, this other bird was there, too. Maybe they got friendly and planned to come back and dig up the money together. Perhaps Davidson did his stretch first, came on up ahead of the other to double-cross him. I think Davidson was working on his own hook when he tried to buy us out. But where would he get the money?"

"I don't think he has it," Charlie suggested. "He was probably planning to pull some slick scheme on us after we agreed to sell."

He turned to Anton. "So, it was your half-brother who lived in the attic and who shot you down the chimney?"

"That ees heem. And now I look for heem and when I find..." Anton's jaw shut with a snap like the bear trap's.

"It's your father's money hidden in the house?" Charlie asked. Then seeing the certainty on Anton's face, he reached a quick decision and looked to Lew, who only nodded assent.

"OK. We'll help you find it, and if we do, it is yours. If there is enough and you want to buy back the family farm, we'll be glad to sell to you—at our cost. But that's up to you."

"I do dees very ting," Anton cried. "I not want you to lose one dollar. I pay you back all you give M'sieur Patton."

"Well, now that we know what we're looking for, suppose we get busy and find it?" Lew suggested.

Charlie spoke next. "I'm afraid we're all going to be disappointed, but we'll try. How much do you think it amounts to?"

"Davidson say twenty-five t'ousand," Anton replied.

"You made a pretty close guess the other day, Charlie," Lew said. "And I don't suppose it will be less—probably more. Davidson isn't the type to tell Anton the full amount."

They searched the rest of the morning. Every joint and crack in the plaster and woodwork was scrutinized. They sounded the spaces between every stud and joist and tore out the wall under the stairs. They smashed through partitions wherever their sounding hammer brought out a different tone. The secret hiding place of the treasure of Henri Ducross, if it existed, defied them.

Doctor Bardeaux drove out to examine Anton's head a little after noon. Much against the Frenchman's protests, he changed the bandage.

Lew was climbing the stairs for the fiftieth time later that afternoon. The sun had started to slide down behind a cloud bank that hung just above the horizon line of timber. He paused at the top step and looked down. Between the riser and tread was a crack, wider at one end than the other. Lew reached for his knife as a matter of habit to probe it. He did not remember if he had given similar attention to that exact crack before. Chances were he had. But as he jerked out his knife, a half-dollar coin rolled from his pocket and hit the step with a clang. The coin spun slowly, rolled sideways, and when it straightened against the upright riser, it slipped through the crack. Lew heard it bounce and roll down to the bottom. But it was the sound it made as it landed that sent his heart pounding. His keen ears caught the faint clink made when coins strike together.

He whooped at the top of his voice. "I've found it! Charlie! Anton! I've found the treasure!"

They both raced up the stairway in headlong eagerness. Lew was pointing at the crack.

"Look there! It's just wide enough to slip money through. It's the slot to the old man's bank. See how the wood is worn back of it? That wear was made by pushing coins—gold, probably—through the slot. They roll down and lodge under the bottom step. Get a hammer!"

Then Lew saw the hammer in Anton's hand and took it. He aimed a short, quick blow at the bottom step. The tread sprang up an inch. The others crowded close, and that hampered his movements.

Before the hammer could land a finishing blow, two bullets smashed through the window and buried themselves in the plaster a foot above Lew's head. Lew dropped the hammer, and Charlie leaped to a front window.

"Gangsters!" he shouted. "Get the guns—quick! They're running across the yard!"

Chapter 10 – The Round Up

Lew threw himself to the floor, broke the lowest pane of window glass with his pistol barrel, thrust the muzzle through and fired at the gang of bootleggers running toward the house. Swinging the pistol like a machine gun, Lew emptied the magazine without really aiming.

He got the desired effect as men scattered and dropped to the ground, worming in behind the clumps of dead weeds and grass.

One of them dropped before the others, throwing up his hands with a sharp exclamation and then tumbling over on his face like they do in the movies. Lew rolled back from the window to load a second charged pistol magazine and grab the box of shells that sat beside his sleeping bag.

By then Charlie was crouched beside the opposite window. He had not fired but waited tensely, watching the men in the yard, only half-concealed but at long range for a pistol shot.

Anton was beating his hands together in helpless frustration. "A gun, M'sieurs! Give me a gun! I can shoot — in the name of Heaven!"

"Get that shotgun in the corner of the kitchen," Lew said. "There are shells in a box on the floor. I hope they're not bird shot."

"Did you hit one?" Charlie asked.

"Just winged him. Anyway, he flopped down with a yell," Lew replied with satisfaction. "If they flank us through the trees, they can rush from the rear. Wonder who fired those two shots through the window? That was a break for us. Otherwise, they might have been inside the door before we knew it."

"Some dope with shaky nerves, I suppose," Charlie guessed. "Wonder what their game is? I don't think they came back just to bump us off. But now that you winged one, they may mean business."

"Suits me," Lew growled. "At last I'm fighting somebody I can see. Those babies out in the grass aren't ghosts."

A sharp volley of bullets smashed through the front wall of the house. After Lew wiped the plaster dust from his eyes he brushed the broken glass from his arms and face. "Anton!" he called softly.

"M'sieur?"

"Watch the back. I think a couple of them are crawling along behind the fence. Give it to 'em if they charge. They may try to set the house on fire."

Anton moved swiftly to the rear room, and Charlie glanced up at the sky. "It will be dark in an hour. Then the real fun starts. We'll have to think up something before that. Why not crawl outside ourselves and shoot from the shrubbery?"

"Too dangerous," Lew replied. "We must hold them out of the house if we can." Then his gun fired twice.

"What was that?" Charlie asked.

"Two got by me; they ran out of sight past the wing. I think they are nearly to the corner. Anton will have to deal with them. Wonder if he needs any help."

"Anton isn't a green hand with a gun. He…"

Boom! The shotgun roared from the rear of the house, and a sharp cry split the air. As they peered out they saw a man run past them straight to the road. Lew lifted his gun and then dropped the muzzle as he saw the fellow clutching his face with both hands.

"Anton must have popped him in the kisser," Lew said. "I guess those shells were bird shot. If they had been number fours, the fellow would have dropped in his tracks."

"There's still one more at the rear," Charlie reminded him.

"And Anton still has half a box of shells," Lew responded. "I'm betting on the Frenchman. But wasn't that a devil of a twist? Just as we get ready to grab the cash, here comes this bunch of yahoos making trouble. That's the way things have been up here from the first night!"

Four figures leaped to their feet and began running in swift zig-zag curves back to the road. Lew lowered his gun in amazement.

"They're running away. I thought they were going to rush the house and finish us off."

"Listen," Charlie whispered.

The steady hum of a powerful motor was coming from down the road. Lew recognized the smooth, muffled roar as the gangster's truck he had stolen and then used to bait them into a wild goose chase.

"Rest of the gang," he muttered. "I suppose these birds came on ahead in the car. They must have parked it down the highway and sneaked up on us. I wonder how many more are in the truck? We've laid two out. There's one back of the house and four that ran off. Makes seven. I hope Blinky is driving the truck alone tonight."

They heard excited voices. Then the motor ceased, and they knew the truck had stopped. From the sounds, a fierce argument was being held. Lew sprang up. "I'm going to make the most of this recess.

I've got a deer rifle that needs a workout. Want yours, Charlie?"

"I'll stick to this pistol. In forty-five minutes it will be too dark to sight either very well, but this will be handier up close. I suspect there won't be any more charging across the open yard. They'll sneak along back of the fence and then rush us at closer range. If we can hold them off until dark, I guess we had better grab the money under the stairs and take to the woods ourselves. Our chances will be better out there than trapped inside here.

"I'm going back to finish ripping up the step," Charlie concluded. "Might as well know what we're fighting for. It won't take long."

He had taken three steps towards the hall when a piercing scream rang through the timber.

Then they heard a terse cry from Anton. "Ees de wife," he cried. "Some of dees devils have her."

The rear door slammed, and Charlie rushed back in time to see Anton disappearing through the timber towards his cabin, brandishing the shotgun. Charlie ran to the door and bolted it from the inside.

"Hurry back and cover your window!" Lew called.

Charlie ran to the front and dropped back down beside the opening. "I pity the gangster who lays a hand on Anton's wife," he said. "Anton will smash his head like a pumpkin."

"Maybe the fellow did it just to draw Anton away? It does leave the rear unguarded."

The group of men milling around in the timber across the road suddenly separated into two groups, and scattering, ran crouched behind the two fences.

Lew's rifle cracked. "Missed," he grunted as he threw a fresh shell into the chamber. "I don't think we can stop them. When they rush the door, we'll have our hands full, all right."

Although both realized their situation was hopeless, neither would admit it. They loaded their pistols and opened a couple of boxes for ready use. Muffled voices sounded from close to the house. The gangsters were pressing in close to the walls, unexposed to shots through the front windows.

Lew crawled to a side window but could see nothing. However, from the sounds it was obvious the men were gathering at the front of the house, half on either side of the door. If the door proved too stout, there were bullet-shattered windows on either side through which they could easily enter.

A sharp whistle indicated the rush was coming. Lew fired two shots through the wall at what he judged to be shoulder height.

Then a new motor roared from outside. Lew took a chance and glanced outside. He saw a motorcycle wheeling into the yard.

"It's Johnny Bass!" he cried.

Leaping from his seat, the rider trained a short-barreled machine gun with drum magazine on the startled gangsters.

A burst of shots kicked dirt into their faces. "Drop your guns!" Johnny commanded. Then he leaned forward, apparently eager to send death crashing into the mob.

They obeyed, knowing full well the efficiency of the death machine in Johnny's hands. The Tommy gun was the weapon of choice in gangland warfare.

Pistols fell from hands and arms reached for the sky.

"You, in the house!" Johnny cried. "Come on out now!"

Lew swung open the door and stepped out with a grin.

"Gather those yeggs' guns," Johnny ordered.

With Charlie's eager help, they swiftly swept the grass clean of automatic pistols and short-barreled gats—the more typical daily gangster weapons.

"Sweet little round-up, isn't it?" Johnny snorted. "An' there won't be any shyster lawyer coming to bail 'em out. This is Wisconsin, and we know how to salt away mugs like these for ten to twenty each.

"Now march," he ordered. "Over there to the truck. And line up in front of it. My finger is mighty itchy. Any bright ideas will be fatal for eight or ten of you."

Lew and Charlie followed the sullen gang. No doubt the gangsters were dangerous men—but now that they had lost the advantage, they acted more like whipped dogs.

Hearing someone running towards them from behind the house, Lew and Charlie swung their pistols but dropped them as Anton appeared, panting. "Everything okay at the cabin?" Charlie called.

The Frenchman swore in French. "One buzzard frighten dees wife. But I get there in time and smash heem over head. He is tied up on the floor, and she is watching with my rifle."

"Good work!" Lew applauded.

Anton regarded the shotgun in his hands apologetically.

"I crack stock, I tink."

Johnny was busy tossing handcuffs.

"You fellows snap them on yourselves while I keep both of my hands on this machine gun. Now you two go get that fellow with a bullet in his leg." Then he looked to Anton. "Big fella, go get the one tied up at the cabin."

Then he looked to Lew and Charlie. "I'm going to need one of you to drive the truck down to the jail while I stay in back covering these rats."

"Gadly," Lew cried enthusiastically. "And look, there's good old Blinky! You'll help me drive, won't you?"

Blinky turned away, too wrathful to reply.

Johnny turned suddenly. "Say, who's that? A fellow just ran from behind the house into the trees. Was there anybody else inside?"

Their faces paled as Charlie and Lew sped towards the building. They had forgotten the money under the stairs, and as they burst into the front room, Lew cried out in bitter disappointment. The bottom stair tread lay in the center of the room, and there was nothing but an empty space where it had been.

They dashed out just in time to hear a powerful car start up on the road. The money was taking flight. Before they could say anything, Johnny yelled, "Watch these babies!"

Then he snapped off the detachable stock from his machine gun and leaped to the motorcycle seat, brandishing the deadly weapon in one hand. With a sputter, the motorbike whirled about and then out into the road. By then Anton had returned and was covering the handcuffed gangsters with the shotgun.

Lew ran for their own car. "Come on, Charlie! We've got to get that cash back!"

Lew had shifted into high gear before he reached the gate. They could barely see Johnny streaking down the road like a comet. They could hear but not see the roadster he was pursuing.

"That's Davidson's car!" Lew yelled. "Just like that guy to sneak in the back door while we were out front handling the gangsters. He must have seen where we had begun to pry up the stair tread. Ain't some guys got all the luck?"

"Not this time," Charlie replied grimly, "not with Johnny Bass on his tail. Look at him go!"

Then a rattle of shots drifted back.

"I'll bet he's shooting out the tires!" Lew cried.

The roadster's speed slackened, and they caught up in time to see it listing dangerously to the left. Then they were close enough to see the deadly gun still poised in Johnny's muscular hand.

"He got both tires!" Lew yelled in delight. "That was some shooting. If our buddy George doesn't stop now, I'll bet Johnny drills him!"

The roadster lurched to a stop, and Lew had to jam his brakes to keep from running into it. Johnny was alongside, pointing the gun in the window. "No funny business," he growled, "or I'll make dog meat out of you."

Davidson stepped out, pale and shaken, hands above his head. And then Lew's eyes bulged as he saw another man step out. Lew slapped Charlie across the shoulders.

"That has to be Mr. X!" he proclaimed gleefully. "If he only knew how anxious I've been to meet him!"

Lew piled out of the car and ran forward. Davidson greeted them with a scowl.

"Another dear friend," Lew cried. "How's the real estate market doing today? Won't you introduce me to your pal, the friendly fellow who mixes dope in a man's sugar and shoots without warning?"

"Cut the comedy and get down to business," Johnny growled. "I'm going back to watch the gang. You take care of these guys. When we look up their records, I think we'll find plenty on that guy," he pointed to Davidson, "and we'll check on the other bird. He's hard enough looking to have a record of his own."

Mr. X appeared unnaturally lean with a hungry face and glittering, shifty eyes. His hands twitched incessantly as he stood glaring at them. A single glance was enough to peg him as a dope fiend.

"Scamper around behind and see if they got anything tucked under their coattails," Lew advised Charlie. "And search the roadster."

When Charlie turned back around, he was holding two heavy canvas bags.

"You can drive the gold back in our car," Lew told him. "I'll walk these birds back. With a little luck, I may even get to tap one of them over the bean with my pistol barrel. If I get real lucky, maybe Mr. X will try another disappearing act, and I'll get to drill him."

By the time Lew got back with his prisoners, Johnny had all of the gangsters lying face-down in the back of the truck. Then Lew helped him lift his motorcycle inside, and Johnny stepped up with machine gun in hand.

When Anton saw Davidson's companion, he stepped up wordlessly and gave him a backhand slap that sent him reeling. Then, dancing on his toes, he poured out a mix of French and Indian, his eyes glowing with a wild look.

Charlie stepped between them. "Calm down, Anton. Johnny will see to it your step-brother gets all that's coming to him. You can take this up with him anytime you want—after he's in jail."

Lew hustled the pair into the truck with the rest.

As the truck drove off with Lew behind the wheel, Charlie whispered in Anton's ear, "Your money is safe in our car. Take it home with you. I've got to follow and then drive Lew home."

Anton lifted the two stout canvas bags, oddly heavy even for their bulk. The contents clinked musically.

An hour later they were back and found Anton sitting on the porch waiting for them.

"Thought you would be home celebrating," Lew said.

"No, M'sieur. I wait for you. We count dees money together."

"It's all yours, old scout," Lew returned. "But we'll help you count it if you wish. Then you better take it straight to the bank."

Anton followed them into the house. Charlie lit the lantern, and Anton dropped the heavy bags on the table. "Dees bags too new; must belong to our fren' Davidson. I tink dee money lay loose under stairs."

Lifting one of the bags, Anton poured out a thick stream of golden coins—a glittering cascade of wealth that overflowed the table top and piled up on the floor.

"Whew!" Lew whistled.

"Count, M'sieurs," the Frenchman urged.

"Come on, Charlie," Lew invited his partner. "Unless we get a job in a bank someday, this is going to be our one and only chance to handle so much dough!"

At last they stood up from the job, nearly an hour later, and Charlie consulted a column of figures.

"Thirty-two thousand, six hundred and forty," he announced. "And every dollar in gold pieces!"

"That's because the old Frenchman was smuggling in Chinese workers," Lew asserted. "They always pay in gold—no bills."

Despite the bonanza, Anton's face never wavered from its serious demeanor. "How much you pay Patton for dees place?" he asked.

"Eight thousand," Charlie replied.

"Count heem out on dees table—eight t'ousand dollars!"

They bent over the stacks of yellow coins and shoved out enough to make the required sum. "Now count out two t'ousand more," Anton ordered. "Dees money, she also belong to you," he said.

And then his face finally broke into a wide smile.

"Gosh, you don't have to do that!" Lew protested.

"Heavens," Anton pleaded, again serious. "Heem not enough?"

"I think Anton really wants to buy back the family farm," Charlie interposed as he saw the Frenchman's face drop.

"I want heem!" Anton agreed.

"And you can have heem!" Lew declared with a grin.

* * *

Two weeks later, Anton and his wife returned from visiting old friends and family in Canada. Charlie and Lew had been watching the place for them, waiting to turn over possession, when late one afternoon Lew looked up and said, "Car coming, and judging from the purr, she's a beaut. Don't suppose any more Chicago real estate men are scouring the country for fox farms?"

Charlie laughed at that, and they both stepped outside for a better look. Lew gasped out loud when the glittering black and silver sedan rolled up before them. It was a thing of shimmering beauty—all of the chrome silver-plated and the body paint a glossy black. Wire wheels with plated metal tire covers glistened from each running board.

A bulky figure stepped out of the driver's side door and saluted them with a grandiose wave.

"It's Anton!" Lew exclaimed. "And look at those clothes!"

It was indeed a nattily clad Anton who rushed up to grasp their hands. His plaid suit of gray and black smelled freshly of the tailor's iron, pressed seams standing out like the prow of a Navy cutter. A full carat diamond gleamed in the red cravat knotted on the bosom of a silk shirt with quarter-inch-wide stripes of pink and green. Anton had blossomed into a vision of sartorial splendor. Then Anton's wife stepped out on the other side of the car, as expensively but much more tastefully garbed in fine furs.

Anton stepped back and lifted the derby from his neatly cropped hair. "How you like heem?" he proclaimed, gesturing toward the car. "Dees baby purr like a bobcat in dees cream jar!"

Later, as Lew and Charlie sat for the last time at the supper table they had built, Lew couldn't stop grinning.

"Well, I guess Anton must have all of fifty dollars left. But boy, I bet the money flew while it lasted. After such a spree, he'll be more than ready to get down to fixing up this big old house and then to the business of raising the silver black fox of Folly Farm."

"After seeing Anton drive up in that machine," Charlie predicted, "I bet the locals will come up with a new name for this place other than the Frenchman's Folly."

Lew agreed with a laugh and then added, "You know, I can't think of a more deserving guy."

The End

The Coffin Cache

Chapter 1 – He's in the Box—Dead!

The Indian glanced down at the two wooden counters in his hand. They were the last of the hundred Lew had given him before he started to buy. One hundred dollars, each dollar represented by a battered blue poker chip, equaled Waweja's fall credit.

Like just about every other native trapper in the North, he was stone broke by the time winter began. He had a stock of dried venison and perhaps a cache of smoked fish, but he needed other supplies while he trapped and shot fur during the months of snow. A few staples— salt, tea, flour, powder and shot for his Birmingham muzzleloader trade musket—these Waweja expected to obtain at the trader's store on credit, said credit being limited by his known ability to trap and then his promptness in clearing the debt each spring.

Waweja was a safe risk for $200 worth of trade in goods and supplies. In a good year, his winter catch of fisher, mink, marten, fox, muskrat and lynx—plus the deer skins—could be conservatively valued at four times that amount, even figured at the low fur prices that prevailed at a northern outpost.

Macanay, the former owner and trader who had sold out lock, stock and barrel to Charlie and Lew, had briefed them concerning each regular customer. Each, it seemed, had peculiarities. Waweja's was that he invariably appeared back at the store in January, asking for a second helping of supplies. In all likelihood, he shared what he got with family and it was not enough to get an extended family through the long winter. It was, therefore, wiser to split his total credit in half and advance one installment at each visit.

Waweja walked to the door and spoke a short command. The woman who had waited patiently outside while he bargained with Lew followed him back inside. Waweja believed in the traditional Northern division of labor. He had finished his part—the bargaining—and it was now up to her to get the goods home. The woman rapidly roped together the largest and heaviest articles in the pile and slung the bundle over her solid shoulders.

Waweja sorted out a few smaller items and stuffed them into a small skin bag as his own share of the load.

"When are we going to get real winter?" asked Lew.

"It will come," Waweja answered. "Black wind. Tonight, maybe the next night. You see. Stay in the store."

Lew glanced out through the opposite window. The sky did look queer, dull gray and streaked with lines of dirty copper color. "Let it come," he replied. "We're ready."

Waweja and his wife had reached the door. "Huh!" the trapper grunted as he passed through, and Lew recognized this as answer.

"See you in January," Lew concluded their exchange.

Lew drew a heavy line under the list of supplies advanced to Waweja. He glanced with much satisfaction at the depleted shelves behind him. Three-fourths of the stock of goods he and Charlie had packed through the wilderness from the boat landing over on the Senesca River had been sold.

Lew shuddered as he recalled those days of torturous labor, the unbearable heat, the mosquitoes and flies that clung to their faces, and that last two-mile portage from the small branch across to the opposite shore of the lake on the near side of which Hazzard House, their outpost store, stood. That labor had changed Lew's opinion of Northern fur traders. This was no easy proposition. It took resources, strength and persistence to successfully stock and maintain a post so far out on the rim of civilization.

Waweja was about the last of their regular customers. Others had started coming as early as September. Now, two months later, fur was already prime and running. The weather was holding just below freezing, cold and dry. A hard 4-inch snow crust had turned the country into a limitless toboggan and dog-sled trail.

"Over $11,000 on the books," Lew reminded himself with pardonable satisfaction. "Figuring the usual loss on delinquents, we should clear $6,000. If fur prices don't hit the bottom of nothing, and if the trappers don't suffer an epidemic of flu or smallpox, we will make twice as much on the furs they sell us next spring.

"To be safe, I'll figure a total of $15,000. Of course, that must cover our own wages for packing, selling and collecting, and we owe about $6,000 to the Van Gorman Mercantile Company. But we ought to take in enough fur by January to square that. Then everything we make will be clear.

"Lew, my boy," he asked himself gleefully, "what are you going to do with all that money?"

As he flipped the cover of the book shut Lew heard the stout stockade gate swing open. He looked out the store door and watched Charlie enter the yard, rifle in hand, pulling a birch bark toboggan loaded with four quarters of meat and a freshly skinned hide.

"He was a good one," Charlie nodded with satisfaction. "A young caribou bull."

"If Waweja is right, we'll need that meat," Lew said. "He forecast a bad storm and warned me to stay in until it was over."

"So Waweja was in this afternoon," Charlie said. "I hope you kept his credit down to the necessities."

Lew only nodded.

"Help hang up three of these quarters," Charlie continued, "and carry the fourth inside. We may have a visitor tonight. I saw a dog sled and driver out on the ice at the lower end of the lake."

"Another prospector headed for the Little Kettle Range," Lew guessed. "How the lure of gold gets them."

"I don't think this man is going to the mountains," Charlie replied. "From the angle at which he struck the lake, I'd say he is coming back from them."

A stout pole some 20 feet high had been planted in the stockade yard. Its sides had been planed as smooth as a plane blade could make them, and then it had been coated with grease. As a further protection against climbing animals, a wide strip of tin was nailed about the pole so it flared out like a collar. Its top held a pair of short, crossed beams with ropes and pulleys at the ends. This was the meat pole.

The quarters were pulled up and tied so they dangled 12 feet above the ground, safe from any kind of varmint or grub-robbing dog that might enter the yard.

As they finished, the pad of dog feet on crusty snow sounded outside the gate. A hoarse command ended the sounds. The gate swung open, and a man entered. Lew caught a glimpse of panting huskies behind him, squatting in their traces, tongues lolling out.

Charlie and Lew were both above average in height, but the stranger towered above them. His thin, lanky body and narrow shoulders magnified the impression of unnatural stature, as did his long, lean arms and legs. None of this held their frank stares so much as did his face. It was badly flushed, cheeks almost crimson beneath hollow, dark-ringed eyes.

He breathed in short gasps as if he had been running. "Howdy," the man began in a hoarse whisper. "Can you put me up for the night?"

"Sure," Lew said. "You look sick. I'd say you had a bad cold."

"You tellin' me?" the man croaked in grim humor. "I suppose this is your store. I'm Hillman, D.A. Hillman."

Charlie responded with Lew's name then his own.

"Bring your team into the yard," he added. "We keep the gate locked, so they won't run away."

"My dogs never run off," Hillman answered abruptly. He spoke to the animals, and they jerked ahead, dragging the heavily loaded sled inside. A queer load, Lew thought, as he surveyed the long, narrow box securely lashed to the frame with a pair of canvas packs tied on top.

"Go in by the stove," Lew offered. "We'll loose the dogs."

But Hillman refused the offer. One by one he released the tired brutes from their Indian-rigged traces. And as he dropped the leather straps, he gripped each animal by its throat with a large hand.

"Lay down!" he growled to each, and then with a final squeeze that brought the beast's mouth open, he slammed it to the ground. When he reached the last dog—a light-furred bitch—it snapped savagely at the outstretched hand. With surprising agility, the man kicked out one of his long legs, and the stiff-soled caribou boot caught the dog squarely in the face. It sprawled backwards with a yelp.

The expression on Hillman's face never changed. He reached down again, gripped the rebellious one by the throat, and repeated his command. This time, the dog cowed to the ground. Hillman then turned to Charlie and Lew. "My team is the best in the North," he whispered in that tortured croak of a voice, "because they know I'm boss."

Charlie shrugged his shoulders as he opened the door of their store, but Hillman did not enter.

"I'd like to set this box inside, near where I'm going to sleep. And that can be on the floor, anywhere that's handy. I'm not soft. This will be the first roof I've slept under in a week. This cold has me worried. Otherwise, I'd not turn off the trail to bother you." The hoarse tones carried more than a trace of arrogance.

"I'll give you a hand," Lew agreed. They cast off the ropes and slid the box over the snow to the doorway. "Say, this is heavy," Lew grunted. "Better help us, Charlie."

The box was finally against the wall opposite the store counter. Lew eyed it curiously as he followed the others to seats by the stove.

The box was 7 feet long, 30 inches wide and a little less than 2 feet high. Hillman slumped down close to the fire. His shoulders were shaking with suppressed shivers. Beads of perspiration glistened on his forehead, cold sweat not caused by the store's modestly heated interior.

Lew lifted the copper kettle that boiled on the stove top and made tea. Hillman gulped two steaming cups without pausing.

"That's better, thanks," he rasped before relaxing into a half-doze while Charlie and Lew began to prepare the night's meal. Charlie sliced thick steaks from the rear quarter of the caribou he had brought in and started frying them. Lew opened a small cupboard beside the stove and set a deep pan of flour on the table underneath. He opened a can of peaches and started them heating on the stove.

Lew mixed salt, caribou fat and baking powder with the flour, added water, and dropped the stiff dough off his spoon in small balls that covered the top of the peaches. Finally, he set the dish in the stove-pipe oven above the stove.

This oven was one of Lew's prizes possessions and favorite inventions. He had cut two round holes in a 10-gallon drum so the pipe passed straight through both sides. There was a hinged door at one end and a metal rack inside to hold a baking pan. When the damper above was turned just right, the pipe passing through the drum gave off enough heat to bake biscuits, pies, puddings or meat.

Hillman roused at intervals to survey these preparations with signs of pleasure on his otherwise grim face. Charlie was turning the steaks for a final cooking when they heard a short hail from outside.

"Sounds like more company for supper," Lew suggested.

Hillman straightened. "A tenderfoot," he muttered, "or he'd know enough to come in without yelling."

Lew knocked the dough from his fingers and went out. Before the half-opened gate stood a single form muffled in mackinaw clothing. A light toboggan heavily loaded sat beside the man.

"Might as well come in, stranger," Lew invited. "It don't cost any more to look from the inside out than from the outside in. There's a fire burning and grub cooking."

"You speak welcome words, my friend," the man replied. His voice was pleasant, smooth, even cultured, although Lew thought it a trifle high-pitched.

"Where are your dogs?" Lew asked, looking doubtfully around. "Or did you pull that load yourself?"

"If your arms and legs felt like mine, you would not need to ask that question," the stranger answered with another smile.

"Where you going?" Lew asked.

"To the Little Kettle Range," came the quiet answer.

"Man, that's 300 miles. You can't pull a load like that over 300 miles of rough trail."

"I'll have to, unless I can buy dogs."

Lew led the way inside. "Slap another steak in the pan, Charlie. Here's another man that ought to be hungry. I guess he's trying out some crazy sled-pulling contest."

"No, I'm not crazy, even if it may look like it. Just suffering a bit of ill luck. And my name's Galt, Doctor Galt."

"He's going up to the Little Kettle gold fields," Lew added. "Pulling a heavily loaded sled by hand."

"I have made a poor start, I admit," Dr. Galt explained. "I left Moose Falls 10 days ago with two men whom I paid to haul my kit on their sleds. This morning, 12 miles south of here, they turned back home leaving me in a rather tight spot. I couldn't give up and return with them, so I bought an Indian's toboggan, loaded my instruments and medicines on it, and came on alone."

The doctor had thrown off his heavy wool cap and was peeling his blanket-lined mackinaw. His face was rather long and sallow. The eyes were of unusual brilliance and set rather widely apart. His mouth was thin, narrow and determined. Short-cropped wiry hair stood stiffly about the top of his head.

"The smell of frying meat reminds me I lunched on a box of crackers at noon," he said smiling, and then sat down beside Hillman. For several seconds he watched the man with sharp glances. Suddenly, he reached out and gripped Hillman's wrist with agile fingers. The other started with a hoarse exclamation, but Galt motioned him back.

"You are not far from pneumonia, my friend," Galt said slowly. "Pulse 112, temperature at least 102. Do you want me to do something for you?"

Hillman grunted. "Maybe after supper, Doc. I'm tough; a cold won't knock me down. But I don't claim this one is any fun."

"As you wish," Galt answered with something like indifference, as though the professional interest aroused by the man's symptoms was as quickly cooled by this reluctance to take treatment.

Galt turned to Charlie. "Do you have a team of dogs you'd be willing to sell, and a sled?"

"We've only the one," Charlie answered, "and we loaned that to one of our trappers who is moving his line into fresh country. But I think you can find dogs at Big-Foot Andre's. He said last week he had extra, and he can build you a birch sled in two hours. Big-Foot lives five miles around the shore of the lake. You can't miss it."

"Fine. Now, can you sell me enough food to last until I reach the Little Kettle Mountains?"

"You goin' up there?" Hillman broke in. "After gold, I suppose, like the rest who tramped 1,000 miles to try their luck."

"Yes, I'm going there," Galt replied evenly. "And after gold. But not to wash or dig it out myself. I will establish my practice there and furnish medical and surgical care for the sick and injured."

Galt turned his keen attention to Lew and Charlie. "I am surprised that neither of you have gone. You are close enough. Didn't the news of a gold strike excite you?"

"Hardly," Lew answered. "It looked too much like a flash in the pan. We have seen a lot of prospectors pass through, and we've seen some of them on their way back, broke and disgusted. I hear a few of the first on the ground did well. But it won't last. Most of the gold was gone before the big rush even began."

"You heard right," Hillman croaked in his husky voice. "It was all over in a month. I know. I've just come from there."

"How was your luck?" Galt spoke.

"Luck?" Hillman repeated with a rumbling laugh that must have torn his raw vocal cords badly. "My luck was good! But I didn't go for the gold, either."

"What did you go for?" pursued Galt, with a trace of insistence in his voice as Hillman slumped down with no sign of speaking.

Hillman looked steadily at the doctor for a moment. Then he said slowly, "I'm Inspector Hillman of the Criminal Investigation Bureau, from Winnipeg. I went up into the Little Kettle after 'Knife' Burke, the murderer. You heard of him, I guess? And I got him—after three months of hard trailing."

"You got him?" Lew cried. "Where?"

Hillman pointed with a long finger. "You're sittin' on him. He's in the box!"

Lew leaped up from his seat like the wood was on fire. He glanced down on the long, narrow box with a shudder. Hillman watched with a sneer on his flushed face.

"My orders were dead or alive," he continued, "and this time dead happened to be handier than alive. The reward is the same either way. That box and its contents are worth fifteen hundred cash in Winnipeg. That's why I wanted it inside." The cold-blooded note in Hillman's voice made his listeners shiver.

"But," Lew objected, "why did you bring him...it...into a warm place? Won't he, er, it decompose?"

Again Hillman laughed. "He's pickled in 15 pounds of salt. Don't worry, he'll keep." The cheerful atmosphere of the room had disappeared with startling speed. Shadows pressed in from the dark corners to stifle the barely burning kerosene lamp on the counter.

Although he fought against them, prickles of fear twitched up Lew's spine. Later, he wondered if these had been a warning of what was to come, a warning of the cloud of terror that later hovered over Hazzard House, when murder stalked the black hours of night, when fear, suspense and danger tested his courage and pitched his hopes headlong into a pit of deepest despair.

Chapter 2 – I Won't Last Until Morning

Supper was a silent meal. Finished, Hillman slowly arose on his long legs. "I'll turn in now. Where do I put my sleeping bag?"

Lew told him, "We have two small rooms with pole bunks in each. You can use one and Dr. Galt the other. Sorry there's but one lamp. I'll light you in and you will find candles in each room.

Hillman stooped over the coffin. "I want to take this in with me," he whispered in his hoarse voice.

Reluctantly, Charlie and Galt helped him carry it. Lew preceded with the lamp, and they stalked like ghostly pallbearers into the first small sleeping room.

They set the coffin on the floor. Lew pointed to a door. "There's your room, Doc."

"Wait a minute," Hillman rasped. "Maybe you better give me something for this cold, Doc."

Nodding assent, Galt opened his leather case and spilled six tablets into his hand. "Two of these every three hours," he instructed. "If you manage to wake up twice before morning, so much the better."

"Call me if you wake first," Hillman said as Charlie and Lew left.

Lew and Charlie spread their own sleeping gear on the floor of the store to sleep. When Lew next sat up in his blankets, he saw dull daylight filtering in through the windows. Charlie was kneeling before the stove, blowing the coals back to life.

Remembering Hillman's request, Lew scrambled into his clothes and walked back to the man's door. He rapped loudly. He could hear thick, wheezing breaths inside, but there was no response. So he rapped again and then called loudly. When Galt finally mumbled something, Lew opened the door and stepped up to the bunk, reached out and shook the sleeping man. That brought results, although of a different nature than Lew expected.

Hillman sat up with a cry; his hand flashed under the blankets, and as he struggled to hold his eyelids open, he raised a flat pistol.

Lew ducked. Then Hillman recognized him and laid the gun down. A grim smile appeared on his lips. "I'm not used to being touched in my sleep. I told you to call me."

Lew forced a grin in answer. "I called you from outside, and you answered. Next time, I'm going to give our guests alarm clocks.

"I have known those things," he nodded to the gun, "to go off when a half-asleep man grabs one."

He glanced at the other door and started when he saw it ajar and black eyes staring at him through the crack. The door swung open and Galt's head appeared. The doctor spoke naturally enough, saying the customary, "Good morning." But Lew knew he had been watching Hillman's room.

At breakfast, Hillman appeared better, his voice less strained. "I feel good," he boasted. "That stuff you gave me done the trick, Doc. My chest is sore and sort of heavy, but I feel strong as an ox."

"The medicine was an emergency treatment," Galt replied, "so you would rest. It gave you temporary relief and maybe brought a false sense of strength. By all means do not start out today. Stay and rest. It is dangerous for you to go on."

"Bunk," Hillman exclaimed. "I'm all right. I plan to mush 50 miles before nightfall."

Galt shrugged at that and turned away. He did not argue, although Lew sensed he had sufficient force of character to ably back any opinion he advanced.

Hillman fed his dogs out in the yard and then the four men attacked a stack of flapjacks and caribou steaks, washed down with huge cups of hot tea.

"If somebody will help me wrangle that coffin for the last time," Hillman declared, "I'll be off."

Charlie and Lew helped him carry the dreadful object out and lash it on the sled. Hillman came back inside and threw down a bill, a rather large one. "No change," he said gruffly. Then he stalked to the door with a brief "so long" flung over his shoulder, and they heard him shout to his dog team.

By then Galt had loaded his toboggan and also was ready to depart. He thrust a hand in his pocket suggestively. "Forget it," Lew said easily. Then he grinned and added, "We'll even up with you when you buy that grub."

"If I can get a sled and dogs I'll be back before noon," Galt assured them as he swung off, jerking the toboggan along behind him.

"Two strange guys," Lew reflected. "I hope we see Galt again, but I'm not itching to handle that coffin of Hillman's again. He sure didn't let it out of his sight. Galt should have left his stuff here and gone after the dogs. He could have saved some pulling."

"Not if he doesn't get dogs from Big-Foot," Charlie retorted. "Then I suspect he will just keep going. The doctor has nerve and determination for a tenderfoot. Well, suppose we start working that caribou hide I peeled yesterday?"

They spread the green skin over a graining log in the yard, scraped off fat and muscle shreds and pared the hide down to an even thickness. As they worked, Lew watched the sky. "I don't like those clouds, Charlie. There is a storm coming." Then he dropped his hand and listened. "I hear somebody coming."

"Galt coming back for grub?" Charlie suggested.

"No," Lew listened intently, "there's more than one sled and at least two teams. Men talking, too." He went over to the stockade gate and opened it a bit. Then he called out, "Look at this, Charlie."

Up from the lake shore straggled three teams of sled dogs. Two men walked behind them, and on the last sled they saw a long, narrow object. No mistaking that. They had handled it too often.

"Goodness!" Lew exclaimed. "Hillman's coffin is back."

"And Hillman's lying on top of it," exclaimed Charlie. "See his hands dangling over the sides?"

A voice hailed them. "Open up. We got a sick man here."

Lew swung the gate wide, and the sled with its gruesome load slipped inside then halted by the store door. One of the men spoke in a rough voice. "What kind of hole is this, anyway? Guys fallin' down woozy in the snow for Spath and me to stop and pick up."

Lew eyed the speaker dubiously. Nothing about him seemed right. His legs were too short for his body. The nose, slightly flattened, looked too small for the face, which plainly was too broad for the cold eyes, set too closely together. The man's shoulders indicated considerable strength, thick, bunchy and also out of proportion. He had drawn off a heavy skin mitten, and Lew saw the fingers were thick and spatulate, covered with short, coarse hair.

Then a mild voice drew Lew's glance to the second stranger. A pleasant contrast from his companion was how Lew regarded him. Just average height, rather slim and thin, long face framing deep-set gray eyes. "We found him flat on his face in the snow," the man said.

"Help me carry him inside," directed Charlie. They lugged the rangy body into the store and laid it gently down on blankets before the stove. Charlie gripped a wrist. The pulse was imperceptible. Hillman's face was ghastly gray, lips slightly drawn back from the teeth. He was breathing so slowly and feebly Charlie wondered if his lungs were actually receiving any air at all.

Charlie straightened with sudden decision. "Lew, run to Big-Foot's and get Dr. Galt. He may still be there. And have him hustle."

"Doctor? What's a doc doing around here?" the short, thick stranger snapped.

"He stayed last night with us," Charlie answered as Lew dashed off at top speed. "So did this man—Inspector Hillman."

"Inspector of what?" the fellow growled.

"Criminals," Charlie said shortly.

"Oh, a dick," came the casual reply. "Well, looks like his inspectin' days are about done."

"Easy, Peak," his companion said. "The man is sick, maybe dying. It's heartless to talk that way."

Peak mumbled under his breath.

And Spath, the other, said to Charlie, "We are on our way to the Little Kettle. We camped for the night about five miles south of here. And it's lucky we did, or nobody might have found the Inspector. He looks pretty bad, doesn't he?"

Charlie didn't reply. He was watching anxiously through a window, wondering if Hillman would even hang on until Lew returned with the doctor. It would be a good hour, at least. What a fool Hillman had been to start out in such condition. He must have been critically ill for days, and now this was the crisis, possibly the end.

Peak spoke, "We better move along, Spath. No use hangin' around this dump."

But Spath demurred, "We might be able to help. Anyway, I want to stay until I know if this man pulls through. We helped bring him in."

It seemed like hours to Charlie before he heard quick steps outside and opened the door for Lew and Doc Galt.

Galt knelt beside the prostrate form. "I feared this," he said. "I warned him this morning to stay off the trail. He has exhausted his strength, perhaps fatally."

Galt opened a small round case, loaded a hypodermic needle and plunged it into Hillman's arm. "If I'm not too late, that should bring him around."

"Powerful stuff if it does," Peak sneered. Galt turned, surveyed the man with blank eyes and then turned back to his patient.

"The doctor was dickering with Big-Foot when I arrived," Lew told Charlie in a whisper. "He was packing up to start for his winter trapline before the Doc arrived. Five minutes more, and they both would have been long gone."

A violent tremor in the unconscious form drew all eyes. Fingers twitched, eyes opened, fluttered, and then went shut.

Galt stood with quiet satisfaction. "He's coming around. Now I want him moved to a cooler place. This is too near the fire."

"We'll make up a bed in the office," Charlie offered.

The original building of Hazzard House had been 30 feet by 50. The store proper occupied a space at the very front, and behind this was the small office. Back of that was the stockroom. Charlie and Lew had found this rather crowded, so they had added a lean-to structure along one side, 28 feet long and 12 feet wide, which was divided into the pair of sleeping rooms with pole bunks. The partners slept there when they were not hosting visitors.

There was a wooden bed with a dried-grass mattress in the office, and on this they placed Hillman's still-sleeping form.

Galt was sorting out more medicine. He called for a cup of water and seated himself beside the bed. The others walked out into the store, and Lew looked out a window then exclaimed, "Look at that snow!"

The snow had arrived in a flurry of swirling flakes, and even as they watched through the window, the dim outlines of the stockade wall slowly disappeared.

"Look at that," growled Peak. "Now we won't get away from here today."

The storm only intensified. The wind stiffened, and in less than an hour was driving icy pellets against the walls of the building.

When Charlie and Peak forced their way out into the yard to feed the three teams of dogs, they found the shaggy animals huddled against a wall in the low, open-front shed. Some quality in the fearful gale had cowed the quarreling that usually surfaces when strange dog teams are brought together.

Hillman was slowly gaining consciousness. Shortly after noon, he was able to sit up and drink a little hot soup. The others dined heartily and perhaps a bit noisily on a meat stew Charlie had started early that morning.

By three o'clock the storm was so heavy and the sky so dark Lew lighted the kerosene lamp. Peak and Spath sat beside the stove playing poker. Galt watched with an inscrutable face, when he wasn't tending to the sick man.

Spath looked up from his hand. "I guess you will have to run a hotel until this snow stops," he declared matter-of-factly.

"A hospital, too," added Peak with an unpleasant chuckle.

"Looks like it," Lew agreed. "There won't be any sled travel to-morrow, and maybe not the next day."

There had been no dusk to warn them of the coming night. It had been dark outside for hours when Lew suddenly realized that it was seven o'clock. Hillman was snoring in his sleep, and Galt decided he should not be awakened for food since rest was even more essential for his recovery.

"He goin' to pull through?" Peak asked indifferently. Spath glanced quickly at the doctor's face, but Galt only shrugged, indicating that the outcome was still undecided. The players continued their poker game, passing small stakes back and forth, neither winning nor losing any appreciable sum.

Suddenly a hoarse sound jerked their startled eyes to the office doorway. They saw Hillman, eyes wild, face contorted. He was trembling, his shaking body barely supported by the doorjamb.

Before anyone could speak, he cried out in a horrible, rasping voice, "Where is it? Where did you hide it? The box! I want it! Where did you hide it? Hurry! Give me the box!"

The others jumped up to settle Galt, but the doctor held them back. "Don't try to restrain him, but bring the box in quickly; that's the only way to relieve him."

Lew cried to Spath and Peak to help, and slipping out the door, they untied the stiff ropes and carried the coffin inside. Hillman still clung to the doorjamb, uttering sounds that were fearful. Only when the box was close and he could reach out and touch it did he permit them to help him back to bed.

Peak was surveying the box with keen interest. "What's in that thing? Must be something precious, him making such a fuss."

Lew turned a casual eye Peak's way. "The box is a coffin. Inside, there's a criminal's body Hillman is taking back to Winnipeg."

The man's expression turned ludicrous.

"What the…" he snarled, staring at the box with bugged-out eyes. Then the surprise was replaced by suspicion, as if he had decided Lew had to be joking. Then, concluding he was not, Peak declared, "You take me out in the storm to bring back a stiff? Why didn't you tie the blasted dick in bed and let him howl. I don't want a corpse in the same house with me."

Lew flushed with slow anger, and for a moment he considered inviting Peak to step outside where there were no corpses. He stifled the impulse and walked silently back into the store. But as he passed through the door he glanced back. Hillman had rolled over to the edge of the bed, and one hand touched the coffin.

"He sure loves that thing," Peak observed, as he followed Lew out of the room.

The stout log walls of Hazzard House quivered under the blows of the storm. Nobody seemed in any hurry for bed. Instead, they hugged close to the stove, listening to blasts of wind that made the indoor air seem much colder than it really was.

Shuffling feet drew their gaze to the door, and again Hillman stood there. Although he clutched the jamb for support, his eyes were calm and filled with reason this time.

Breathing heavily, he panted, "I want to say something. Don't stop me, Doc. I'm goin' back when I'm done. I got a hunch I won't last 'til morning. Maybe I'm wrong. But I got to say this while I can."

Galt was on his feet, and now he slipped by the trembling form into the office and returned with a cup. "Drink this," he commanded, holding it to Hillman's lips.

Hillman gulped with difficulty. The medicine seemed to give him strength, and he continued, "You all been good to me. I'd have cashed in sooner if you hadn't helped. So I'm goin' to do something in return. I'm alone. No folks. If I kick it," he tried to smile, but the attempt was ghastly, "all I got is yours. I give it to you for helping me. For all to share and share alike. Help me back now, Doc."

Galt steadied the shaking form and guided him back to the bed. He returned a minute later and sat without speaking. Peak was staring at the office door with deep concentration. Spath idly turned cards over with his fingers.

Finally, Peak whispered, "What did the dick mean? What's he givin' us?"

Nobody answered until the silence grew oppressive. Then Lew said briefly, "I don't really know."

"We better go through his duffle and see," Peak proposed.

Blank silence again, until Galt replied, "In all decency, we might wait until the man dies." His voice was edged with disgust.

"Now don't get snooty with me, Doc," Peak retorted. "I suppose what Hillman is givin' us includes the boxed-up stiff. What a legacy. You may be able to use your share, Doc. Cut it up and experiment. What'll you give me for my end?"

With a strong effort Charlie suppressed his loathing for the man and explained. "Hillman says the corpse is worth a fifteen hundred dollar reward. If that's right, he is handing us a nice stake. Blamed good pay for the little trouble he has caused, and I appreciate his intentions."

"Winnipeg is a long way off," Spath said mildly. Silence again filled the room.

Galt yawned, "I'm going to turn in."

The others started to their feet, too.

"Use the same room, Doctor," Charlie anticipated his question. "Spath and Peak can sleep in the front room where Hillman spent last night. Lew and I will camp on the floor again. We can hear Hillman if he gets worse or needs anything."

"Call me if he does," Galt ordered.

Outside, the wind still battered the stout log walls of Hazzard House and whipped snow against the frosted panes of glass, howling and shrieking. Inside, the fire burned low. Sleeping men turned heavily between blankets, and the lamp burned dim on the counter.

Lew sat up in bed, struggling with the anesthesia that stupefied him whenever he slept indoors. Had he heard something besides the wind? Or had he dreamed the sound—a sound like the short, quick gasp of a man struggling for air.

His senses cleared. The wind quieted in a sudden lull, and then Lew's muscles went tense. There was no mistake. Something had moved out there—a sound like something brushing along the wall, the faint squeak of a floorboard.

Lew sprang up, turned the lamp high and walked into the office. For a moment all was shadows. Then his eyes cleared before the glare. Hillman was lying facing towards the opposite side of the bed. Lew flashed his lamp over the room. Nobody there, nothing unusual. Or was there something about the sick man?

He bent closer, and some quality in the open mouth, the clenched hands and open, staring eyes made him gasp. He straightened and cried out loudly, "Charlie! Doctor Galt! Hurry!"

Charlie rolled out instantly and was beside him. A moment later, Galt appeared and Lew pointed down. Galt turned the still form over on its back, gripped a wrist and listened with his ear to the motionless chest. "Yes, he's dead," came the verdict.

Spath stumbled in, rubbing his eyes. Behind him waddled Peak's thick form. "What's up?"

"Hillman is dead," Galt announced quietly. "I am afraid he strained his lungs and his heart past the breaking point."

"When did it happen?" Lew asked.

Galt covered the lean hand outside the blanket with his own, then carefully flexed the fingers. "Within the last few minutes."

Lew felt his scalp prickle. "Good gosh," he breathed, remembering the gasp that had brought him out of his sleep.

Lew did not forget that moment for years afterward: the raging storm, the smoky lamp throwing shadows about the little room, and five men staring somberly down on the bed and its deceased occupant. He became aware that his toe was jammed against something hard, looked down and saw the wooden coffin shoved partly under the bed.

Lew shivered and then walked swiftly into the store, kindled up the fire and sat beside it. The others joined him. The presence of death blasted all thoughts of sleep, yet many a minute passed before a word was spoken.

Peak finally said, "Bein' an heir of the departed, I'm wonderin' just what my legacy is worth."

"You would," Lew could not help saying.

"Why not?" Peak demanded with a good humor that surprised them all. "I never saw the guy before. I'm not sheddin' any tears over him; neither are you. He's dead, and before he kicked off he gave me a share of his stuff. Now I want to know what that is."

"I'm afraid Hillman's entire estate is the corpse in the coffin," said Galt. "I know he is not wearing a money belt, which he would be if he carried any great sum."

"Well, well," said Peak. "So you been lookin' around on your own hook, eh, Doc?"

Galt flushed then said sharply, "I merely discovered that in the routine of treating him."

"Anyway, let's take a look-see," insisted Peak. He regarded them defiantly. Then, as none of them offered to join him, he disappeared into the room of death.

Shortly afterwards he came back. "Nothing in his clothes but this beat-up old pistol and $32," he said with a snort of disgust.

"Now I suppose you want to open the coffin and look in there?" Lew suggested. "Maybe there's a watch in the corpse's pocket."

Peak refused to take offense. "That's a good idea, young fellow. I'm going to do just that. The stiff is our only hope if we're goin' to cash in. But before I lam off as far as Winnipeg with a stiff, I'm going to make sure the box isn't loaded with rocks." Lew turned away in disgust, but Peak spoke coolly. "Where's a screwdriver?"

Charlie hesitated then went behind the counter and picked one out of the hardware stock. Peak grabbed it, helped himself to the lamp and disappeared. The others looked with inquiring eyes at each other then followed one by one, drawn by dreadful fascination. Lew alone stuck in his chair, immovable.

He heard Peak grunt as he worked on the screws. The heavy lid scraped across the box's top. Lew could not repress a shudder as silence filled the little store, and then...

"Dang," he heard Peak gasp. "So that's it! If I didn't suspect..."

Chapter 3 – Someone Murdered Him

Lew ran into the room. He saw four tense faces staring down. The lamp in Spath's hand shook as he endeavored to hold it so the yellow light fell into the coffin.

Lew pushed among them, crowding men to either side as he advanced. Instead of a corpse embalmed in salt, his amazed eyes saw rows of short fat sacks, packed tightly and wedged with braces of wood so none would shift about.

"What is it?" he asked.

Peak spoke with a sudden snap of his mouth. "Gold! Gold from Little Kettle!" His voice grew shrill with greed. "Hillman wasn't no inspector. He fooled us all. He was a prospector. He used this coffin stunt to hide his haul."

"You sure it's gold?" Lew asked. "Opened any of the sacks yet?"

Peak's eyes glared disdainfully. His hands darted to a sack. Frantic fingers loosened the string, spread open the mouth. They leaned closer still, and a queer murmur swelled from their throats. The glittering dust seemed to reflect a sinister yellow over their features as they hovered above the coffin cache.

"It's gold, all right," Charlie whispered.

"And we share it equally," Galt breathed.

At these words, something like a blast of air cooled Lew's heated cheeks. Some tingling quality illuminated the ether about him. He looked quickly to right and left and saw that the others were watching him and each other with strange, shifting looks.

Lew could not suppress a shudder. Thousands of dollars' worth of gold given to five storm-locked men in a lonely trading post—by a dead man who still lay on the bed behind them.

Peak spoke first. "Well, you guys—speak up. What do you say?"

"Say?" Spath spit out. "I never expected to be so lucky."

"I'm not sure whether it's true or a dream," confessed Galt.

"And I call it pretty decent of Hillman," said Charlie.

"Can that stuff," Peak growled. "Of course we're all thankful and such. Maybe if we had known what was in the box old Hillman wouldn't have lasted this long."

He chuckled quietly over this for a moment, until he noticed the stony glare in Charlie's eyes. "Now don't get sore. I was just jokin.' But how are we goin' to divide the stuff? So every man's satisfied?"

"We have scales," suggested Lew.

"Them hay weighers?" Peak guffawed. "Don't make me laugh. I've seen Indian trader's scales before, and I wouldn't want to weigh sand on 'em, much less gold."

"Why divide it?" Charlie spoke up quickly to choke off the angry retort he saw forming on Lew's lips. "Why not let it be as it is? Then when the storm clears we can all go together and haul it to the nearest bank. Let them value the lot. Then we split the money itself."

"Sounds sensible to me," Galt agreed.

But Peak glared with aroused suspicion. "What? You two pairin' off against me already? Who's goin' to watch this stuff all of the time and see that nobody sneaks out a handful? Handfuls of gold run into money, you know."

"Go easy, Peak," Spath cautioned. "I've only known you three days and these other men less than 24 hours, and I'm not worrying. There isn't any cause to get suspicious. Why quarrel over such wonderful good luck? If there is fifty thousand in the sacks, which there could be, that makes $10,000 for each of us. That's a real stake, and nobody has to sneak more than his share."

But Peak shook his head doggedly. "You can't sell me on that. I want my share now so it can't shrink. And I'm not going to take my eyes off it until I'm sure."

Charlie stepped forward, quietly shouldered Peak aside and laid the lid on the box. "Sink those screws," he ordered Lew, disregarding the suspicion in Peak's features.

Lew obeyed.

"The only way," Charlie said, "is to seal this box so no one can open it without the knowledge of the rest."

"And how you suppose we do that?" Peak demanded.

Charlie did not answer, but walked back to the store and returned with a ball of stout linen fishing line.

"There are five of us," he continued quietly. "We will tie the lid down with five separate pieces of cord. Then each man will seal one of the knots with a waxed imprint. It will be impossible to lift the lid without destroying all five cords, and since no man can duplicate more than one of the original seals, the gold will be secure from tampering. Even two or three men can't conspire to rob the others without them knowing it."

Everybody considered this in silence.

"I call that clever," Galt finally praised.

"Suits me," agreed Spath.

Peak grunted, "Guess it'll do until we think of something better."

Charlie cut five pieces from the ball of cord, and with their help, passed each about the length and width of the box and tied the ends. "Now," he said, "I'll soften this wax over the lamp, drop a soft blob on the knots, and every man will seal it in turn. I'll use my monogram watch charm for my seal."

Galt produced a small jeweled knife. Lew held out a round object. "It's my American Trappers Association button. I don't think any of you have one, too."

Spath slipped a ring from one finger. But Peak only glared and growled, "That's okay for you guys. But I ain't got a thing on me."

"Then use your thumb," Charlie advised coldly. "You ought to know that no two men have the same thumb print."

"What ya' mean by that?" Peak asked quickly. But Charlie was busy with his stick of wax and paid no attention.

"Now, gentlemen," Galt spoke with a trace of sarcasm in his voice. "Now that we have disposed of what the dead man gave us, suppose we give some attention to his body."

"What the devil can we do with that?" Peak demanded. "Nothing until the storm stops."

"The disposal of the body is only a secondary matter," Galt returned. "Of course we must give him a decent burial as soon as we can. But I am thinking of something more important. We must make a report of his death, its cause and the exact time and date. This information must be filed with the authorities at the earliest possible hour. Do you know where the nearest coroner lives?"

Charlie shook his head. "None within a couple of hundred miles to my knowledge."

"What's biting you?" snapped Peak. "What you goin' to mess around with coroners for? The man's dead, ain't he? We didn't kill him, did we? He died from being sick. We'll roll him in the ground, set up a wooden cross, and let it go at that."

"We will not," asserted Galt. His voice was even but cold as ice and sharp as a steel knife edge. "I am a registered physician. I won't be a party to any such infraction of the law. We will write a complete statement of this unfortunate affair, giving every detail, and then we will all sign it as witnesses. We will make two copies, one for the coroner's office and one for the police. Then, if any question ever comes up regarding Hillman or his death, no finger of suspicion can be pointed our way. We will have done our duty."

"Oh, all right," Peak growled. "Since you're so crazy about the job, you take it on."

"I expect to," Galt answered dryly. He asked Charlie for paper and drew a fountain pen from his pocket. "Did anyone notice the exact hour we found Hillman?" he asked.

"I did," Charlie said. "I looked at my watch, anticipating something like this. It was 15 minutes after 2 o'clock when you pronounced him dead."

"This is Friday morning," pursued Galt. "You saw Hillman first on Wednesday afternoon, a few hours before I came. Right?"

"Correct," affirmed Lew.

Galt's pen drove steadily over the paper. He wrote for so long the others became restless.

"Deal up the cards," Peak growled to Spath, and they began to play poker again. Charlie walked to the office door, hesitated a moment and went inside. Out in the storm-whipped yard a dog howled, a long melancholy wail that turned the eyes of the players instinctively to the room where Hillman's body lay.

Spath shivered then whispered, "He knows his master is dead."

At the words, Peak swore luridly. "Whatcha' mean by that tripe?" he snarled. "Tryin' to scare us? Talk sense or shut up."

Looking quickly at the man, Lew thought, "If Spath had intended to frighten one of us, then he succeeded."

Galt laid down his pen with a sigh of relief. "I have finished," he stated. "Now I suggest that each of you read the statement carefully and check me on anything I have missed. Then we will all sign."

"And who's goin' to keep the paper?" Peak demanded.

"I will," Galt told him. "I am the doctor on the scene, and I will assume that responsibility as one of my duties."

He handed the paper to Lew, who read it slowly. He saw the statement was plain and clear. It recorded Hillman's first appearance, his stay Wednesday night, Galt's warning to rest before resuming his journey, Hillman's second appearance with Peak and Spath, the progress of his illness, Galt's prescriptions for it, and finally the death, with the doctor's professional record of cause and time.

But Lew saw the record did not once mention Hillman's gold or his queer way of carrying or disposing of it. He held his own counsel on this odd omission and handed the paper to Peak, who read scowling, with Spath looking over his shoulder. Then Lew called to Charlie, who was still in the room of death. After Charlie had finished, he handed the paper to Galt and went back into the office.

Galt spread the statement out on the table and affixed his signature to the bottom. He motioned the others over and Spath signed next. Peak clumsily scrawled something below Spath's name, which Galt scrutinized closely. Lew had stooped over, pen between his fingers, when Charlie stepped abruptly into the room.

"Don't sign it, Lew," he ordered crisply. "It is false—a lie."

Someone in the room inhaled so sharply it made Lew wheel around. Galt was staring at Charlie, his cheeks pale. Peak and Spath were no less amazed, and they stood waiting for Charlie to explain.

Charlie stepped closer, and looking into the doctor's eyes, said distinctly, "Hillman did not die of pneumonia or a strained heart." Lew moistened dry lips. Something clicked in his brain; his memory flashed back to that moment he had sat up in his blankets just before they had found the dead man. Again in his mind he heard that short, quick gasp that had jerked him awake; he also heard the soft brushing sound of something moving in back of the log partition. And Lew knew what his partner was going to add, yet he waited with thumping heart and prickly skin for the words: "Hillman was murdered."

Total silence. Then, from Galt, "How do you know?"

"I have been in there examining the body," Charlie said carefully and precisely, "something I always supposed a physician did when death comes. I turned back the blankets looking for something that might further identify the man. I opened his shirt, since people sometimes carry a locket or tag about their neck. Soldiers in the last war did, and Hillman could easily have been a serviceman. I found nothing that would shed light on his past life, but I did find something that told me how he died. I found," he hesitated a moment, "finger marks on his throat. He was strangled."

"My gosh!" Lew gasped. He glanced at Galt. The man's face was the color of dead ashes, and his lips were parted as though breathing had suddenly become difficult.

"So," Charlie continued, "I think you are just a bit premature in signing that statement."

Galt squared his shoulders, passed a hand over his face as if clearing his mind. "How do you know the marks were finger bruises, and how do you know they were made tonight?"

"They are fresh, made a few minutes ago, and even now slowly fading as rigor mortis comes. I have seen strangulation finger marks before. There is no doubt in my mind about these."

Galt seized the lamp and strode into the office, the others at his heels. He bent close and slowly examined the lean throat. Then he faced them. "Those could be finger marks. They could have been made less than an hour ago. But there is no proof. So far as them fading after death, as you say, I know of no medical authority for such a thing."

"Neither do I," Charlie retorted. "But that is my opinion, and I'm sticking to it."

Galt continued, "His heart and lungs were in bad shape; they could have killed him. In fact, I still think they did. He had pneumonia in each lung—almost always fatal without hospital care. I saw the clenched hands, open mouth and bulging eyes, but these are usual symptoms of heart attack. I can alter my statement, of course."

"I think in your own mind that you agree with me, Doctor," Charlie went on gravely. "But even so, I am afraid you have missed the vital point, as have the others."

"You mean…" Galt suddenly faltered. For the second time that night his cheeks and lips turned pale.

"Exactly," Charlie lowered his voice. "If Hillman was strangled, as I have no doubt he was, someone in this house murdered him."

Dead silence followed that. Galt wheeled about and left the room. Back in the store, he paused beside the table, picked up his written account, crumpled the paper with trembling fingers, and cast it to the floor. "That changes it all," he said.

"Yes," Charlie agreed. "Hillman's body must not be buried until we know. It must be preserved exactly as it is until we can notify the police and get them here to take charge.

"And what's more," he added grimly. "The box of gold must remain sealed until this crime is solved. Under no circumstances can we attempt to divide it."

Peak started up at that. "What the devil you mean? Wasn't the dick half dead already? Doc here says he was, and Doc ought to know. How do you know those are finger marks on his neck, and if they are, that they croaked him? You amateur detectives make me sick."

"Just the same, Peak," Charlie told him sternly, "what I say goes. This post belongs to my partner and me. We don't intend to let any detail of this business be mishandled—no matter how bad you want to get your hands on the dead man's gold."

"I guess I ain't the only one that wanted it," Peak growled, sinking back into his chair.

"Everybody keep calm," admonished Spath, speaking for the first time since Charlie's news had gripped them all so deeply.

"Peak, you behave. These men are, in a sense, responsible for the safety of their guests, and for the keeping of the law in this region. I suggest we send an Indian or that one of us go to the closest police post. In the meantime, we will leave everything in that room just as it stands now and wait for an officer of the law to come and take charge. It's the only thing we can do."

"If I'm mixed up with a gang of murderers I want to watch my gold," Peak objected. "If he's right," Peak added, glancing at Charlie, "none of us will be safe in our beds."

He eyed them truculently. When no man answered, Peak flared out in a burst, "I'm going to take my share now!"

But Charlie stepped quickly to his side before he could move. "I don't think you mean that, Peak," he said slowly, poised on the balls of his feet. "There are several reasons why I think you don't. One of them is a question I now ask you.

"Tell us, will you, how you happened to be the only one with moccasins on when we ran into Hillman's room and found him dead? Moccasins that were laced and tied."

Peak's chair tipped backwards as he leaped to his feet with clenched fists. Lew edged a trifle closer, watching the man's face work. "What do you mean? You sayin' I killed him?" Peak bellowed.

"I'm not accusing you or anybody else," Charlie answered evenly. "I'm just asking you a question. How did you get enough time to lace those moccasins?"

With a mighty effort Peak regained control of himself. "That's easy," he said with an ugly laugh. "I always sleep in these. Look at them. I had them made for wearin' nights. Ask Spath, he knows."

"That's right," Spath affirmed. "Peak wore them every night we've been together."

Peak laughed again, a nasty sound. "Got any more questions — or guesses, gumshoe?"

"Not now," Charlie replied, and the look he sent Peak across the room seemed to sober him like a splash of ice water.

Dawn was breaking. The fall of snow had lightened, but the wind still beat with fierce blasts against the outside walls, and they knew impenetrable drifts were piling up across the trails.

It was time to make breakfast, and Charlie walked back to the stockroom and began to slice steaks from the hunk of caribou meat.

Lew whispered, "You think one of them killed Hillman?"

"Of course," Charlie assured him, "and so do you. Nobody has entered Hazzard House."

"Who?" Lew asked with a glance over his shoulder.

"I wish I knew," Charlie replied. "Lew, we're in terrible danger—just as Hillman was. Don't you see? Split it five ways and you get ten thousand. Split it four times, or only twice, and the piles just keep getting bigger."

"What can we do?" Lew muttered. "If we knew who it was we could act. But now we must sit and wait for them to act."

"I think I've got a pretty good clue," Charlie began slowly. "Something that happened when I told you Hillman had been strangled. You remember—" He ceased speaking and held a finger to his lips. Then he pressed them close to Lew's ear. "Somebody moved out there. We mustn't whisper together. The murderer will be watching. Don't show a sign of suspicion—not if you value your life."

He picked up the pile of sliced meat and they went up front to the store. Lew opened the cupboard and tilted the flour can.

"Darned if the flour isn't almost gone," he tried to talk normally. "We'll have to open another sack."

"I'll get it if you'll bring in some snow to melt for tea water," Charlie offered. Their water came from a spring several hundred yards away, but neither of them cared to wade deep snow even for so short a ways unless it was necessary.

Lew hurried out and scooped up two pails of clean snow. He looked carefully around. There was no sign of a track about the building or stockade wall. Lew ran back in and set the snow on the stove where it would melt.

Charlie had not brought the flour and neither of the others was in sight. He waited nervously a minute and then called, "Can't you find it?" But he knew the flour was piled up in 50-pound bags in plain view. There still was no answer, and a chill of fear smote Lew. He started back at a swift walk. He wanted to run, but he feared to appear ridiculous if nothing was wrong.

Lew glanced in the first sleeping room as he entered the office. Spath was leaning over, rummaging in a packsack. He heard somebody stropping a razor in the rear room, and then a low cry burst from his lips. Charlie was lying on the floor, motionless, his head jammed against the wall and a 50-pound sack of flour beside him.

Peak appeared in the doorway, razor in hand. "What the devil..." he began. Spath was behind him peering over his shoulder. And when he saw Charlie he repeated Lew's involuntary cry. Lew turned to them.

"Where's Galt?" he demanded. But as he spoke he heard footsteps, and wheeling, he saw Galt entering through the office door.

"Somebody hurt?" he asked quickly.

Chapter 4 – You Did It...You Devil!

Lew instinctively clenched his fists as the doctor advanced. Then he remembered Charlie's warning not to show suspicion, and he turned and knelt beside his prostrate partner. Galt knelt on the opposite side and asked, "How did this happen?"

Lew forced himself to answer calmly. "I don't know. I came back here and found him like this. Where were you?"

Galt returned his gaze with surprise. "I was in the office when you went through. If you had looked to the right you would have seen me. I was standing by the bed."

His slim fingers went around Charlie's throat feeling for heartbeats. Lew watched, struggling with a mixture of emotions: fear for Charlie, anger against whoever had been responsible for the attack, and reluctant admiration for the doctor's calm mien.

"Didn't any of you hear him fall?" demanded Lew.

Peak shook his head. "I was workin' my razor on Doc's strop," he said. "It made the only noise I could hear."

"I heard him moving something around," volunteered Spath. "Once I thought he dropped a box. That must have been him falling."

"I heard nothing," Galt added. "But I was thinking about Hillman, and when I concentrate I don't hear small sounds. Besides, I was up in the store for a moment. He may have fallen then."

"He isn't—dead?" Lew's lips barely sounded the word.

"No," Galt assured him. "But knocked unconscious."

"Looks like he slipped and fell and hit his head on the wall," Peak suggested hopefully.

"Charlie is pretty sure on his feet," Lew objected, careful to suppress the suspicion he felt.

"There's a bruise starting just above the forehead," said Galt. "Help me turn him over," and he ran quick fingers over Charlie's head and neck.

"That appears to be the only injury," the doctor added. And despite Lew's conviction that Charlie had been the victim of an attack, he could not help wondering if he might be mistaken. Could his partner have slipped? Could he fall hard enough to be knocked unconscious?

Then, at Galt's suggestion, they carried Charlie out to the store and laid him carefully on his blankets.

"Can you give him something to bring him around?" Lew asked.

But Galt gravely said, "He may have a fractured skull. A stimulant then would be dangerous. The only thing is to wait. We will try cold applications on his head." Gathered in a tight circle, all waited in silence, staring down at the unconscious form.

Lew strove to view the event with a cool, collected mind. But disturbing thoughts were racing through his brain like water through rock-walled rapids. If Charlie had not fallen, then who had crept up behind and struck him down? Galt had said he was in the store for a moment, then in the office the rest of the time. But Lew reflected that he had only the man's own word for this. That was all he had for any of the others' actions—merely their statements. Each man had been alone in a separate room when the attack had occurred, and each had been only a few steps from where he found Charlie.

Lew reviewed the position of the doors that opened into the office and stockroom. Galt could have cat-footed in behind Charlie and struck him. Spath would not have seen—he was bending over the packsack, his back to the door when Lew hurried past. Neither would Peak have noticed the doctor—for Peak was in no position to look into any part of the stockroom.

Had Peak struck the blow? The chances appeared equally good, perhaps better. Peak could have crept around the door, struck quickly, and gotten back to his stropping without having missed more than a few strokes. Neither of the others would have noticed. Partitions and opened doors blocked Spath's view, and Galt, by his own admission, had stood with his back to the doorway, examining Hillman's body.

Spath? He could have tiptoed into the office without much chance of Galt seeing. It would have required soft moving, but then Galt said he always lapsed into a sort of deep study when he concentrated on anything. Besides, Galt had been up in the store once. That would have made it easy for Spath, and yet Lew could hardly bring himself to believe this of the mild-mannered man.

It was a puzzle. Each of the three had opportunity, and none could check up on another's actions. Still, Lew reflected, he might be worrying uselessly. Galt had found only a bruise above the forehead, a natural result of a head striking a wall.

He felt that the others were watching him and in a sense waiting to see what he would do, so he tried to act naturally, to keep all signs of suspicion from his face. That was all he could do. He had no foundation for accusing anyone of anything, and he felt that further questioning would only antagonize them, shed no light on the affair and, in fact, make matters worse.

But his heart sank as he watched the still face of his stricken partner. If Charlie did not recover—what would he do?

Lew glanced out a window. The wind had abated, but heavy snow fell steadily, clogging the trails. No prospect of leaving soon. And he shuddered at the thought of being confined here with three strangers, one of whom might be a killer, and a corpse.

An hour passed. Spath and Peak finally returned to the table and resumed their game of cards. Galt did not leave the position he had taken beside Charlie; he only moved to renew the cold packs that Lew handed him to lay over the patient's forehead.

Another hour dragged by, and then Lew's heart jumped at Galt's words, "He's coming around."

Lew almost shouted with relief when he saw color returning to the waxy cheeks. The white, bloodless lips parted, and Charlie groaned, turning his head feebly. Charlie was coming back, would soon be able to shoulder part of the burden of fear and distrust that was slowly crushing Lew's courage.

With a strong effort, Charlie sat up.

"How do you feel, old-timer?" Lew asked, forcing a grin. But Charlie fell back on the blankets with another groan.

"He isn't able to talk yet," Galt interposed. "I'll give him a weak stimulant now."

The drug brought more color to Charlie's cheeks. His breathing became stronger, and ten minutes later he struggled up to a sitting position for the second time.

Lew could not restrain his eager questions. "What happened? Did you fall in the stockroom? How…"

And then Lew faltered, unable to continue, for Charlie was staring at him with eyes utterly devoid of understanding. Something in those eyes made Lew shudder. They were expressionless, lifeless.

"Can't you talk?" Lew whispered. And then he would have given almost anything to have taken the words back. Charlie's lips parted, and he laughed, a senile sound that chilled Lew's blood.

Charlie scrambled to his feet, laughed again and stumbled away, arms hanging loosely at his sides. He faced them from a corner of the room, and backing into it, squatted on his heels.

"What's the matter?" Lew gasped.

"He's batty, off his nut," Peak declared. "That knock on the head made him silly." He surveyed Charlie with wonder.

Lew could not stand it any longer. He rushed to Charlie. Grabbing his shoulder, he shook him and shouted, "Snap out of it!"

Charlie screamed, a cry shrill with terror, and struck his hand away. Then he pressed farther back into the corner, striking out wildly and crying gibberish. Lew drew back, saw the drooping mouth and fearful eyes; then he covered his own eyes. He could not bear the sight. "This is terrible," he heard Spath say. "The fellow is an idiot."

Lew turned to Galt. "Could a blow do this?" he demanded.

Galt nodded. "He may recover, may even wake up tomorrow morning entirely rational—or he may not." Seeing the spasm of pain that shot over Lew's face at the implication, he stopped speaking.

Lew backed away, slumped in a chair and covered his face with shaking hands. "What will I do?" he groaned in a voice too low for the others to hear.

Charlie had gradually lapsed into a calm silence. He crouched, pressed against the converging walls, watching them with quick, sharp glances of fear.

Galt whispered, "Pay no attention to him. He doesn't want to be noticed—it makes him fearful."

Lew nodded assent and tried not to stare at the remains of a once-strong, clear-thinking man.

An hour later—Lew could never say how it passed—Charlie was seized with a sudden sense of duty. He ambled across the room and poked a stick of wood in the stove. Then he picked up the shaved birch broom and swept scattered ashes up from the floor. Peak dropped a card, and Charlie stooped and recovered it for him.

When Charlie seized one of the pails and started to the door, Lew sprang up, determined to stop him, fearing he might get lost in the snow. But Galt restrained him with a hand on his arm. Charlie stepped outdoors and came back with a pail of snow. Then he ambled back to the corner, backed into it, and crouched, facing them.

"God help me!" Lew cried. "I'll go crazy if he doesn't stop that."

"That won't help," Galt said, in sharp warning. "Don't watch him. Look the other way. Don't do a thing that might excite him. He might turn violent, you know."

And then Lew remembered that this terrible happening had driven all thought of food from his mind, that they had not eaten breakfast and that it was nearly noon. He pulled himself together and began to work, cooking meat, flapjacks and tea. He noticed that Peak had dropped the cards and was staring at Charlie with a queer look, eyes drawn back under overhanging brows.

They sat down to eat.

"Shall I call him?" Lew whispered, but Galt shook his head.

"Put a plate in his usual place and then ignore him."

They ate slowly, Lew swallowing with difficulty. Every mouthful seemed to choke him. Charlie watched closely. Something was stirring in his dead brain. He crept closer with short, furtive moves, reached out suddenly, seized his heaped plate, and with a silly sound of triumph scuttled back to the corner and crouched there, wolfing the food.

Lew got up abruptly, pushed his plate back and walked out of the room. The sight was unbearable. But he remembered that Charlie needed his help now more than ever. He must not fail; he must guard him as he would a child against further injury. Charlie had helped himself to a steaming cup of tea, and drinking it, had burned his mouth and cried out like a hurt rabbit.

Peak swore with vehemence. "That will drive me nuts, if he keeps it up. Can't you give him something, Doc, to put him to sleep? Maybe he'll snooze this crazy jag off."

Charlie finished eating, carried his plate to the table and gathered up the dishes. "He still knows enough to work," Peak observed. "If that is the way a crack on the bean works, I know plenty of guys that could use one."

With Lew's help, Charlie did the dishes. He still avoided contact with his partner and the others, shrinking back whenever they approached. Then he disappeared through the door into the office. Lew followed after a few minutes and found Charlie in the first sleeping room, arranging the blankets back in order. And as Lew watched him from the doorway, he noticed that Charlie's hand stole up to his head every few moments. The fingers carefully rubbed over a spot that seemed to hurt. Suddenly it flashed over Lew that he was rubbing the back of his head, not the spot in front that had been bruised when he fell. The back of Charlie's head hurt. Like another flash came the significance of that. He had been struck on the back of the skull, a blow that had pitched him forward against the wall, a blow that shocked his brain so badly it went imbecile when he regained consciousness.

Lew advanced slowly. "Let me see, Charlie," he asked.

But Charlie sprang away with a cry that wrung his partner's heart, and Lew turned back with clouded eyes and returned to the store. As he sat, outwardly calm and unruffled, red-hot thoughts were burning across his brain: Hillman strangled. Charlie struck a murderous blow from behind. Who would be next?

Peak started towards the door, "Guess I better feed the dogs," he said. Lew sat watching him disappear, heard the door slam shut, and then for some unaccountable reason suddenly felt that he should accompany the man. He glanced about. Spath was hunched over in his chair, almost asleep. Galt was immersed in deep thought and did not even glance up as Lew rose to go.

Lew rounded the corner of the building and found Peak standing motionless, back toward him before the dog shed. Lew advanced swiftly, and peering over the man's shoulder saw him turning something over in his fingers. Lew's jaw set as he recognized a handmade leather blackjack, laced with rawhide and loaded with shot. Just the weapon to pitch a man unconscious on his face and crack his skull.

Lew uttered a snarled, "So you did it, you devil!" He drew back his fist to strike but Peak jumped forward, and something in his face when he whirled about stayed the blow Lew had aimed at his jaw.

The man was startled, he could see that plainly, but there was something else in Peak's eyes, a look of perplexed wonder, that made Lew hesitate.

"Don't get excited, young fellow," Peak growled. "And don't do something now you'll be sorry for later. I found this thing in the snow just now. I saw where something had been pitched in this drift not that long ago, and I dug it out. An' now I don't know whether I'm glad I did or not."

"I can't swallow that, Peak," Lew snarled. "You came out here to hide it, and I caught you before you could. I had you tagged for Hillman. And now I know you slugged my partner. You think I'm going to let you get away with that?"

He braced himself for the fight that seemed inevitable, which he really welcomed. But it did not come.

Instead, Peak's eyes grew weary, it seemed to Lew, and they still held a trace of that look of perplexity that had so surprised him.

"Be your age!" Peak advised harshly. "Use your bean. If I had wanted to hide this thing, you suppose I'd carry it out here and stand around lookin' at it? And keep on lookin' when you crawled up behind me? I heard you shut the door and come out. I ain't exactly a fool. No, if I had wanted to ditch this, I'd have kept it until night and then put it away for good."

"But if you didn't—who did?" Lew asked.

Peak surveyed him sullenly. "I dunno," he finally answered. "Maybe Galt beaned him. Maybe Spath did it. Maybe you. But I can think of reasons why none of you did."

"I would be interested to hear them," Lew replied.

Peak glared at him before he spoke. "You'd hardly knock your own partner silly, although you had a chance. And I can't see Doc carryin' a billy around. He's got drugs and surgical knives he's more handy with. Also, I never saw Spath whip a dog or speak a harsh word to one, let alone a man. It don't seem like him to pull off something like this."

"Which leaves you," Lew suggested evenly. "Just the sort of thing a rough guy like you might do."

Peak blinked rapidly, but kept control of his temper.

"I knew you'd say that. And I may end up thinkin' I did do it, if such queer things keep on happening. I tell you, I thought that stuff about Hillman bein' choked was bunk. I didn't believe it. Don't know as I do for sure now—but I'm worried. I saw your partner rubbin' the back of his head like it hurt, yet Doc says the only rap he got was in front. And now I find this," swinging the blackjack suggestively. "An' I don't know what to think!"

With a quick move, Peak tossed the weapon over the stockade.

"What did you do that for?" Lew demanded.

"Plenty of reasons, all good," Peak retorted. "The only fingerprints on it now are probably mine, and this business ain't over yet, young man. The fewer weapons layin' around, the better."

Abruptly, Peak swung about, and without feeding a dog, walked back into the store.

Lew gave the animals their dinner, thinking fast as he worked. Peak was showing a new, almost startling side. The man acted worried, or was he putting up a good bluff?

He had talked Lew out of his determination for a showdown over the blackjack, got around the issue very neatly, Lew realized with chagrin. "Darned if I know what to think," Lew finally exploded. "But just the same, I keep an eye on Mr. Peak. He bears watching."

Lew did not know how he got through that day. Spath and Peak played poker on and off, and Peak seemed reluctant to meet Lew's eyes or address him directly. Galt had taken to pacing restively across the floor with monotonous steps that grated on Lew's nerves. Charlie crouched in the corner most of the time, jerking whenever he caught someone's eyes on him.

Night fell and they ate again, a mockery of a meal. Lew forced down some food and watched the shadows play on the wall behind the table. He turned his head when Charlie crept out of the corner, snatched his plate and devoured the food with animal noises.

After supper, Peak became restless to an almost unbearable degree. He started up nervously, paced back and forth, and gnawed at thick, rough fingernails. Finally, he spoke. "I'm goin' to bed. I'm tired, but I can't sleep. Can you give me a dose that'll put me out, Doc?"

Galt glanced up. "I can give you a mild sedative," he replied, and he opened the small case and measured powder in a glass. Filling the glass half full of water, he handed it to Peak.

Peak drained the stuff in a single gulp and set the glass down. He walked over to a window and tried to stare out into the night. A moment later, he stepped to the door, opened it and thrust his head outside. "Dang," he exclaimed. "Snowin' just as bad as ever."

"We have all missed sleep," Spath said. "I'm going to turn in myself, and I think you should follow our example." He followed Peak, and Galt yawned and left a minute later.

Lew sat by the stove. He wondered if he could persuade Charlie to lie down on his blankets, and decided the best way to do this was by his own example. And while he spread out the beds his thoughts strayed to Peak. Funny Peak should suddenly show nerves. He wasn't the type, the sort that needed a sedative to sleep. Peak should be able to lay his bear-like body anywhere and doze off.

Lew thought of the storm, the persistent snow that bottled them up and which was surely, relentlessly, heaping additional barriers to deter any escape. He opened the door and lamp light streamed out through the opening. It was still snowing steadily.

Lew glanced down on the ground. Something he saw sent the blood racing through his veins. A small hole in the snow, just such an opening one would make by spitting out a mouthful of water.

Lew bent down, took another look and backed inside.

"Clever," he muttered. "Peak drank Doc's medicine and went immediately to the window. He didn't swallow the stuff but held it in his mouth. Then, later, he opened the door, spit it out and turned around to tell us how hard it was snowing. Clever, but not quite clever enough."

As he prepared for bed, Lew muttered to himself, "Peak wanted us to think he was asleep tonight—and I'm going to find out why."

Charlie was closely watching his preparations and finally shambled out from the corner, seized his own bed roll and jerked it around to the end of the counter. Habit had finally prevailed. Charlie pulled off his shoes and lay down to sleep.

Lew had determined to stay awake all night if necessary, but it wasn't long before he felt his eyelids dropping. Soon, he realized it was impossible to stay awake, so he crept out of his blankets and tiptoed back of the counter. There, he procured a spool of black thread and two stout pins.

Creeping back to the doorway leading into the office, Lew stuck the two pins firmly into the log ends forming the door frame at a height 18 inches above the floor. He tied the thread to one pin, drew it across the opening behind the other pin and led the thread over to his blankets, broke it from the spool, and tied the free end to his little finger. Confident that no one could enter the store without waking him, Lew lay back and was soon asleep.

A sharp tug on his finger aroused him.

Chapter 5 – He's a Homicidal Maniac!

Lew wiggled his little finger and found that the thread tied to it was broken loose. He lay listening and looking out into the dark room, wondering if somebody had really come through the doorway or if a movement in his sleep had parted the thread.

His eyes slowly became attuned to the gray interior of the room until they penetrated to the dim outlines of the counter some 12 feet away. He cautiously raised his head. Was that a patch of shadow at the end of the counter? Was someone standing there, motionless, staring at him with colorless eyes?

Lew's hand crept up to the pistol under his rolled-up coat. A violent burst of wind smote the store door until it rattled. Instinctively, Lew's eyes turned toward the sound, and when they flashed back to the counter he thought the shadow had vanished.

He sat up, gripping the gun. He must know if someone had entered the room. But he preferred to find out without awakening any suspicions. The intruder's errand may have been harmless, to get a drink of water. And Lew was remembering Charlie's last warning: "If you value your life, don't show that you suspect anyone."

Lew slid out of his blankets and stepped toward the counter. A sound froze him motionless; he waited with raised pistol. Then he realized what he had heard. Charlie was turning over in his bed. Lew crept out through the doorway into the office.

He stopped at the door of the first sleeping room to listen. Heavy breathing sounded from inside, and he felt sure it was coming from two men, which would account for Peak and Spath. Moving on, he entered the stockroom and crouched beside the door leading out of it. He heard breathing, almost a wheeze. That accounted for the doctor.

Lew stole back, stretched a second length of black thread across the doorway, and with the loop again about his finger drifted back to sleep thinking he must have imagined that shadow watching from across the room.

Morning came without further alarm. Charlie was sleeping soundly, and Lew moved quietly about, building the fire and setting out food and utensils to start breakfast.

Finally he heard someone stir and was not surprised to see Peak approach quietly. But he almost started up when the other sat very close beside him and leaned forward to bring lips near his ear.

"I didn't intend to say nothin' about it, but dang if I haven't got to tell somebody," Peak began. "Last night I didn't sleep very much."

"I know," Lew replied. "I heard you come in here."

"When I stood by the counter?" asked Peak, not the least abashed. "Yes."

"I thought you did. You was breathing naturally when I passed the door, then all of a sudden you stopped."

Lew waited, making a mental note to keep right on breathing naturally when awakened in the night.

Peak continued, "I faked that drink of dope Doc gave me." He paused, but Lew did not say, "I knew that, too." Lew had decided it was wiser not to display such an aptitude for finding out things.

"I wanted everybody to think I was goin' to sleep," Peak went on. "I spit the stuff out the door. Then, about 10:30 or so, I got out of the bunk and came into the office there. I spent most of the night sittin' close to Hillman's corpse and the gold."

Lew shivered as he thought of that grisly watch in the night. Peak went on, "I thought I might learn something. If you or Galt or Spath had picked out last night for funny business, I was going to have a ringside seat."

"Well?" Lew whispered.

"Nothing happened. I sat there for several hours, and then something did happen. I got the worst jolt I ever had, and I ain't no soft chicken. My scalp still twitches when I think of it. I was sitting there half asleep when I just knew somebody was in the room beside me."

"Go on!" Lew was interested now.

"I had been squatting on the floor not far from the wall where your partner got socked on the head. I looked up, and here in the door or right beside it, I saw eyes lookin' into mine. Someone sitting there as silent as a cat lookin' at me for I don't know how long!"

"What did you do?"

"I blinked to clear my head, and then when I looked again, he was gone. I guess I must have rubbed my eyes to make sure they wasn't foolin' me, and that gave him a chance to sneak."

"Sure you didn't dream it?" Lew asked.

Peak glared at him. "I don't dream, young fellow. As I said, you was breathin' along natural until I passed the door, and then I figured something woke you. I stood beside the counter waitin' for a blast of wind to cover any noise I might make, and while I stood there I made up my mind to find out whose bunk was empty. And I did."

"Whose was it?" Lew snapped.

"Your crazy partner. I felt down with my foot and his blankets were empty. He was gone out of them."

Lew's mouth dropped open. "Why, it couldn't have been Charlie. Just after you left I heard him turn over in his bed."

"You heard him crawlin' back in it, you mean," Peak said shortly.

Odd thoughts began racing through Lew's puzzled brain. Peak sitting up to watch Hazzard House. And then Charlie watching Peak. Could he believe that? It might be true. Charlie's warped brain could be reverting back to instinct. Night watches? Could it be?

But what seemed more probable was that Peak had built up an elaborate alibi to cover his own actions—to conceal his real motive. Suppose he had come in the store to attack Lew? And hearing Lew's natural breathing stop, he had realized he might be awake. Foiled of this murderous purpose, he would retreat and concoct a tale of Charlie being gone from his blankets.

Peak laid a thick hand on Lew's knee. "But that ain't all. I got something else. I don't know yet why I picked you out instead of the rest, but here goes. While I was watchin' out last night, somebody came over to my bunk."

"How do you know that?"

Peak surveyed him through narrowed, cunning eyes. "I ain't clear dumb even if I act it. When I left I laid my moccasins on edge— two feet out from the bed just where somebody who came monkeyin' around would stumble over them. When I got back they was still sittin' up on edge, but they had been moved."

He waited to see the effect of this statement. But Lew sat outwardly calm, waiting for him to finish.

"Don't you get it? Somebody stumbled over the moccasins. And then set them up again on edge thinkin' they could fool me. But they couldn't, for I had laid the strings in a neat coil on top of the toes, and when I found them the strings were straggled to the sides."

Peak stared full into Lew's eyes. "Someone was over at my bunk in the night," he said coldly, "and I want to know why."

Lew considered this for a minute. Peak was more clever than he appeared. "Do you think it was Charlie?" he finally asked.

"Must have been," Peak answered gruffly. Then he got up and walked to the window with elaborate indifference, his face a mask of disinterest. He surveyed the falling snow and spoke. "Will it ever stop? Lord, but I want to get out of this place."

Lew silently seconded that notion. Then he heard Charlie move and whirled about, suddenly remembering Galt's words: "He might awake some morning, clear-minded and sane as ever."

He watched his partner eagerly to see if the miracle had occurred. But then his heart sank as Charlie opened the same dull eyes and sagging mouth.

Galt appeared in the door with Spath just behind. Charlie appeared more eager to work now than before, and he busied himself with Lew at breakfast, performing tasks with a sort of detached unconcern that showed such actions were merely the result of many years' experience and habit.

"Something happened last night that startled me," Spath said as they sat down to eat. "Either I dreamed it or else somebody came and leaned over my bunk. Was it you, Peak? Did I snore too loud?"

"Never heard you snore yet," Peak grunted. "You probably ate too much supper and dreamed it."

Galt had been watching Charlie with what seemed professional interest. "I thought he might be better this morning, but I see he's just the same," the doctor finally told Lew.

"Can't something be done?" Lew asked.

"Perhaps an operation," Galt answered. "Pressure on the brain may be causing this. An operation could relieve the pressure. It is dangerous, and chances are no better than even for success."

"When this storm lets up," Lew declared, "I will take him to the best hospital in the land."

"That ain't a bad idea, rushin' out of here," Peak agreed. "I say as soon as we can travel, we put Hillman's body and the gold on a sled, and all of us mush down to the police post and have it out there. What's the use of waitin' here to send them word?"

"I'm for anything that will hasten Charlie's recovery," Lew cried. Spath and Galt nodded assent. All approved Peak's plan.

"I'm goin' in and look over my legacy," Peak said suddenly. "Want to come along?" His gesture included them all. The three men rose from the table and followed him into the room where Hillman's body lay covered with a blanket. Below it on the floor sat the wooden cache filled with sacks of virgin gold dust.

Peak bent over and tugged at each of the five cords. Every seal was tight and secure. "Okay," he grunted, and they turned silently about and filed out. Lew kept his eyes resolutely away from the cold form on the bed. His nerves were close to the breaking point already. This enforced confinement with a corpse made him unusually suscep-tible to the accumulating strain piling upon him.

Lew decided he must stay busy, even if he had to repeat the same task over and over again. So he began to rearrange the stock of merchandise on the shelves behind the counter. He regrouped food, toys, clothing and cheap ornaments, bringing in fresh cartons from the stockroom to fill depleted slots.

Peak and Spath had resumed their poker game with a calm that irrationally irritated Lew, and Galt stood with his back to the room, gazing out through the window at swirling snow. Lew brushed dust from a shelf, felt a sharp sting, and exclaimed aloud when he saw he had ripped his hand on a protruding nail.

"I'll fix that up," Galt offered and hurried off with professional zeal for his kit. He opened it then lifted a puzzled face. "My scissors are missing," he declared.

Peak looked up, mildly interested. "You're lucky to have any-thing left in this dump," he said, but nobody paid attention, being thor-oughly immune to his crass comments.

"I saw them here yesterday," Galt continued. "Nobody borrowed them, did they?"

"Never mind," Lew interrupted. "Use my knife." But Galt in-sisted on looking again with minute care, again without any result.

"What are you trying to do, Doc? Work an alibi so you can stick us in the gizzard with the shears?" Peak grinned.

Galt flushed with anger at that and then shrugged and bound up Lew's finger in silence.

Lew returned to his work. He moved things about slowly, shift-ing them again and again in an attempt to make the job last as long as possible. Finally, he had to admit that nothing more could be bettered, and he emerged from behind the counter.

The day wore on, noon passed and afternoon brought so thick a gloom that Lew lit the kerosene lamp. Peak's face had acquired a deep flush and Lew suspected the man was drinking. He had been wander-ing about the room, disappearing back through the office and out again. Suddenly he appeared before them.

"Find your shears yet, Doc?" he asked in a disagreeable voice.

"No," Galt replied evenly.

"Well," Peak sneered, "I know where they are."

Galt glanced at him. "Where?"

"Sure you don't know?"

Galt ignored the question.

"I know something else," Peak went on, his voice turning ugly. "And I'm going..." He broke off and turned to Lew. "Say, that lamp of yours is going dry." Lew saw the flame slowly dying. He grabbed it up and walked to the kerosene can behind the counter.

What was Peak going to tell them? Lew removed the chimney and as he did his eyes chanced to fall upon Charlie crouched in the corner, staring at him with a look of queer intentness. Lew blew out the dying flame and pitched the room into darkness.

"Hang it!" he exclaimed. "I hadn't ought to have done that. Get me a candle, will you Peak, so I can see to fill this?"

He heard footsteps coming towards the office door. Somewhere by the stove a chair pushed back. "Better strike a match to find your way," Lew admonished.

Then a sharp cry rang out, followed by a heavy thud and Spath's voice crying shrilly, "Someone light a match! Quick!"

Lew sprang out into the room, fumbling through his pockets. He jerked out a match and struck it.

Galt and Spath were standing close beside him, tense faces staring into the black doorway of the office. But before Lew's eyes could pierce the gloom, the match flickered out, like a sudden breath had found it.

This time it was Galt who spoke. "Something's wrong! Hurry!"

Then Lew remembered a box of thick candles among the goods he had sorted that morning. He groped back to the shelf, located the box, and with shaking fingers lit one.

Holding it high overhead he moved slowly toward the office. Galt and Spath pressed in behind.

At the threshold he stiffened, horrified at the sight in the narrow circle of light. Just beyond the doorway a man lay on the floor, hands sprawled and legs drawn up underneath in an unmistakable posture of death. A dark stain slowly spread along the worn floorboards.

Galt was speaking, trying to keep his voice calm, "Fill your lamp at once. We can't see well enough by that."

Lew ran back to the counter, stuck the candle upright in a blob of its own wax, and poured the lamp full of fuel. With both candle and lamp flooding the room with light, they advanced fearfully to where Peak's body lay.

Galt bent over, fingers passing swiftly over the man's back. He ripped up the flannel shirt, heavy and wet with blood. "Stabbed in the back! Two times, and each through the heart!"

Galt rose to his feet, and Lew saw the long, white fingers trembling as with ague.

Suddenly Lew thought of Charlie. He ran back into the store and sighed with relief when he found his partner staring at him from the corner. The doctor came back from the office and stood watching the broken figure crouched there.

Spath was almost sobbing in agitation. "Peak killed. Who's next? What will we do?" He repeated the same cries over and over, wringing his hands despairingly.

Lew surveyed them with narrowed eyes. This time there could be no mistake. This murder was indisputable. He glanced from Spath to Galt. What was Peak going to tell them? Was it something the murderer did not dare let him say? Had Peak sealed his own death warrant with his final words? It looked that way.

He couldn't let things go on like they were.

Gradually a plan formed in his mind. He would get his gun, get the drop on both of these men and force one to tie up the other. Then he would bind the second himself, keeping them confined until the storm passed and he could send for help. That was the only course open. How he wished Charlie were able to back him with his customary strength and clear thinking.

Galt spoke sharply to Spath, "Shut up, man. Stop whimpering. We have work to do. We have got to stop this ghastly business."

Lew advanced a step. "How are you going to stop it?" His voice was quiet, but anyone who knew Lew would have sensed the underlying intensity.

"How?" Galt said. "I know who stabbed Peak, and so do you. It was him!" And he pointed an accusing finger directly at Charlie.

"What?" Lew cried. "He never did it. It was..." Lew stopped himself before finishing the sentence. He started to say, "It was one of you two." But he decided that was unwise. He was not yet ready to show his hand. He must get his gun, first.

Galt's long arm swept the lamp up from the counter. He stepped forward and thrust it toward Charlie's shrinking face.

"There's blood on his shoe!" Galt's voice shrilled triumphantly.

Lew's reluctant eyes followed the man's pointing finger. He saw a dark stain on the edge of one shoe, a stain that glittered in the lamp

180

light. His heart began to thump with a queer, strained rhythm and cold perspiration wet his forehead.

"He will murder us all if we don't stop him," Galt said. "He's become a homicidal maniac!"

Chapter 6 – Three Sacks Are Missing

Lew quickly stepped between his shrinking partner and Doctor Galt. "You're crazy yourself! He isn't that kind!" he said defiantly.

"Not when he was sane," Galt retorted. "But he isn't sane now. His brain is tortured by the pressure of a fractured skull. His mind and judgment are distorted. There are cases on record where a brain injury has turned gentle, harmless men into murdering fiends."

That left Lew shaken. The plain truth in Galt's words and his loyalty to Charlie struggled for supremacy. He, too, had heard of such cases, yet he could not believe anything like that of Charlie. His pal for years—a murderer? Never! Lew grew calm and also firm in his determination to stand by Charlie to the last.

And, naturally, he seized upon the first defense that entered his head. "Where's the weapon?" he asked. "What killed Peak? You better find that before you accuse anybody."

But Galt merely glanced at Charlie and replied, "He had plenty of time to dispose of it. There were minutes of total darkness, you know."

With a strong effort Lew overpowered his repugnance and stepped over to Peak's body.

"Bring the lamp," he said, and Galt carried it to him, both leaning over to examine the gaping wounds in the blood-soaked back.

"Small, sharp blade made them," Lew muttered. Spath edged close, trembling so badly Lew felt pity for the man. He appeared completely unnerved, his face white and fingers working nervously.

He spoke with reluctance. "Could scissors have done it, Doctor?"

Lew straightened at that and said, "Of course! This doesn't look like knife work. Peak was stabbed with your scissors, wasn't he?"

"It is possible the scissors were used," Galt admitted. "They are very sharp."

"Then why accuse Charlie? Peak was killed with your instrument. Is there any reason why I shouldn't accuse you?"

"Two very good ones," Galt shot back. "You forget that I missed them this morning. Someone had taken them from my case."

"I recall you saying that," Lew retorted. "But why Charlie? Why not Spath, or me? Seems to me like a maniac with homicidal impulses would want an axe or a club."

Galt shook his head. "Not necessarily. An insane person may act sly. He may control his murderous impulse in order to obtain a particular weapon and the chance to use it. This is perfectly in accord with the theory of such cases. Also," Galt added, "you haven't heard my second reason. If the man is innocent, how did he get fresh blood on his shoe?"

That floored Lew. He glanced with a shudder at the incriminatory evidence. How had it got there? But his faith in Charlie was only shaken for a second, and he rallied quickly to the defense.

"There's a murderer among us," he admitted, "but it isn't Charlie. He didn't strangle Hillman, and he didn't hit himself over the head. Whoever did those things killed Peak."

"There's no proof that Hillman was strangled," Galt snapped.

"I remember you tried to gloss that over," Lew shot back.

"I did nothing of the sort!" Galt retorted. "I did what any medical doctor would do, and I still maintain Hillman probably died of pneumonia and a bad heart. There is no proof, either, that Charlie was hit on the head. He could have slipped and injured himself."

"Maybe you'll tell me next that Peak stabbed himself in the back?" Lew gritted.

"No," Galt's voice was shrill. "There is no doubt of this one—it's murder. And everything points to your partner as the murderer. If he kills another of us, you will be responsible."

"Why me?" Lew growled.

"Because you refuse to see the facts. Because you won't agree that he must be tied and kept under guard until we can break out of this prison. I warn you, Charlie is now a homicidal maniac. If you permit him to stay at liberty, you share his guilt."

"I got to think it over," Lew muttered, shaken by the vehemence of Galt's proclamation.

"That's better," Spath interposed. "Nobody will sleep tonight. I know I won't. And we will be safer together. Safety in numbers, you know. In the morning we can decide what is best to do."

Galt shrugged, not appearing convinced. But he made no protest. He glanced at Peak's body. "We should move that," he said.

Lew and Galt picked it up and laid it on the office floor close to the bed and the box of gold. Spath did not offer to help but huddled close to the stove with averted face. Lew glanced around the room. Two dead men and a fortune in gold. Where would this end?

Back in the store they sat silently, three sober men wrestling with their own thoughts. Spath suddenly jumped up, babbling in fright. "I'm not going to wait. I won't stay here to be killed. I'm going now!" He seized his hat and coat from behind the stove and rushed for the door.

They caught him struggling at the gate, trying to open it. Then he stumbled back, shaking from the sudden exposure to the cold. "I can't get it open," he whimpered. "There's four feet of snow against it."

"Come back in and sit down by the stove like a sensible man," Lew told him. "If you get through the gate, the trail outside will be just as bad. You won't make the first mile."

"But I'll be killed if I stay," the man groaned. "I've got to go tomorrow morning. I must!"

Back at the stove, silence fell again over the little group. Charlie moved slowly out of his corner, creeping closer to the heat. Galt watched him with suspicious eyes, muscles tensed for fast action, or so it seemed to Lew.

Charlie finally slunk off to his blankets, but sleep for the others was out of the question. Lew had shoved his chair close to the office door from where he could watch each of the others rest without turning his head. The hours dragged on. Spath smoked nervously; Galt leaned forward, brooding with set features.

Lew felt himself dozing, and he jerked his eyelids open in sudden panic. It would never do for him to sleep. He must stay awake, must watch for the menace that hovered over Hazzard House.

But his eyes grew increasingly heavy with the monotony of the night, and despite his determination, he started up some moments later with the guilty conviction that he had been sleeping for several minutes. His surprised eyes saw Galt on his feet by the stove. Lew jumped up, a look of alarm on his face.

"I'm making tea," Galt told him quietly. Lew saw that he held the kettle in his hand. "It will help us stay awake."

Spath straightened up and Lew suspected that he, too, had drifted off. Galt set cups beside the steaming kettle, poured and passed them around. Lew gulped the hot drink greedily. It soothed his cramped, tired muscles and sent a glow of comfort over his body. He saw Galt arouse Charlie and press a cup in his hand with kindly insistence. His heart warmed to the man at the act. Maybe they could get together in the morning and fix up things so everybody would be satisfied?

Galt refilled his cup and Spath's then sat down and began to talk. He spoke of the storm, speculating on how long it would last and how they could force a way through the drifts. And the last thing Lew remembered was the doctor talking steadily in his grave tones.

When Lew awoke he started to his feet. He had fallen asleep after all, for hours, too, as morning was breaking outside. Then he gripped the chair. He was dizzy, light nausea seizing him as he ruefully thought that sleeping beside the stove in a hard chair was not the best way to obtain much-needed rest.

He glanced at the others. Spath was slumped over with head and arms resting on the table. Galt leaned back in his chair, lips parted and breathing noisily. Charlie was on his blankets at the end of the counter, seemingly asleep like the rest.

"I'm no good," Lew told himself. "I meant to stay awake and watch and I bet I slept most of the night."

Galt opened his eyes, stared blankly about. "I must have been asleep," he said.

"Everybody was," Lew admitted. Spath slept on, and Lew eyed him doubtfully. He needed the table to prepare breakfast. Finally, he leaned over and shook Spath firmly. Spath muttered thickly, half-raised his head and then slumped forward.

Lew shook him again, roughly this time, and the man sprang to his feet, swayed unsteadily and glared wildly around. Then he laughed. "My head feels like a barrel."

"That's because you slept sitting up," Galt told him.

After the morning meal Galt broached the subject that Lew dreaded but knew must come.

"Despite the danger, we all fell asleep last night," the doctor said. "We are fortunate in coming through unharmed, but we mustn't take another chance of that sort. What are we going to do with Peak's murderer?" Lew flushed at the implication. Galt's insistence on Charlie's guilt was beginning to make Lew suspect him, but he did not say this. Instead, he decided to postpone the issue of Charlie's liberty as long as he could, so he said, "Yesterday morning Peak examined the gold. Maybe we better follow his example and look it over."

"Nonsense," Galt retorted. "The gold is all right. How could it be otherwise?" Then he frowned as he realized Lew's evasion of the question he had just asked.

Lew found an unexpected backer in Spath, who seconded the proposal. Galt followed them reluctantly into the office. Keeping his eyes turned as far as he could from the two stiff bodies, one on the bed and the other on the floor, Lew pulled the coffin-shaped box out into the middle of the room. He plucked at the cords that sealed the screwed-on lid against tampering.

"All okay," he announced as he jerked the last string. The wax seals were undisturbed.

But Spath leaned forward. "Didn't that last one seem loose?"

"Only a little," Lew agreed. He tested it once more. Yes, there was more slack than seemed usual. With a sudden resolve, he grasped the box, and signing to Spath, rolled it over bottom side up.

Both cried out in surprise. "Look! Somebody's cut and tied them back again!" Lew remembered there were no knots whatsoever in the cords when Charlie had placed them there.

Spath pulled out a knife and cut them away. "Get the screwdriver, quick," he ordered with surprising energy. Lew brought the tool and attacked the screws, the others bending eagerly over, watching and waiting. The lid was free now and he thrust it aside.

"Three sacks missing," Lew cried. "There were fifteen at the start; now there's twelve!"

Spath started to go shaky again. "I'll go crazy if I don't get away from here," he finally said.

And Galt answered deliberately, "I think it was Peak."

Lew shot an astonished glance at him. What made Galt think it was Peak? And then he remembered the night Peak had stayed up to watch in the office, and he mentally agreed with the doctor. Peak could easily have cut the strings, removed the lid and the three missing sacks of treasure. He could have tied the strings on the bottom of the box where they would go unnoticed, and all the time the seals would remain undisturbed. But why would Peak take only three sacks? He couldn't make sense of that at all.

Then Spath, calmer now, said, "If Peak took them, they're still in the house somewhere."

Lew wanted to add, "So is the murderer," but he held his peace.

Galt replied, "They are still here, no matter who took them." And Lew glanced at him with suspicious eyes. Then Lew bent over, replaced the lid and drove home the screws. He picked up the wax sealed cords and tossed them away.

"Those are no good now," he told them. "I'm going to shove this box under the counter, and I'll sleep beside it tonight and every night that we are here. Nobody will get any more of our gold." While neither of the others seemed to relish his proposal, neither objected aloud.

Spath helped him move the heavy box, now lighter than before, over the floor and out into the store.

"We can look in Peak's outfit," Lew suggested. But in his heart he doubted they would find anything. This piling of mystery upon mystery was forming a puzzle that he could not solve.

They searched diligently through all of Peak's belongings, even searched in the bed that supported Hillman's body, but all without success. The missing gold was not in the bedrooms nor in the office. Lew even searched all of the goods in the stockroom and store, the entire stock. The gold had simply vanished without a trace.

Lew was alone in the stockroom, still searching aimlessly, when he glanced up to see Charlie crouching against the wall, watching him with those dull, vacant eyes.

A sudden impulse seized Lew and he crossed over swiftly, laid his hands on the stricken man's shoulders and started to speak. But Charlie jerked back in alarm. Even as Lew spoke soothingly, he retreated with so wild a look of fear Lew stopped.

Lew groaned, "If only you could speak, could remember what happened the day before yesterday and tell me. One of them is a killer and a thief. I'm liable to go insane myself and shoot them both if something doesn't break soon."

In the store, Spath was looking eagerly out the window. "I think it is clearing up," he cried. "The wind has dropped, and the sun's coming out. Maybe we can leave tonight."

But Lew doubted this. "The sun may settle the snow somewhat, but it will still be too deep for travel," he said.

Yet the storm had stopped. That much was clear, and by noon, the sun was blazing in the southern sky, fringed by bright, fair-weather clouds. At three o'clock they could see where heaped-up snow had softened, was even melting and undoubtedly settling.

Spath grew cheerful, childishly elated. Every few minutes he peered out of the window. "I am going tomorrow, for sure," he repeated after each inspection.

Lew's spirits also rose with the anticipated reprieve. How fine it would be to get out of the dark log rooms. But he shrank from what the trip might ultimately bring. These killings would have to be investigated; each member of the party would be a suspect under the law, with Charlie bearing the heaviest burden of all. Would they just lock him away for killing Peak?

Lew didn't know, but the thought of Charlie in an insane asylum left him shaking with dread.

Night fell, and it brought back the tension that the unexpected sunshine had melted along with the snow. Galt stood up and announced, "I'm sleeping in a bed tonight, and I'm going to lock both doors. I advise you to follow my example. This will likely be our last night here, and I wouldn't take any chances."

He turned to Lew then looked at Charlie. "You will expose yourself dangerously if you occupy this room with him."

"I'll risk it," Lew replied, stung into quick defense of his partner. "I've faced many dangers beside him, and he has never failed me."

Galt tossed up his hands at so foolish a resolve. Then he disappeared and later Lew heard him bolt both of the doors to his room.

"I'm going to turn in, too," Spath said. "I think Galt's advice is good. Why don't you come in and bunk with me?"

Lew declined, little suspecting how bitterly he would regret that before morning. He kicked off his shoes and rolled between the blankets without undressing. Outside, he could hear softening snow dropping from the building's roof.

Lew did not know how long he slept but found himself suddenly awake, every nerve tense, each muscle quivering with dread. And he knew instinctively someone was bending over him. He could feel the play of breath on his face as he lay staring up into the gloom.

Fear gripped Lew completely. A spell seemed to hold his arms powerless at his sides, and the flesh of his breast crawled as if anticipating the fatal blow descending.

With a supreme effort Lew broke the fear that paralyzed him, and with a desperate jerk flung his body over and away from the descending blow. A sharp pain shot through his shoulder, his brain reeled and he dropped into a bottomless oblivion.

The sensation of dull, gnawing pain slowly forced itself on Lew's senses. He struggled to break through the thick fog that separated the worlds of anesthesia and sensibility, and after several attempts, his eyelids fluttered open. His first impression was surprise at the changed aspect of the room. A dim glow had spread through it, and in the subdued light he saw a dark figure bending over him.

Terror gripped him again, and he flung up both arms to ward off the next blow. But he could see and recognize the face peering into his. His throat went dry and his tongue swelled until he could only croak in a caricature of speech.

"Charlie! What are you doing? You wouldn't ..."

Unable to finish, Lew struggled to roll aside. Then every muscle relaxed as both of his wrists were gripped in firm, strong hands, and he heard Charlie whisper in his old confidence-inspiring voice.

"Be quiet, Lew. Let me fix that shoulder. Then we're going after the fiend who stabbed you. He's been diabolically clever, but I've got his number now."

Chapter 7 – He's an Expert at Murder!

"Yes," Charlie quietly repeated, "he has been devilish. But we've got him now. I nearly caught him when Peak was killed. That's how I got the blood on my shoe. But I was just a second too late. Tonight, he nearly got you, Lew.

"It was my fault. I tried to stay awake, but I have missed so much sleep I just couldn't. I drifted off, and he slipped in and stabbed you. But I stopped him before he could strike again and kill you."

Lew drank in the words with eager amazement. Now he found his voice. "You aren't crazy, Charlie?" That, despite all the astonishing things Charlie was saying, gripped him hardest.

"Never was," Charlie replied, the flicker of a grim smile on his lips. "That was just a game. I think I played it rather too well. You almost fell for Galt's homicidal maniac stuff, didn't you?"

"I guess so. Don't put me through anything like that again."

Charlie pressed his good shoulder with a sympathetic grip.

"Well, it was mighty lucky for us both that I wasn't knocked dead in the stockroom. If I had been, we'd both be where Peak is now."

"How did it happen?" Lew whispered.

"Nothing much to tell," Charlie replied. "I heard a slight sound behind me, and before I could turn something crashed down on my skull. All I saw was a million stars before I passed out. When I came to, I lay with my eyes shut, thinking hard. I believed Hillman had been strangled. Then came the attack on me. There was a killer among us, and I knew he would keep on until he alone claimed all of the gold."

"He has made it halfway to success," Lew replied wryly.

"Then I had an inspiration," Charlie continued. "I decided to act like the blow had crazed me, for two reasons. First, the murderer would not try to finish the job. He had figured I was too smart, you know. That's why he picked me as the next to go."

"He didn't lose any time, either," Lew muttered.

"My second reason was better. If I could make him believe me crazy, he would have nothing more to fear from me and wouldn't trouble to watch me. That would give me a chance to keep an eye on all of them until I could pick out the murderer. How did I play the insane role, anyway?"

"Too realistic for me," Lew said, shivering at the memory.

"I had my eye on Peak at the start. He seemed the logical choice, just the type who would resort to violence. But when he was killed, I knew I was way off."

"Who is it, Charlie? Tell me."

"Don't you know?"

"It's either Spath or Galt, of course. I suspected the doctor, because he was eager to pin it on you."

Charlie held something out on his hand. "Ever see this before?" It was a short, thin wisp of gray fur.

"It looks familiar. Sure—that's one of the squirrel tails from Galt's fur vest."

"Right. After you were stabbed I heard you groan. That woke me, and I was on my feet in a second. But he was too quick. Only one hand caught something, and that was this squirrel tail."

"Then it is Galt?"

"Yes."

"Why didn't you just run him down?" Lew asked.

"I was following when you groaned. I was afraid you might be bleeding badly, so I turned back. I knew he couldn't get away. As I struck the match to light the lantern, I heard a door somewhere back there close softly."

"What did he stick me with?" Lew asked, tenderly touching the bandage on his shoulder.

"The scissors that killed Peak. They gave you a nasty flesh wound, but it should heal." Charlie held up the long-bladed instrument. "A very deadly weapon in skilled hands," he added.

"I'm afraid I can't do much to help you," Lew said. "I can hold a gun on Galt, but that's about all. Let's go and get him."

Charlie glanced at his watch. Then he motioned Lew back.

"It is four o'clock. Perhaps we should wait until daylight. He can't get away, and we won't sleep anymore tonight. It may be safer for us to tackle him then."

"I suppose he has locked himself in," Lew said.

Charlie walked softly back through the office into the stockroom. He was back in a moment, and nodded. "Door bolted on the inside."

They sat in silence for several minutes. Lew started up at a sudden thought. "We forgot about Spath. Is he in danger? Maybe Galt will creep into his room and finish him while we sit here waiting."

"I didn't think of that," Charlie admitted and went straight to the door of Spath's room.

"He's okay," he said when he returned. "I can hear him snoring away. I don't think Galt will do anymore tonight. He knows we are awake and watching. He may think I did not recognize him, may even believe I am too addled to tell anyone if I did. It was dark, and he isn't likely to miss the squirrel tail I yanked from his vest. He may try to bluff it in the morning. In fact, that's all he can do without openly attacking all of us, and that's not his style."

"Here's what we do," Lew suggested. "We aren't police officers, but we have to act in their place. In the morning, we'll watch for our chance. We'll go on like nothing has happened. You play crazy as usual, and when we get him where he can't strike back, we'll stick a gun in his face and tie him up. Of course, he's got to be handled carefully. When a man has killed twice, he isn't going to be squeamish about bumping off some more people. They can't hang him any harder or higher for four than for two, so Galt will strike back like a cornered rattlesnake, if we give him the chance."

"That's sound thinking," Charlie agreed. "We won't tell Spath before we act. All you need do is handle the gun. I'll draw Galt's fangs. But if it becomes necessary, shoot—and shoot to kill."

"Don't worry," Lew said grimly. Then his features relaxed. "Gosh, it's good to have you working with me again. This business was getting worse at every turn, and I couldn't think fast enough to keep up with things. First you get knocked out, then Peak killed, part of the gold disappears, and then this attack on me."

"About that missing gold," Charlie began.

"Do you know anything about that?" Lew interrupted eagerly. "You said you stayed awake at night to watch. Peak told me he saw you watching him the night before he was killed. Did you see him take those three sacks?"

"I saw..." he stopped at the sound of footsteps from an inside room. "Sssh! It's Spath," he whispered. "Remember—not a word."

Lew held his place beside the stove, and Charlie darted back to his blankets. The door opened and Spath stepped in. "Anything wrong?" he asked. "I heard you talking."

"I guess I was just talking to myself," Lew said with a wry grin. "I been doing that a lot lately. It's a bad sign, too. When a fellow starts talking to himself up North, it's time for him to clear away to where there are more people. This strain and worry has about got me."

"It has been awful," Spath agreed, "and you have had a heavier load to bear than the rest of us. But you can't be any more pleased to leave than me. Can't we start this morning? I know the snow has melted a lot; I could hear it falling off the roof and the trees all night long. At times the sound kept me awake."

"We can't tell until we go out and walk around," Lew replied. "But we're going to start just as soon as we have a good chance to get through." As he talked he was wondering how Spath would take the news Charlie and he would soon break.

Charlie sat up in his blankets, yawned, and gave a good imitation of one just aroused from sleep. He moved over into his favorite corner and sat staring with the slack mouth and lifeless eyes that had wrung Lew's heart before. Lew could see a certain element of black humor in his partner's pose, now that he knew it was not genuine.

The minutes passed. Lew started to cook breakfast, moving slowly as he favored his wounded shoulder while trying to conceal the fact that he was injured. Going to the stockroom for a can of fruit, he held an ear close to Galt's door but could not detect any sound. He began to wonder just how things would turn out.

"What's the matter with Galt?" he finally asked Spath. "Usually, he is the first man up for breakfast."

Spath glanced up quickly. "That's right. He usually beats me."

"Guess I'll call him," Lew tried to make his voice sound casual. He went to the rear door and tapped. "Grub's waiting, Galt," he called. There was no reply. Lew began to wonder if the man really was inside. Had he escaped through the window last night?

He pounded heavily on the door, shook and rattled it. Then he returned to the store with a pale face. "He won't answer," he told Spath.

"Maybe he took some of his own medicine," Spath suggested so pointedly that Lew glanced at him in surprise. "Some of that stuff he gave us night before last."

"What do you mean?" Lew demanded, although he began to think he knew exactly what Spath was talking about.

"Galt drugged us in that tea he made. Had he ever volunteered to help with the cooking before? Course not. But he made some tea. He even gave your partner a cup. Everybody in the house was laid out except him. He was playing some game then."

"But what sort of game?" Lew asked, even though he thought he knew. He believed Galt had left some evidence, something he had to destroy or change without the others knowing. It was a simple matter to give them a drug and work while they slept. He had even made sure that Charlie got his dose, too.

Spath shrugged in answer to Lew's question as though he suggested one man's guess was as good as another. Suddenly Lew began to feel a disturbing fear. Something didn't fit right, and it all hinged on Galt's uncanny silence in the back room.

He ran outdoors with the sudden resolve to discover if Galt had escaped through the window. But the heavy bars on the outside were firm and solid. The glass was steamed over on the inside, and he could not see anything through it. Lew ran back through the wet snow and burst in through the door.

"He didn't get out the window," he cried. "He must be in there."

And then Charlie sprang out of the corner, his face determined. "We must force the door," he said crisply, and disregarding the look of amazement that flooded Spath's face, ran swiftly to the locked door. Lew was at his heels, and Spath came stumbling along several feet behind. Lew had glanced at Spath when Charlie cast off his mask of insanity, and it was obvious Spath had just received a shock.

"Help, Spath," Charlie cried, pushing Lew aside, for he was in no condition to bust in a bolted door. Their shoulders crashed into the door. It trembled but held. Again, they smashed against it with every ounce of weight and strength they had.

"Once more; it's just giving," Charlie grunted, and backing off three steps, they ran at the tottering door. This time the fastenings inside snapped off and they fell through the opening. Charlie was on his feet in an instant. "He's dead!"

Galt lay on the bunk with one hand trailing down over the edge. Clasped in the fingers was a small, flat pistol. And in the doctor's temple they saw a round, red-rimmed hole from which a thin trickle of blood thickened on the waxen face.

"He shot himself," Lew whispered. Spath retreated to the door in a panic. "How terrible! What will happen next?" he cried, almost incoherently. He trembled and covered his face with shaking hands.

"That's a twenty-five caliber pistol," Charlie said softly. "The falling snow outside and the heavy door would just about muffle its report. That's why we didn't recognize the shot." He touched the hanging arm. "Stiff. He has been dead several hours."

"He shot himself after he came in…" and Lew hesitated before finishing his sentence. Maybe Charlie was not yet ready to let Spath know about last night.

Charlie had stepped back from the bunk. He stooped now and

picked up a tiny object. It was a spent shell, the shell that in all probability had killed Galt. He glanced towards the door leading into Spath's room. It was locked on the inside, same as the door they had broken down. "Let's get out of here a minute," he advised. "We need something hot in our stomachs. Come on, Spath," he added, touching the shaking figure's shoulder. "You'll feel better after a good, hot drink."

Spath followed mumbling, "Another one dead? When will it end?" Then, after he had drained a large cup of tea, he regained his composure. "It's all over now, isn't it? I mean, Galt killed Peak and then committed suicide. We're all safe, aren't we?"

Spath turned to Charlie, suddenly aware of the transformation that had occurred. "But you? You were insane yesterday. What cured you? This shock?"

"Hardly," Charlie replied. "I wasn't exactly crazy, although I might have been if this business had lasted any longer. No, I was playing a game. I didn't even tell Lew, for fear he might give it away unintentionally. I pretended I was crazy so I would have a better chance to protect myself and watch all of you."

Spath regarded him intently. "Had you discovered that it was Galt before that ... that back there?" He pointed to the rear room.

Charlie nodded.

"How ghastly," Spath mumbled.

"We'll try to leave at noon," Charlie stated. "It will be hard to break trail through the snow, but it has settled enough to try. We have three teams of dogs, and they can take turns in the lead."

"We've got a load for each sled, too," Lew said slowly, picturing in his mind the grim procession they would form, hauling three corpses and a box of gold.

Charlie pushed back his plate and stood up. "I'm going back and pack up Galt's outfit," he said. Lew volunteered to help.

But Spath shivered and said, "If you don't mind, I'll pass."

Charlie went back and bent over the dead man. "See," he said to Lew. "Galt had his fur vest on. And one of the squirrel tails is missing. Just as I thought. That is one of the things I wanted to check on."

"Good gosh!" Lew exclaimed. "There's no doubt of it, then, is there? He killed Peak and tried to kill both of us."

But Charlie did not reply. He was examining the door that connected with Spath's room. The bolt was home. He turned back and stared at the bunk with its grim contents. He pulled the spent shell casing out and examined it closely. Then he sprang forward and grasped the trailing arm that still held the gun. He plucked the weapon forcibly from the stiffening fingers. And when he looked up at Lew, his eyes glowed. He motioned with his hand. "Shut that door, Lew." His voice was harsh but low.

Surprised, Lew shoved the door softly shut and then turned back to Charlie. "What is it?" he asked. "Why do you look that way?"

But Charlie was muttering to himself. "He's an expert at murder, alright. And just for this little thing, I never would have known."

"What are you talking about?" Lew demanded.

"Hush!" Charlie admonished. "Be careful. We aren't out of this yet. Galt didn't kill himself. He was murdered!"

Chapter 8 – Luck Didn't Fail Us

Charlie's statement that Galt had been murdered and had not died by suicide seemed incredible to Lew.

"That's impossible," he finally said.

"Why?" asked Charlie, his features hard as he studied the stiff form on the bunk.

"Look around," replied Lew. "Everything points to suicide. Both doors of the room were bolted on the inside. The window is barred. The gun was still in his hand."

"I know that," Charlie said. "Yet there is something wrong. Something that makes me question the gun and the locked doors."

"I don't see what that can be."

"This spent shell," said Charlie, indicating the tiny cylinder. "Get this, Lew. Galt lies on his back, head towards the wall. His right side is on the outside. Now, suppose he grips the gun in his right hand, which he naturally would being right-handed, raises it and fires into his temple. Where would the ejected shell go?"

"Let's see," Lew bent over to examine the pistol. "Right side ejection, the shell would fly over into the bunk."

"Then why was it lying in the middle of the room, on the opposite side from which it would kick out of the gun?"

"I get you now," Lew whispered fiercely. "The shell should be in the bunk. But hold on. Suppose Spath did shoot Galt. The pistol would be held just the same, and the shell would still fly into the wall. The fired shell still ends up in the wrong location, whether it's murder or suicide. I don't see what you've proved."

"Listen, and you will," Charlie said. "Galt was shot at close range. But if Galt had shot himself, he would place the muzzle against his head—suicides always do. But where are the powder burns?"

"There aren't any," Lew had to admit.

"That's what started me thinking," went on Charlie. "Even a small bore gun like this leaves some marks of the hot powder gas. I see only two reasons for their absence."

"Let's have them."

"First possibility, the gun was fired at a distance of 5 or 6 feet. We can dismiss that, for the lack of light and the location of the bunk make that impossible. Even in good light, it is hard to shoot a small gun like this with such accuracy. The second possibility, the one I believe, is the gun was wrapped in cloth to muffle the sound. That would eliminate powder marks even if the gun was held very close to Galt's head."

"You win," Lew admitted. "A murderer would muffle the gun to deaden the noise; a suicide wouldn't."

"Exactly," Charlie replied. "And, of course, when he unwrapped the gun so he could set it in Galt's fingers, the shell dropped out on the floor, where we found it."

"There are still the locked doors to explain," Lew reminded.

"I know. But suppose we line up the evidence on both sides? First, the position of the spent shell. Second, the lack of powder burns. Both indicate murder to me. Now, opposing these, we have a room with doors locked on the inside. A tough nut to crack, and until we do, we can't prove this wasn't a self-inflicted death."

"Something else," added Lew. "That squirrel tail you jerked from Galt's vest. He is wearing it now. How do you explain that?"

"Easy," Charlie said. "Galt wasn't wearing the vest when he died. The murderer put it on when he came to attack you. Then he slipped it back on Galt."

"Might as well call him by his name," Lew said dryly. "If Galt was murdered, Spath did it."

"Sure. I figure Spath shot Galt in the night. Then he put on the dead man's vest and came for you. I believe he intended to plant one of the tails in your hand after he killed you, to throw suspicion on Galt. After that, I would be the only one left, with no one to dispute his version of the tragedy, and remember, he thought I was insane. Who's to say what fate might have befallen me?"

"The impressive part is that after I frightened him away, before he could make sure he had finished you off, he was cool enough to slip the vest back on Galt's dead body."

"I just can't see Spath as such a cold blooded killer," Lew demurred. "He's so mild and good-humored. I just can't see it."

"You put too much in appearances," Charlie said. "So did I, at first. So did Galt. Peak's roughness naturally made him the suspect. Spath, in the meantime, was building a clever image with his mildness and his fright, which is exactly what a cunning murderer would do."

"Still, you've got to explain these locked doors," Lew challenged.

"That is exactly what I intend to do. I don't think Galt would let

Spath into his room and then go and lie down to be shot. There are no signs of a struggle, and the doctor wouldn't submit without a fight. No, Galt was asleep in his bed when he died. I'm sure of that."

Charlie lapsed into thought.

"Spath is devilishly cunning," he resumed a minute later. "If he gets away with this, he's safe. We can't prove Galt didn't shoot himself, and the other murders will be hung on him. Spath will be free of suspicion and will get his share of the gold just the same. There's only three of us now, so the share will be considerable."

"And on our way out, some 'accident' could happen to eliminate one or both of us," Lew added slowly.

"Sure," Charlie replied. "Spath wants the entire fortune for himself. Now that he has gone this far, you think he will divide it with us?"

Charlie walked over to the door. He slid the heavy bolt back and forth in its socket. "Anybody could shut the door and then lock it from the other side. All he would need is a piece of cord, like this." He picked a length of string from the floor, doubled it, and slipped the loop over the bolt's knob. "Watch," he said.

He entered Spath's room and closed the door behind him, shutting it on the doubled cord. The string tightened, and with a faint click the bolt slid home. Then the string slipped through the crack and disappeared. Lew pushed the bolt back, and Charlie opened the door.

"See?" he asked. "Now I need to figure out how he opened the bolt from the outside." Charlie's jaw snapped shut, and he stood staring at the peeled log partition between the two rooms. Then he darted back into the stockroom. When he returned, he carried a piece of heavy wire some 2 feet long.

"Lock the door behind me," he directed. "I think I know how Spath got in here." He was almost shaking with excitement as the door closed after him. Lew slid the bolt home and waited. He could hear soft, furtive sounds; then the end of the wire projected through a crack in the wall. The crevice between the logs was narrow, barely wide enough to admit the heavy wire. He saw that Charlie had bent a flat loop on the end.

Now the wire started to curve, to bend in an arc, and Lew breathlessly watched it approach the protruding bolt knob. It touched the knob, slipped off and then described a tiny circle as Charlie endeavored to catch it again. Then the loop quietly settled over it.

Lew knew Charlie was pushing, using his dexterity to back up the bolt. It moved a little then stuck. Lew saw the door shake gently, then with a smooth click the bolt slipped back and the door opened.

"Satisfied?" asked Charlie.

"Let's go get him," Lew said grimly.

"He's probably armed, so take it easy," Charlie cautioned.

"Maybe he has cleared out already?" Lew offered hopefully.

"He wouldn't leave without the gold," Charlie replied. "Not after going to the steps he has already taken."

Lew turned and grasped the stockroom door latch when a sharp cry sounded behind it. Then, they heard Spath cry, "Fire! The storeroom's afire! Help! Quick!"

Lew flung the door open. The room was filling with smoke, and through the cloud he saw Spath standing in the opposite doorway, waving his arms and pointing into one of the far corners.

They leaped towards it, stumbling over heaps of boxes and bags.

"Here it is, in this bale of clothing," Charlie gasped, coughing as the black smoke rolled up in his face. He jerked at the bale and flung it over. "Help me drag it outside," he ordered.

Lew bent over to help and grasped the bale with his sound arm. Forgetting Spath in their excitement, they hustled the smoking mass to the door. The room was opaque now, filled with a stinging, biting vapor that smarted eyes and lungs.

Charlie bumped into the door and recoiled in surprise. It was shut. He pushed against it but it did not open, and he knew that it had been locked on the outside. In his distrust, the former owner of Hazzard House had installed locks on all inside doors.

"We're trapped," he told Lew grimly. Flames burst out of the smoldering bale. "It's kerosene. Spath knew his game was up. He set this fire so he could get away. Didn't I say he was devilish?"

Charlie leaned back and then crashed his body into the door. It shook but held. He stepped back for another lunge, but as he crouched, ready to leap forward, there was a sharp crack outside and a bullet ripped through the wood, passing the spot where his head had been a moment before. "Get down," he ordered fiercely.

They lay flat on the floor. The smoke was not so thick there, but gradually it was becoming heavier as it was rolled down from the ceiling. Lew knew he couldn't stand the stuff much longer.

"We have to break out, gun or no," he said. "We'll suffocate in here, and the building will catch fire soon. We might as well be shot as smothered and burned alive."

Charlie was crawling away to search among the goods, toppling boxes. Finally, he found what he sought. He thrust an axe in Lew's good hand.

"Try the other door," he said. "Stay behind the log wall and work one-handed. I'll cut through here. He can't cover both of us."

"All of the guns are out there," Lew groaned.

"If you get through first and see him, sling your axe at his head," Charlie snapped. He raised his own tool and sent it crashing into the door. Again and again he struck, half-blinded by the smoke. As he worked, he grimly thought what a fool he had been to allow Spath this literally golden opportunity to get away with all of the gold.

Another smashing cut swung the door open. Charlie staggered through with poised axe, but the room was empty. Smoke surged after him and filled the room quickly.

"All clear," he shouted to Lew. His first brief glance had showed Charlie the door leading from the store was also closed. Up came his axe again.

A volley of pistol shots came from across the yard. For a moment they wondered if Spath had encountered someone in the yard and was battling with him. Then Lew knew.

"The dogs!" he cried. "Spath's killing the dogs so we can't follow him on another sled!"

Crash! Crash! Charlie's axe went home at each blow, and the door sagged. Another blow flung it open. They shoved through and ran for the front. Smoke poured in after them. Charlie flung open the front door and saw the yard empty. Spath had escaped.

"He had his own team outside ready to go and then came back and finished the remaining dogs." Lew gritted as he ran to the rack where their rifles hung.

"Wait!" Charlie yelled. "We've got to get that burning bale outdoors before the building goes up in flames."

Lew seized the water pail and dashed back into the stockroom to pour its contents on the blazing mass. The fire was doused, and between them they slid the smoldering thing through the office door, across the store floor, and out into the snow in the yard. Charlie looked around the corner of the building. One glance showed the slaughter of the dogs. Every animal was dead or crippled.

"Snowshoes and rifles, Lew," he called. "We'll get him, alright."

"You know he took the gold, too, and that will slow him down," Lew shouted back.

As Charlie loaded his rifle. Lew donned cap and coat. Both

donned snowshoes.

Soon, their web-clad feet were pounding across the yard. The heavy gate swung open, and they looked eagerly ahead. A fresh trail led out through the timber, following the bank of the lake. Gripping rifles in clenched fingers, they settled into a swift, relentless pace in pursuit of the fleeing murderer.

Although the trail was partly broken, soft wet snow soon clogged the meshes of their long, slim shoes, weighing down each step. The first flush of confidence that they would overtake Spath began to fade as they covered mile after mile without catching sight of him.

"He can't keep this pace up long," Charlie grunted. "The dogs are fresh, but they'll wear down shortly. Then we'll gain."

But he realized that things were not going to be so easy. Spath was not the man to permit them to just run him down without striking back. He would lay in ambush.

"We'll have to quit this blind pursuit," he panted. "Spath may send the team on and wait for us behind a tree. Then he can pick us off. We must separate. You take a line 200 yards on that side of the trail and I'll do the same here."

Lew nodded and swung off to the left. They kept on steadily, but the going was slower in unbroken trail, and their speed dropped.

At the top of a huge, bowl-shaped depression their trails met. The dog team trail followed straight ahead downslope towards a narrow but deceptively deep body of water the Indians had named Warm Spring Lake. "Spath has gone straight on," Lew said. "We'll each take one side of the rim and meet again on the opposite side."

But when they drew together 10 minutes later, they stared at the snow before them. It was unmarked, completely bare of tracks.

"That's queer," Charlie said. "We should have cut his trail here for sure."

"He may have turned back," Lew suggested. "Hazzard House is empty now, door wide open, and it would make a safer refuge than the open timber."

Alarmed at the thought, they whirled about and started down the long, gentle slope, headed straight for Warm Spring Lake.

"Keep to the edges," Charlie warned. "I don't think the center ice will bear our weight." Then, with a jolt, he suddenly realized the real reason they had not cut Spath's trail on the other side of the lake.

Lew clutched his partner's arm with an involuntary cry. Out near the middle of the tiny lake, they saw a raw, gaping hole. Coming across from the opposite side, the fresh trail of a dog team led straight into the open water. And that was all.

They stared for a minute then silently turned back towards home. Two hours later, they stumbled through the stockade gate, spent.

"How deep is Warm Spring Lake?" asked Lew. "Suppose we could salvage the gold?"

"The Indians claim it has no bottom," Charlie replied without a trace of emotion in his voice. "We might get a deep sea diver to come up and try."

"Our luck has slumped," Lew mourned. "Usually something turns up to save it."

That brought Charlie to his feet. "It's going to now," he declared. Then he laughed. "In all of the excitement, I clean forgot to tell you. I started to tell you about it last night—this morning, rather—before Spath came in the room."

"Go on!" Lew urged.

"I was suspicious of Galt Saturday, the time he made tea for us, so I didn't drink any. I poured mine out under the edge of my blankets. Spath was right about it being doped. After he put you all to sleep with the stuff, Galt went in the office, opened the box, and took out three sacks of gold."

"So it was him," Lew cried. "I thought Peak did that."

"Galt was a pretty square shooter," Charlie continued. "Note that he only took a fifth of the sacks, his rightful share. And then he hid them. Cleverly, too."

He paused, and Lew reached down on the floor and picked up a heavy shoe. "If you don't finish the story right now without any more halts, I'll fire this at you," he threatened.

"As I was saying," Charlie continued, "the doctor showed real cleverness. If he had shown half as much in suspecting somebody besides my humble self of stabbing Peak, he might still be alive.

"He opened the case of canned beans under the counter, took out three cans and put the sacks in their place. Then he threw the beans out over the stockade and nailed the lid back down on the case. I saw part of what he did and heard the rest."

"And I suppose he was going to buy the case from us when he started out," Lew said as he grabbed the box in question. He pried off the cover and peered inside.

"Yep, safe and snug," he declared. "Luck didn't fail us after all."

He lifted the plump sacks up onto the counter and regarded them with shining eyes

"One thing isn't clear, though," he added. "How did Spath get on to the gold? And why did he kill Hillman that night? Hillman had given everything of his to us in case he died, but nobody knew how valuable it might be."

"That puzzled me, too, for a while," Charlie continued. "We will probably never know all of the details, but I believe Spath was in the office snooping about, and Hillman must have talked aloud in his delirium and gave the thing away. So Spath started in on his murder spree then and there. If it hadn't been for Hillman's fixation on his gold, he, Peak, Galt, our dogs, even Spath would still be alive."

The pair now regarded the glittering content of the heavy little sacks in somber silence, their earlier enthusiasm tempered by realization of the terrible toll human greed and deceit had wrought.

The End